BURNING SECRETS

DEADLY SECRETS TEXAS TRILOGY - BOOK 2

DENISE DIANA HUDDLE

Copyright © 2024 by Crimes & Passion, LLC. All rights reserved.
Editing by Laura Barth
Proofreading by Beth Attwood
Cover design by Damonza.com
Contact email: denise@denisedianahuddle.com

ISBN: 979-8-9858912-4-9 - Paperback
ISBN: 979-8-9858912-5-6 - Ebook

In honor of Sherry Arrant

CHAPTER 1

THE PERCUSSION WAVE shook the ground under Adelaide's feet. For a split second she thought it was a bomb. Jerking her head toward the mill, she didn't see flames—not yet, anyway. But she was half a mile away, and the explosive force had been strong enough to rattle her field equipment. Then the sirens sounded—endless, blaring loops of wailing tones designed to induce brain-rattling panic in anyone within earshot. It worked. Adelaide knew what those sirens meant. Get upwind. Get.Up.Wind. GETUPWIND.

She looked up at the neon-orange wind socks that surrounded the mill. They were all pointing south like a circle of perfectly aligned glow-in-the-dark sentinels. Unfortunately, they were all pointing directly at her.

She put her hand in the air and studied the sway of the tree-tops, estimating the wind speed at twenty miles per hour. Images of the road map she had been reading only a few minutes before flashed through her mind. At this distance, there was no time to get into a hazmat suit. Mercifully, so far all she could smell was the pervasive odor of the pines. But the hairs on the back of her neck were ramrod straight, and her heart was racing.

Adelaide scooped up her gear and threw it in the open hatch-back of her Explorer. She jumped into the driver's seat and hit the ignition. As soon as the engine sprang to life, she punched the button to shut down the AC, turned south on the two-lane caliche road, and floored it.

The speedometer swept past seventy-five as the SUV fish-tailed on the gravel road. The slipping tires kicked up a spray of limestone pebbles that clattered against her undercarriage as they joined the massive dust cloud she was leaving in her wake. She couldn't see a thing behind her, and she was quickly losing visibility out her side windows as the nebula of powdered caliche enveloped the SUV. She could taste the limestone dust sneaking through the vents. *Damn it. The car isn't sealed.*

The farther she got from ground zero of the contamination—whatever it was—the better. Assuming the wind conditions held steady and she didn't total the truck in the process, she should be okay. Problem was, she was still speeding downwind.

The steering wheel jerked in her palms as the Explorer bounced over the ruts in the gravel road. For now, outrunning it would have to do. But pretty soon, she was going to need to cut east or west. Then, she would have to find a way to head due north and upwind. She recalled an east-west farm-to-market road she had passed earlier. Fumbling for the map, she pulled it into her lap and shot a glance at the X she had marked that morning. Sweat dripped from her brow, but she didn't dare turn on the AC. God only knew what was in the air.

As she came into a curve, the sign for the farm-to-market popped into view. The knots in her shoulders relaxed if only for a moment as she mopped the sweat out of her eyes. Holding the steering wheel in a death grip, she managed to slingshot the truck around the corner without ending up in the bar ditch. She pushed the Explorer through five kidney-bruising eastbound miles on the unpaved road before the interstate appeared on the horizon.

Finally back on pavement, she did the math. She placed herself roughly thirteen miles southwest of ground zero. That should be safe. She hit the AC button on the dash and jacked the fan to full speed. Three Texas highway patrol cars zipped past her, their sirens whelping, undoubtedly headed to the mill.

Adelaide swung into a rest area and screeched to a stop. She bailed out of the dust-covered Explorer and rushed to the tailgate. Hauling the heavy emergency bag out of the back of the SUV, she swatted at a mosquito on her neck. Even a toxic plume couldn't slow down Texas mosquitoes. Another squad of sirens sped by on the highway as she made a beeline to the ladies' room.

Once inside, she scrambled through the laborious process of unpacking and putting on her Level A hazmat suit. Getting into the suit was no small undertaking. Doing it without help made it even harder. But she had no choice—she needed to be as ready as possible when she got to the site.

She carefully pulled the suit on over her clothes, shoved her feet into the chunky rubber boots, and duct-taped the suit to the boot tops. Then, she prepped the gloves, face shield, and her self-contained breathing apparatus. That was as ready as she could be and still drive. As she left the ladies' room, she caught sight of herself in the mirror—a frumpy green space invader. Pushing through the doors into the scorching East Texas heat, she thought, *Good thing I'm headed to an industrial accident, not looking for a date.* Hefting her bag on her shoulder, she made tracks back to her car.

Halfway across the parking lot, she caught sight of movement near the back of her truck. Squinting, she made out a stocky white bull terrier belly-crawling out from under her Explorer. Free of the car, the dog waddled a few steps and sat down by the left rear tire.

As she came closer, Adelaide saw the dog was sitting by two high-top tennis-shoed feet that were sticking out from underneath her bumper. The dog barked two quick yaps as she approached. The high-tops telescoped out from the shadows of the undercarriage. They were attached to a man who quickly got to his feet. He began brushing off his hands and dusting off his clothes.

What the hell? Adelaide marched right up to him. As she got closer, all she could think was *Wow!* About six foot three or four, he was beautifully proportioned and well muscled. He was wearing a black T-shirt and black jeans. The clothes fit just tight enough in all the right places. The effect was topped off with medium-brown hair in one of those devil-may-care messy-but-oh-so-hot styles, and his cobalt-blue eyes definitely qualified as a lethal weapon. He had the whole bad-boy-next-door thing down to a science.

Another passing siren jolted her out of her reverie. Hot or not, she didn't like this guy around her car. Anyway, she didn't have time to waste on pleasantries.

"Excuse me…would you mind telling me what you're doing under my truck?"

He was staring at her. Awkwardly, he stuck out his hand. Adelaide didn't move. When she didn't reciprocate, he dropped his arm.

"Uh…I am so sorry, ma'am. I'm Brock Emerson. This is Rufus." As if on cue, the dog pointed his egg-shaped nose to the sky and emitted a single, deep-chested bark. The man smiled. "We were just making a little pit stop when Rufus here got spooked by those sirens." He held up the collar and leash dangling like an empty hangman's noose. "He slipped his leash and hightailed it under your car." She looked down at the dog as it toddled closer to his owner. He fidgeted a little and went on to fill the awkward silence. "He was not at all interested in coming out. I finally had to crawl under there on a rescue mission."

Following his gaze, she looked down and realized she was parading around a roadside picnic area dressed like a chartreuse Michelin Man. "I'm a chemical engineer. There's been an incident at the mill in Pine Grove. If you'll excuse me, I'm in a hurry."

He smiled as he backed away doing the "I surrender" thing with his hands. "No problem. Sorry for the confusion. You drive safe." Then he winked at her.

*Winking? Honestly. Why is it that gorgeous men so often feel compelled to push it with such adolescent ridiculousness? Probably because those absurd little pre-mating rituals evoke just the response I'm feeling right now…*which was a warm, tingling sensation that could make bad ideas seem really tempting. Times like this she remembered that pulling herself off of the dating merry-go-round wasn't that bad…and it was certainly less confusing.

She walked past him with a cursory smile and heaved her bag into the cargo area of the Explorer. Sliding her breathing apparatus, face shield, and gloves onto the front seat, she jumped in and headed back north—upwind, toward the mill. As she sped down the highway, she forced herself to put the handsome stranger out of her mind—or gave it her best shot, anyway.

Approaching the road that ran to the plant, she slowed down for the detour local law enforcement had set up. Lowering her window, she passed her Environmental Protection Agency credentials to the Nacogdoches County deputy manning the roadblock. He inspected the laminated card carefully. Satisfied, he spoke into his radio and waited for a response before he moved the barricade and waved her on.

The road to the mill allowed an approach from the upwind side to the northern entrance of the property. Black smoke was oozing up from the horizon. A malevolent plume was forming to the south carrying the toxins in the direction from which Adelaide had just come. Her mouth was dry, and her heart was racing. She was so hot in the heavy suit, she could feel the sweat running down her back and chest. It was always scarier when you didn't know what you were dealing with. She could hear her blood pulsing in her ears. Her palms were sweaty on the leather steering wheel as she struggled to calm herself. She needed a clear head.

Just north of the main mill entrance, she saw the collection of response vehicles parked outside of the scene access-control point. Only the fire trucks had been allowed inside the mill property.

She parked the SUV, secured her equipment, and headed to the makeshift barricade.

Oddly, the Fairfield County sheriff's deputy manning the entrance wasn't wearing protective gear. She offered her credentials to him. He reviewed them but made no comment—and no move to wave her through.

Adelaide spoke into the microphone inside her breathing apparatus. "I'm a chemical engineer acting as a special consultant to the Dallas office of the EPA's on-scene coordinator. I happened to be working in the area when I heard the alarms. I came straightaway to see how I can assist. I need to speak with the scene commander."

He folded her ID case and handed it back to her. "You don't need that getup. This isn't anything besides a kitchen fire in one of the admin offices."

"Deputy, I heard a sizable explosion followed by toxic-release warning sirens. Chemical sensors that detect airborne toxins trigger those sirens."

Shrug. "Suit yourself." He chuckled at his own joke.

Adelaide was not amused. "May I please see the scene commander?"

The man smirked. "Well, he's a little busy right now."

"I'm sure he is. However, if you would be so kind as to raise him on the radio and let him know that I'm here, I'll go to him."

"No one is being admitted to the property. How about you leave your card, and he can call you later?" Nasty smile.

Okay. Being polite hadn't worked. "How about I call the EPA's on-scene coordinator in Dallas and tell him that since the local scene commander is unavailable, maybe EPA should helicopter over some federal agents to come and help out?"

The deputy straightened his posture and unhooked the snap on his holster. "Ma'am, please step away from the barricade. If you insist on attempting to enter this area despite my warnings, I will be forced to take you into custody."

Tapping the button on the chest of her suit with her gloved hand, she set her communication system to the central command frequency and spoke into her microphone. "This is Adelaide Reese with the office of the OSC of the EPA. I am at the access-control point. I need to see the scene commander or his deputy. The scene access-control officer—" she squinted through her face shield to read his name tag "—Deputy Jackson, has denied me access." She saw Jackson redden as her voice came through his emergency response radio.

Her radio crackled. "Scene commander. Stand by."

Shortly, a golf cart pulled up to the main gate and disgorged a man in street clothes who walked toward the barricade.

"I'm Darren Blackwood, the manager of this facility."

After countless town hall meetings and depositions, she knew exactly who Darren Blackwood was. And he knew good and well who she was, too—though he didn't let on.

"This fire is restricted to an administrative area of the plant. It began when someone left a stack of paper napkins too close to a coffeepot during an employee birthday celebration. We have secured all potentially toxic or flammable materials, shut down all plant operations, and evacuated the facility. There are no injuries. The internal fire suppression system is operating properly. The fire is under control, and we expect to have it fully extinguished shortly."

He was talking too fast, and his eyes were darting around like a fly avoiding a swatter.

"Mr. Blackwood, paper napkins do not explode when left near coffeepots. The warning sirens that sounded—" she looked at the watch taped to the arm of her suit "—forty-two minutes ago are activated by sensors that detect the presence of potentially life-threatening airborne agents. I am here to see how I can assist."

Just then, another golf cart pulled up. Adelaide recognized the man walking toward her as Remy Stone, the local counsel for the paper mill. As he inserted himself between Adelaide and the plant manager, he slapped the executive on the back. "I've got this, Darren." Blackwood scurried back to his golf cart.

The lawyer reminded Adelaide of a car salesman trying to unload the biggest heap on the lot. "Ms. Reese, you don't need that silly suit. This is much ado about nothing. We've got ourselves a little kitchen fire here. Everything's under control."

Under control? Is this guy out of his mind? He's standing in front of a burning paper mill. "Sir, with respect. You are in no position to make that assessment."

"Well, what I am in a position to do is to ask you to answer the call that should be coming through to your phone just about now."

As if on cue, Adelaide's phone rang, the blaring tone ricocheting around the hood of her suit. She hit her chest button to answer the call. Momentarily, she heard the good-old-country-boy voice of Brett Pierce, the head of the OSC from the Dallas office. "You've sure got those folks at the paper mill in a twist."

"Right now, plant personnel report a Class A fire. However, we've got the risk of developing a Class B involving flammable fuel. Never mind all the paper stored here."

"Yeah. Well, the paper's not our problem. The other flammable fuels might be. Is it true that you are acting as an expert witness for plaintiffs that are suing that mill on a toxic tort?"

She could feel her anger rising like the toxic plume. She clenched her fist in the bulky glove as she struggled to maintain her composure. "Yes, sir. That's true. But that's irrelevant. I came here because I was following protocol."

"You and I know that, but they think you're sneaking around, using the fire as an excuse to look in their underwear drawer. For now, I want you to stay out of their hair. But stay close in case I need you. Meanwhile, I'll get some of our boys up in a chopper and let them take a look. I can't afford to have the OSC tied up in some conflict-of-interest mess with these yahoos. And keep that suit on until you're clear."

"Got it."

With that, she turned and marched back to her truck. She could feel the smug, self-satisfied grins like a hail of poison darts bombarding her back as she walked away. She got in the Explorer and slammed the door. *What a complete waste of time!* Dealing with bullheaded men like these just served to reinforce her decision to stay in the no-dating zone…

But as she drove away, an image of the hot guy with the cute dog crept back into her mind. Damn it! She didn't have time for men…no matter how cute their dogs were.

CHAPTER 2

SHE PULLED THE face shield off, tossed it on the passenger's seat, and started the car. Once on the road, she hit the voice command button on her steering wheel. "Call Ava Lawson." She waited while the phone dialed and rang.

"Polymer Lab. Dr. Lawson."

"Hey, Dr. Lawson, head of the Polymer Lab. This is Adelaide Reese, MS—your local polluters' favorite punching bag. What's cookin' on your Bunsen burner today?"

"I'm brewing up a potion to turn the assistant dean into a frog. Wanna help?"

Adelaide laughed. "Can you make an extra batch? Hell, can you make enough to turn the whole damn management team at East-Tex Consolidated into a swamp full of toads? Wait a sec... someone already did that."

Ava chuckled. "Bad day on the eco-battlefield?"

Ava listened patiently while Adelaide told her what had gone on. "So EPA's got choppers up?"

"Yeah. I just got a text from Brett. They should be over the mill in half an hour. Damn stubborn good old boys. You know, there are rare moments I think maybe I should try dating again... then something like this garbage happens, and I remember how men just can't handle women in science. They all want happy little homemakers to take their crap, wash their laundry, and birth their babies."

Ava laughed again. "I totally get you, but apparently they're not all like that. This year, I've got a grad student whose über-hot husband is staying home to raise their kid and working a night job to support them while she gets her doctorate. He had the whole crew over for dinner last week…torched crème brûlée for dessert right at the dinner table. So they're out there. I'm not sure where, but they're out there."

Adelaide shook her head. "Yeah, I guess they are. We just never see them because they're living in a far-off land with the Easter Bunny and Santa Claus. One thing's for certain, we know they don't work in the ass dean's office at Travis State University in the beautiful Piney Woods, and they sure as hell don't have anything to do with East-Tex Consolidated."

"Yea verily, sister. You got that right." Then Adelaide heard her friend talking to someone in the lab. "What? Just hold on. I'll be right with you…" Ava said. Then, "Ad? You still there? I've got to run. I think one of the students is really trying the frog thing. Later." And then she was gone.

Ava Lawson had been her best friend since first semester at MIT. Ava could always make Adelaide feel better, even after the crappiest of days…like this one. In short order, Adelaide pulled the car into the parking lot of the glamorous Swiss Chateau Inn & Suites and parked. At least today was over and there was a hot meal and a bubble bath in her immediate future. Plus, there was always hope that Ava would pull off the frog thing.

CHAPTER 3

ADELAIDE REESE WAS smart and very easy on the eyes. In another world… He shook his head to clear it. This was *not* another world. This was the reality of high-dollar litigation. No matter how smart or how beautiful she was, this was work, and Brock never mixed business and pleasure. Still, it would have been easier to keep his distance if she had looked like a refugee from the East German shot put team instead of the beauty she was.

Rufus stood up, stretched, and muzzle-bumped his master for a treat. Brock pulled a cookie from the bag he kept in the console, and the terrier snarfed it down in a single bite.

Brock absently scratched the dog's ears as he reminded himself to be very careful with this one. She was no fool. If she'd taken a room at the Evergreen Motel in Pine Grove—which happened to be owned by Remy Stone's sister-in-law—he'd have been inside her room weeks ago. But instead, she had chosen a corporate-owned chain hotel in another county, with good security and interior entrances, outside the reach of the Fairfield County sheriff and his deputies.

He watched her carefully lock her truck and use her key card on the side door closest to her room. She was still in the suit, minus the face shield and gloves. He admired her long wavy black hair. Her creamy, soft features were pierced by her dark-brown eyes. Stopping himself as he began imagining what treasures were concealed under the plastic suit, he settled in to wait.

As he sat in the hot truck, his mind kept wandering back to his last job in Milwaukee. How could it have gone so wrong? He kept running it over and over in his mind…trying to figure it out. He'd worked undercover for his whole career, and he was one of the best. There was a substantial demand for his services. The pay was great and only getting better. Who would have ever thought he would be pulling down a quarter mill a year by the time he was thirty-five?

Lately, though, he wondered if he'd been pretending to be someone else so long, he'd forgotten who he really was. Maybe he never really knew to begin with. Sometimes it seemed as though cover stories and reality were blending together like an oil slick sliding over the surface of a crystal-blue sea, contaminating the once-clear water. When had he lost track of the lines? Maybe he'd crossed one without knowing it. Maybe he'd crossed it so long ago that he couldn't even remember where it was.

The subjects of undercover operations were always pissed when his true identity was ultimately revealed to them…*if* it was ever revealed to them at all. Sometimes he just disappeared into the night, leaving them mystified that somehow their enemy had learned all their secrets. Other times, he watched their jaws drop as he strode past them to the witness stand or appeared at a deposition, having been summoned as a surprise witness by his real name. In all those years, he had never really cared what they thought. The people he was paid to get close to were usually drug dealers, embezzlers, thieves, or some other kind of miscreant who needed to be shut down. Whatever they got, he figured they had it coming.

But sometimes—rarely—the subjects were just ordinary, decent folks who happened to stumble across something that the client didn't want them to know. Like a widower accountant with three little kids who noticed something screwy in a pattern of chemical orders and couldn't leave it alone. Then the world quivered on its axis.

And sometimes, they were gorgeous chemical engineers just doing their jobs.

Rufus yapped, jarring Brock from his reverie as Adelaide came out the same door she'd gone into a few minutes before. Now wearing jeans and a cotton blouse, she headed out walking down Main Street. The night air was still and oppressive. Brock could feel his T-shirt sticking to his back. He hooked Rufus's lead to his collar, and the dog emitted a soft grunt as he and Brock climbed out of the suffocating heat of the truck and fell in behind Adelaide.

Trading the hazmat suit for jeans and a shirt was a substantial cosmetic improvement. Brock tried to never think of his subjects as real people. He imagined they were just characters in a play. But, professionalism aside, he couldn't help notice how the jeans hugged her shapely hips and the blouse clung to her torso leaving just enough to the imagination. He kept a good distance as she strolled down Main Street, pausing occasionally to look in the shop windows. Eventually, she stopped at the local barbecue joint.

On weeknights in cosmopolitan Nacogdoches, travelers ate at Babe's. It was that or mystery meat from the roller grill at the Kwikee Mart. Adelaide picked her way through the crowd loitering on the sidewalk until she reached the hostess desk. Brock hung far enough back not to be noticed but close enough to listen in. Adelaide was met by a smiling blonde Texas-cheerleader type that Brock had gotten to know over the past months.

"Table for one, please."

Darlene considered the electronic seating chart. "Inside or patio seating?"

"Patio seating? It's over ninety degrees out here."

Darlene offered a perplexed look. Adelaide sighed. "I'll take inside, please."

The response elicited a bright hooray-for-the-home-team smile. "Well, okeydokey. We're running right at a two-hour wait for indoor seating. You're welcome to wait out front if you'd like. There are some benches." She passed Adelaide what looked like a cross between a hockey puck and a highway reflector. "We'll page you on that when your table is available."

Adelaide looked at the device and back at Darlene. "Two hours? For barbecue? You're bound to be kidding."

"No, ma'am. All the churches have choir practice tonight. Most of 'em just got finished. Besides, we're the only place in town open for dinner during the week."

Adelaide let out another sigh. "How long for patio seating?"

"Oh, we can do that right now. But you'll have to join our private club. The patio is technically part of the bar, and only members can go in the bar. County rules. The membership is five dollars."

Just then, Darlene caught site of Brock. A broad smile came across her face and she waved. Maybe he should have stayed farther back, but he figured this was as good a time for his approach as any. Plus, the idea of wrangling an excuse to spend some time with Adelaide Reese over dinner wasn't exactly a hardship…

"Hey there, Darlene! How're the ribs tonight?"

Darlene beamed. "Good, as always!"

He leaned on the hostess podium. "Do you have room for me and Rufus out on the patio? We're starving."

"Absolutely." Darlene turned to Adelaide with a decidedly frosty air compared to her animated exchange with Brock. "Ma'am, did you decide on patio seating or do you want to wait?"

Working to seem unconcerned with Darlene's exchange with Adelaide, Brock monitored them with his peripheral vision. Adelaide shook her head, shifting her focus from Brock and Rufus back to Darlene. She stammered just a bit as she regained her composure. "The patio will be fine."

Darlene grabbed two menus printed on brown paper bags, two baskets of bread, and a couple rolls of silverware encased in disposable plastic bibs. She winked at Brock and said, "I'll see you out there."

"You got it," Brock said. As he turned to walk away, he did a double take on Adelaide. "Excuse me, but don't I know you from somewhere?"

Adelaide cleared her throat. Her voice was smooth and rich and just deep enough to be Lauren Bacall sexy. "I believe we met at the rest stop earlier today."

As he transitioned his face from *I don't have the foggiest idea what you're talking about* to *Oh, my God, was that you?* he let loose with a high-wattage smile of recognition. "I'm sorry. I didn't recognize you without the suit."

She produced a polite, socially appropriate smile. "No problem. Occupational hazard." She started after Darlene with a brief nod. "Have a nice evening."

"I'll see you over there. Rufus can't go through the dining room, so we take the outdoor route. Catch you in a few."

Adelaide nodded casually. Darlene led her to a table just outside the dining room. Brock observed from around the corner as the hostess unceremoniously tossed a menu, breadbasket, and silverware roll on the table and said, "Enjoy your meal," with all the warmth and enthusiasm of a toll-booth operator.

Once free of Adelaide, Darlene scurried to meet Brock and Rufus. After seating them on the edge of the patio, she fussed shamelessly over him, hanging on his every word while giggling and flirting. She petted Rufus nonstop.

Brock pulled a small sack out of his backpack and handed it to Darlene. "You're always so nice to me and Rufus…making sure we don't starve. Rufus brought you a little present."

Darlene looked surprised and blushed bright red. She opened the bag and extracted a Dallas Stars T-shirt. She beamed. "Oh, my gosh…it's great. You know how I love my Stars." She held it up and admired the kelly green shirt.

Brock smiled. "I thought you might like it. You're so great to us…we just wanted you to know how much we appreciate it."

They chatted for several minutes until the restaurant manager walked by and spoke to Darlene briefly before continuing his rounds. Apparently chastised, she hustled back to her hostess station.

Adelaide studied the menu while she waited for a waitress to appear. Brock slipped Rufus a treat, pointed behind his menu to Adelaide, and whispered, "Chair." Rufus waddled over to Adelaide's table, hopped up on the wrought iron chair, and stuffed his head into the basket of sliced white bread. Leaning his spine against the wicker back of the chair, the dog settled on his haunches like a bear, draped his front paws lazily on his belly, and munched on his ill-gotten booty.

Brock was not far behind, arriving just as Rufus gobbled down the last morsel of Wonder Bread and licked his chops. Brock grabbed Rufus by the collar and hooked the lead to the metal loop bearing his tags. As he wrestled the terrier out of the chair, he caught a whiff of Adelaide's perfume. It was flowery and fresh and clean. He could even smell the scent of her shampoo. His mind drifted to images of her coming out of the shower… *Whoa, cowboy! Have you lost your mind?* He forced himself to concentrate on his job.

"I'm so sorry. He loves meeting new people."

"Isn't there some regulation against pets in restaurants?"

"Well, they sort of make an exception for me. We're staying over at the Tall Pines. The TP doesn't have a restaurant, so I have to eat somewhere. Darlene's good people. She finagled a deal with the manager. We come in every night. I sit over there on the edge of the bricks, and they pretend that Rufus is outside the dining area. They have a steady customer, and I don't starve."

Adelaide nodded and went back to her menu. "Well, enjoy your dinner."

Brock called to Rufus, who steadfastly refused to get out of the chair—probably because Brock was subtly giving him the hand signal for *stay*. Brock finally made a show of picking the animal up and hauling him back to their table on the opposite side of the patio. No sooner had Adelaide folded her menu and set it aside than Rufus jumped right back onto the same chair and snatched another slice of bread out of the basket. Brock was right behind him.

"He seems pretty committed to sitting with you. Would you mind if we join you?"

Adelaide hesitated. She reached over and ruffled Rufus's ears.

"Who am I to argue with this little beast?"

Brock walked back over to where he had been sitting. *Chicks love a cute dog. Works every single time.* He picked up his menu, water glass, and breadbasket and carried them to Adelaide's table. *So far, so good.* "Here's some fresh bread. Guaranteed free of dog slobber."

The waitress walked up, cocked her hip, and produced a flirty little smile for Brock as she reached over and petted Rufus. Her attention to Adelaide was considerably less welcoming. "You decided yet, ma'am?"

"I'll have the sausage plate with iced tea." Adelaide handed her the menu. "Thanks."

"And I assume you fellas are having your usual?"

Brock smiled back. "You got it, Betty. Thanks." Betty slipped her pen behind her ear, tucked her pad in her apron pocket, and walked away.

Adelaide watched the waitress sashay toward the kitchen and turned back to Brock. "You seem to be quite the fixture around here."

He took a sip of ice water. Something about being this close to Adelaide Reese had his heart beating a littler faster than usual. "We got here a couple of weeks ago. I'm a journalist."

"Sounds interesting. Who do you work for?" She leaned back in her chair. Rufus reached out with one of his front paws and tapped her hand, and she turned to him. "You feeling neglected, buddy?" She adjusted her chair so she could scratch his ears. The dog nuzzled up against her, his head against her chest. Brock found himself thinking about what lay under that white cotton blouse…and what it would feel like to do a little nuzzling himself. He caught himself and hoped to God she hadn't noticed him looking. Another sip of water. "I'm freelance. I'm hoping to sell my story to a national publication."

"That sounds great, but what could a journalist possibly find to write about in this corner of the world—especially that could take more than two weeks or that might interest a national publication?"

"I write for environmental magazines—like the ones published by Greenpeace and the Sierra Club. There's a lawsuit going on in the next county over involving a paper mill that's trashing the local water supply. Bunch of dead wildlife, stinky water wells, sick kids, and so forth. Headed to federal court. Somebody's got to talk about these things, or the bad guys get away with it."

Adelaide nodded noncommittally, but he was certain he could see in her beautiful brown eyes that she wasn't as noncommittal as she would have him think. He found himself tamping down the urge to try to pick her up. If things were different, he'd be scrambling to get her on a date for sure. But things weren't different. This was work, and it was important for him to find out what Adelaide knew. And he had to make sure he didn't push too hard doing it. He continued casually. "So, what brings you to the Piney Woods of beautiful East Texas?"

"I'm a chemical engineer. I'm doing some consulting work."

Consulting work? She's not a blabbermouth, that's for sure. "Well, I was hoping I'd run into you again after we met at the rest area today. I realized why you were all suited up when I finally got back here and heard on the local news that there was a fire up at the mill. You work for East-Tex Consolidated?"

She shook her head. "No. I'm a special consultant to the Dallas office of the EPA's on-scene coordinator. I reported as required when I heard the sirens, but the local authorities declined EPA assistance."

"All dressed up and nowhere to go."

She shrugged. "Less work for me."

Betty arrived with their barbecue plates along with a bag of scraps for Rufus. Adelaide and Brock dug into their meals while Rufus gnawed diligently on a pork rib that Betty fished from the bag for him.

He'd called into the office earlier trying to get more details about the explosion besides the public hokum the mill was releasing about a fire in one of the break rooms, but nobody had heard anything besides the official party line. *Right. Exploding napkins.* In between mouthfuls, Brock asked, "So, have you heard anything about the cause of the fire or if any contaminates were released?"

She shook her head. "Not a thing. These events can be nothing. A fire in an admin area that never comes near any hazardous materials...or they can be five-star horror shows that require county-wide evacuations and months—or even years—of cleanup. You never can tell. Since there were no evacuations, maybe it was nothing."

"Or maybe those ecoterrorists at East-Tex Consolidated didn't order any evacuations because they just don't give a damn about any of the people living downwind of the mill and figure the bean counters will sort it out when the cancer cases start showing up."

Adelaide smiled neutrally. "Well, there's that."

Tight-lipped and naturally suspicious. Tough combination. They ate some more. When they finished their meals, Betty cleared their plates and left their checks.

Brock wadded his napkin up and tossed it on the table. "So, what kind of work does a chemical engineer do around here?"

"I look at drainage and water quality." She looked at her check and dug in her purse for her wallet. Brock reached out for the vinyl folder.

"It would be our pleasure to pick up dinner. After all, Rufus here did help himself to your breadbasket."

He felt a tingle run up his arm as his hand brushed hers. He'd been trying hard to ignore the energy between them all night. He wondered if she could feel it, too. If she could, she was doing a good job of disguising it.

She picked up the folder. "Thank you, but that's not necessary. Nice meeting you." She briefly scratched Rufus's ears again. "Good night, pooch."

As she pulled her purse over her shoulder, he caught her eye. He felt a wave of warmth rise in him as she let her eyes linger on his for a couple of beats before she nodded her head and walked to the cash register.

He told himself it must have been his imagination when he thought he caught her sneaking a glance back at him while she waited for the cashier to ring up her check. Catching himself, he shook his head to clear it. *Get your head in the game, pal! You're undercover for the defense in a multimillion-dollar federal lawsuit. Keep your hands in your pockets and do your damn job.*

Waiting until she was well out the door, he tossed some bills on the table and fell in behind her.

CHAPTER 4

ADELAIDE CIRCLED THE courthouse again. *Damn!* The car immediately in front of her took the very last parking space on the county square. Admitting defeat, she headed four blocks down to the bank and parked the Explorer.

As she walked toward the high school, Adelaide found herself looking around for Brock Emerson. Considering what he was writing about, it seemed unlikely he'd miss the monthly community meeting about the water situation.

Despite her best efforts, she hadn't been able to completely rid herself of thoughts of him. Bad enough, he had a great face and was built like Michelangelo's *David*, but he also had a voice like whiskey and warm honey. She reminded herself she was definitely off the market…but what harm could a little fantasy do?

She spotted him with Rufus as she walked up the sidewalk to the high school. Her cheeks warmed as her pulse picked up. As she got closer to the school, she noticed he was visiting with Betty, the waitress from Babe's. And she felt just the tiniest pang of… what? No…not jealousy. Couldn't be. She shook her head. *You are not doing this…you're working. You need to concentrate on all the sick people in this county and find a way to nail the bastards that are killing them, not flirt with some hotshot charmer who probably makes it a point to split before sunup.*

She felt a blast of cool air wash over her as she pulled open the glass door to the auditorium. The space was filling up fast. Four hundred theater-style wooden seats sat in rows running back from the stage. Volunteers from the American Legion were setting up folding chairs, which were filled as soon as they hit the floor. The clang of the metal echoed off the painted cinderblock walls of the auditorium. Adelaide inhaled the smell of hormones, chalk, and day-old laundry that permeates every high school in the world. Tonight, it was blended with the cloying odor of chronic fear and bone-crushing fatigue that clung to the crowd like mildew on an old window unit.

The monthly town meetings had been mandated by the city council in the earlier days of the pollution talk. Attendance at the gatherings had steadily ballooned as word of the drinking water contamination morphed from gossip to fact. Since the lawsuit against East-Tex had been filed, the monthly meetings had become a chance for angry citizens to rail at the plant management, who still vehemently denied any responsibility for the contamination. The mill fire had turbocharged the already-growing anxiety and was blasting attendance to never-before-seen levels.

Addison Raines's firm was Adelaide's client. Raines was the lead litigator for the plaintiffs who had, three months before, filed suit against the parent company of the paper mill.

In the course of her work, Adelaide had gotten to know almost all of the plaintiffs personally. Their stories were heartbreaking and getting worse all the time. Addison was the lawyer, and these were his clients. But they were *her* people. Adelaide was the one who had been working with them for months before coming to stay in Nacogdoches full-time for the past month. Addison came in and out, but he was working out of his office in San Antonio. To the plaintiffs, Adelaide was the local face of their representation.

Like all plaintiffs in pollution cases, these folks were sick and scared and outgunned by a corporation that was killing them. She and Addison were their only real hope of getting clean water and any meaningful medical help. And, like all of the cases she worked on, Adelaide would do every legal thing within her power to help them. She understood their suffering in a way no one else could, and she was determined to help them salvage what they had left and avenge what they could never get back.

Raines had staked out two chairs on the second row for himself and Adelaide, just behind the seats reserved for the mayor and the city council. As she made her way through the crowd to the front of the auditorium, a tall man in a mill uniform jostled her, almost knocking her down as he pushed past her. Struggling to stay on her feet, she snapped, "Hey! Watch where you're going."

The man turned and gave her a nasty sneer. "You're the one who needs to watch yourself. You and Mr. Lawyer-Man."

Before Adelaide could respond, Brock Emerson stepped between them, facing the blond man. His mellow voice took on a razor-like quality. "Nah. The lady's right. You're the one who needs to watch yourself." There was a silent moment of tension. The big guy looked around. He wiped his mouth with the back of his sleeve, bared his crooked teeth in a wicked smile, turned, and walked away. Brock looked Adelaide up and down. "You okay?"

She shook it off, adjusting her suit jacket before she answered. "I'm fine. But thanks for…stepping up." She looked him over. He was decked out in cowboy boots, blue jeans, and a snug black T-shirt. The shirt featured a cartoon of a smiling Earth and read, Don't Be Trashy. His firm pecs were outlined through the shirt. She caught herself and hoped to hell he hadn't noticed her looking. *Stop ogling him!*

He smiled at her like they'd known each other since kindergarten. "What's a nice chemical engineer like you doing in a place like this?"

"Working." She reached her row and stowed her briefcase and bag. As she leaned past him, she caught a whiff of something spicy and woodsy…and very male. "Cute shirt," she managed.

He smiled and held her eyes with his. She was a sucker for blue eyes.

"Glad you like it." He looked around. "And how do you figure into this zoo?"

She swallowed hard. Brock Emerson caused a lump in her throat every single time he got near her. And, no matter how hard she tried to make it clear she wasn't interested, he wasn't taking the hint. Maybe because, as much as she wanted to deny it, she *was* interested…*way* more interested than could possibly be good for her. She reminded herself she'd dropped out of the dating scene for a reason. *They're either shameless players or want to marry Dolly Domestic.*

"I'm an expert witness for the plaintiffs."

He raised an eyebrow. "Well, don't I feel like an idiot, rambling on about the litigation over dinner. I never had any idea…"

She straightened her blouse. "Don't worry about it. It wouldn't have been appropriate for me to discuss the case."

Brock looked over toward Addison Raines. "Is that the lead litigator from Raines & Raines?"

She followed his gaze. "One and the same."

"I've been hoping for an interview. Could you introduce me?"

She shrugged and gave him a "suit yourself" look. "I'll be happy to introduce you, but I can tell you now—he's not big on the press."

"Never say die. I'll take what I can get."

Adelaide cut down the row and made her way around to Raines. Brock followed. When she found a decent break in the conversation, she made the introductions then added, "I met Brock at Babe's last night when his dog jumped on my table."

Brock shook his head. "Rufus needs some work on his manners."

She spied a white dog hair on his shoulder and, without thinking, plucked it off while she said, "Speaking of, where is the beast?" Adelaide had to admit the little bread hog was pretty cute.

With a wry smile, he checked his shoulder for more hairs and then locked eyes with Adelaide again. "Betty from the diner is watching him just outside, trying to teach him what fork to use." Suddenly aware of the lawyer and the mayor, Adelaide cleared her throat.

Brock surveyed the room. "Looks like you're drawing a crowd."

The mayor handed him a copy of the agenda. Shaking his head sadly, he said, "There's more every month. The calls to the citizen hotline at city hall are off the charts."

Adelaide nodded. "I remember the early meetings back in the winter. I used to park right across the street. Tonight, I had to park four blocks down at the bank. I think some folks are parking all the way down at the Winn-Dixie and hiking in."

Brock looked around. "Yeah. I think most of them are here to see what Arthur Wesley has to say about the fire."

The mayor shook his head again. "Poor Arthur. First the lawsuit and now the fire…what an awful time to be in charge of safety and compliance for East-Tex Consolidated. I bet he wishes he and his wife had taken his EPA pension and moved to Alaska after he retired last year."

Just then a rail-thin woman tapped Adelaide on the shoulder.

Adelaide turned and saw her sunken face, the dark circles under her eyes, and the turban she wore over her bald head.

"I was hoping to catch you tonight."

Adelaide gently squeezed the woman's frail arm and stepped aside with her. "Hey, Grace. How're you doing? Dan told me you were having a hard time with the new chemo."

Grace nodded. "They started it last week. It's rough, but the doctor thinks it may help. The insurance company is refusing to pay for the new anti-nausea medicine. Do you think Mr. Raines could make a call for me? I can't get anywhere with them and neither can the doctor's office. I'm so sick, I can hardly eat at all."

Adelaide smiled. "Damn straight we'll call them. We'll get on it first thing in the morning." Opening her briefcase, she extracted a folder and rummaged through its contents as she spoke. "Now, you're seeing Dr. Voss, right?"

Grace nodded. Adelaide pulled out a form and fished a pen out of her jacket pocket. "I'm sure Addison already has a HIPPA release for you, but let's just get another one so he doesn't have to dig through the files in the morning. Dr. Voss's receptionist can be pretty tough on rule-following."

Grace smiled weakly and signed her name with a shaky hand. Adelaide put her arm around the woman and gave her a gentle squeeze. "I'll text you after Addison makes that call in the morning. If he's tied up, I'll make sure one of the staff attorneys does it." As she tucked the form back into her briefcase, she saw Brock watching her...with those cobalt eyes. Damn it. She needed to concentrate on the meeting. There were many more clients here who would have come specifically to get her to help them with individual problems. Plus, she needed to help Raines dissect the technical babble coming from the mill about the fire. No matter how good-looking and charming Brock Emerson was, she had work to do, and she didn't need any distractions.

"Well, Brock, thanks for stopping to say hello, but I'm going to have to ask you to excuse us. We need to get situated for the meeting."

Brock nodded and smiled. "Sure. No problem." He turned to shake hands with Raines and the mayor. "I'd love to interview you gentlemen for my article. It could be a great opportunity to shine a national light on what East-Tex Consolidated has done to your town and your clients." With that, he handed them business cards then walked to the back of the auditorium and took a seat, but not before he casually placed his hand on Adelaide's back as he squeezed by her. She was sure she could feel a heated imprint of his hand long after he walked away.

The mayor looked at the card and shook his head. "Jeez. Now we've got an out-of-town reporter sniffing around. Just what we need to boost those falling property values—a national piece about what a toxic wasteland Pine Grove is. As if things weren't bad enough, the plant has to practically explode before our very eyes. You could hear those alarms halfway to Dallas. I left the store and went straight out there when I heard them. Those bozos wouldn't let me in. One of the deputies actually threatened to arrest me if I crossed that barricade they had set up."

Adelaide nodded her head. "You're in good company. Some no-neck bully named Jackson threatened me, too."

Raines shook his head in disgust and then turned to Adelaide. "Did you hear anything from Brett Pierce about the air quality samples they took yesterday?"

She shrugged. "Yeah. We talked late last night. The samples our guys took from the helicopter were clear. Same for samples from some local monitoring stations. Whatever set off those alarms was dissipated before the OSC helicopter got on scene."

Arthur Wesley walked up and shook hands with Adelaide and the two men. The mayor glanced down at the agenda, did a double take, and looked up at Wesley.

"Arthur, why in the world is Darren Blackwood doing the piece on the fire? You're the safety and compliance officer—the one with the technical degrees. Why are we going to listen to Darren Blackwood toe the party line when you could actually explain to us what's going on?"

Wesley shrugged, jammed his hands in his trouser pockets, and looked at his shoes. "Darren's the plant manager. If Corporate decides he's the one to do the dog-and-pony show, he's the one to do it. Between you, me, and the lamppost, Corporate would just as soon that I was on an extended assignment in Zimbabwe tonight, but Darren asked me to be here, so I'm here."

Raines looked over his shoulder at the burgeoning crowd. "He seems like a nice enough guy. Sometimes I don't know how he lives with himself."

Adelaide was stunned. "Arthur, you mean to tell me Darren Blackwood is going to answer to the city council about the fire without a presentation from the chief safety and compliance officer for the mill?"

He nodded. "That's the deal."

"Please tell me at least you prepped the technical portions of the presentation. Darren has a frigging accounting degree from Lamar State. He doesn't know the difference between an organic compound and an organic carrot."

Arthur Wesley gave her an ironic smile. "What technical portions? I guess I would have had to prep them—if there were any. But since there aren't, my services were not required. What I *can* tell you is that I am honored to have the privilege of supervising safety and compliance for a corporation that always places the health of its workers and the safety of the communities surrounding its plants ahead of profits." He rolled his eyes at his own sarcasm.

Adelaide shook her head in disbelief. "Those pinheads have one of the top environmental engineers in the country on staff, and they send some yahoo bean counter to hoodwink the community about how they didn't almost turn us into Three Mile Island yesterday. Honestly, Arthur, I don't know how you stand them."

He shrugged. "Oh, Adelaide, it's always a pleasure to be part of the effort at East-Tex Consolidated, where we are working hard today to make a better tomorrow," he said, sardonically quoting a local public service announcement for East-Tex.

The mayor checked his watch and buttoned his suit coat.

"If you good people will excuse me, I need to get this show on the road."

Adelaide moved to take her seat. Before she sat down, she snuck a casual glance toward the back of the auditorium—telling herself she was just looking to see if Grace had stayed for the meeting or gone on home—when she just happened to spy Brock Emerson. He'd apparently been watching her. When they made eye contact, he winked. She felt a zap of awareness sizzle through her veins and groaned inwardly at her own foolishness.

CHAPTER 5

MAYOR ELIAS CASE climbed the steps up to the stage and assumed the podium. He thanked everyone for their attendance and introduced the plant manager. Several boos were heard from the crowd. Darren Blackwood walked up to the microphone. He was a tall, skinny, middle-aged man who was showing the signs of strain. He had dark circles under his eyes and carried himself with the slumped posture of the truly exhausted.

Blackwood's voice was a defeated monotone. Brock was reminded of the grainy old films of POWs in Vietnam reciting false confessions in robotic voices emanating from expressionless faces bearing hopeless, blank stares.

Blackwood went on to sing the same old tired song about the paper napkins and the coffeepot. Then he summed up with some happy spin about how well the mill had handled the whole situation. *What a bush-league operation. These idiots have been running that same riff, almost word for word, to anyone who would listen since the damn fire started.*

Not surprisingly, the auditorium erupted as citizens shouted their inquiries at the stage. *Why do clients do stupid crap that makes their lives just that much harder?*

Blackwood stared out into the angry crowd with a bewildered

look, cleared his throat, and spoke softly into the mic. "I'm sorry I won't have time for questions tonight." With that, he exited through wings of the stage and disappeared.

Brock watched as Adelaide leaned over and whispered something to Raines. The woman was no dummy. No doubt, she realized what a can of ham it was. Her long black hair fell over her shoulders as she shifted back in her seat. He imagined himself running his hands through that hair, feeling its silky softness as he… His reverie was interrupted by shouts for Arthur Wesley that echoed through the room.

Wesley had been born and raised two counties over. By placing a qualified engineer with EPA credentials and local roots in charge of safety and compliance at the plant, East-Tex had hoped to quell growing community outrage against the mill. Apparently, even Arthur Wesley couldn't stop East-Tex Consolidated's unrelenting quest for the almighty dollar.

Wesley didn't take the stage but stood and faced the crowd. He spoke loudly, without the mic.

"Ladies and gentlemen, I am so sorry to tell you that I have not been authorized by my employer to participate in the presentation tonight. So I won't be able to answer your questions. I know you folks are worried, and I don't blame you. As the safety and compliance officer for the mill, I am in charge of conducting our own internal investigation as to the cause of the fire and filing all of the resulting reports with EPA. By way of a public service message, I would like to point out that every bit of information that EPA has about the fire—and the mill in general—is public record. As citizens, you can obtain that information simply by going to the agency's website and making a Freedom of Information Act request for all of their data regarding any aspect of mill operations you want."

A ripple of interested chatter spread through the crowd at the mention of the FOIA requests. When it died down, Wesley, unable to completely disguise his regret, said, "I wish I could do more for you folks tonight, but that's all I can say right now."

With that, he turned and sat back down in his chair. As he did, a tall man in the back with white-blond hair yelled out, "Tree hugger." A burly man with a long black beard sitting next to him shouted, "Turncoat!" As the hecklers gathered steam, several other men wearing clothes with mill logos stood and started waving their agendas and shouting at Wesley.

"Don't forget which team you're on!"

"Shut up before you get us all fired!"

"Get out of town!"

The mayor scurried to the stage and spoke into the microphone.

"Gentlemen, take your seats immediately or leave this meeting! We are here to learn information, not threaten our fellow citizens. I will not allow this problem to turn us against each other. Being frustrated is not an excuse for thuggery."

The group of men stormed out the back doors of the auditorium. The crowd eventually quieted down after the doors swung shut behind the rabble-rousers.

The mayor introduced a professor of public health from Lamar University in Beaumont. His message was clear—if it comes out of a tap in Fairfield County, don't touch it. When the man left the podium, the mayor stepped back up.

"Well, folks, that about does it for this month's town hall meeting. Before we go tonight, we need to get through the Families in Need list."

The crowd fell silent. Mayor Case called on a local clergyman. Reverend Billy Henderson from the First Baptist Church came forward. He adjusted his reading glasses and cleared his throat. "Please help us, Dear Lord. Here goes with tonight's list…"

The list went on for what seemed like an eternity. Brock had been showing up at these meetings for several months, always in a different disguise—strolling among the crowd, eavesdropping on conversations, clandestinely assessing and reporting on local sentiment—even before he and his journalist persona had been put on the job full-time three weeks ago. Brock was part owner in InfoGlobal Investigations—not to mention its star undercover operative—and East-Tex was one of their biggest accounts. He hated to knock any team he was on, but any idiot could see the number of folks with sick family members was growing. Brock was hardly a sentimentalist, but the monthly reading of the Families in Need list would have been heartbreaking to Attila the Hun.

When you looked around that auditorium, it was impossible not to at least wonder if the mill had something to do with it. The whole damn town was getting sick. He'd worked these jobs for ages, and he had always been on board with the party line. But now, after Milwaukee, he kept wondering if he was on the right side. He cleared his head. A job is a job…do it and get paid. But he still hoped to hell this misery wasn't his client's fault. He didn't think he could bear being a party to all the suffering of the families in need.

After the reverend finished his list, the mayor thanked everyone for coming and closed the meeting. When Adelaide and Addison Raines stood from their seats, Brock made his way toward them as casually as possible. Various of their clients congregated around Raines to discuss the night's events. Others descended on Adelaide with more requests for help, just as the woman she called Grace had done earlier. She carefully made notes of each of their issues on her legal pad and promised them return calls or emails as soon as she could get to their problem. Her voice was calm and reassuring, and she was patient with even the most difficult and needy of the clients. *Jesus. She's beautiful, decent, kind…and I'm hustling her like some mark in a Ponzi scheme.* What the hell had happened to him? What had he become?

After visiting with the last client requesting her help, Adelaide edged toward a group of citizens who seemed to know Arthur

Wesley or his family. Gathered around him in a tight knot, they peppered him with questions about the fire. Discreetly, Brock sidled up where he could hear better. He noticed Adelaide doing the same while pretending to listen to the clients chatter at Raines. Wesley was circumspect and vague while being as sympathetic and understanding as possible.

A woman Brock recognized as Darren Blackwood's assistant worked her way up to Wesley. She put her hand on his elbow and took him aside. They were still where Brock could hear them. He watched as Adelaide casually adjusted her position to improve her reception. She needed to work on her technique, but she wouldn't be half-bad as an undercover. Brilliant, beautiful women with balls and field skills were hard to find.

Blackwood's assistant looked upset as she cleared her throat. "Sir, I'm sorry to bother you. Mr. Blackwood has asked me to tell you that he needs you to cover the senior staff meeting in the morning. I don't know any details, but I'm guessing that his son has taken a turn."

Wesley winced. "Of course. I'll handle it. Just let me check my schedule. I may need you to cancel something for me." He pulled an old-fashioned burgundy-leather appointment book out of his shirt pocket. He flipped to the proper page and shook his head. "No. I'm good. I don't have anything until later tomorrow afternoon when I'm meeting with the contractors about the fire damage. Does Darren want me to call him when I get out of here?"

"No, sir. He said something about the ICU, and I don't think they let anyone have cell phones in there. I just told him that I would get it handled, and he hung up."

"Can you email me that PowerPoint we worked on in his office this afternoon? I'll need that."

"Certainly, sir. I'll take care of it as soon as I get to a computer." With that, she was gone.

Apparently, the local townspeople gathered around Wesley had heard the exchange as well as Brock had.

An older woman shook her head. "I feel so sorry for that child. He's got the seizures and the leukemia."

A middle-aged woman with a helmet hairdo said, "I can't imagine how Darren works for those people. He knows good and darn well what that plant is doing to all of us—it's killing his own son, plain and simple."

A younger woman holding a baby chimed in. "Well, good, bad, or indifferent, that's how he's getting health insurance for that child. If, God forbid, my kid had cancer, I'd work for the devil if it was the only way I could get his treatment."

Helmet Hair spoke again. "Don't get too excited about that insurance. My husband used to work over there. That coverage they're so proud of is almost worthless. What I hear is that about half the cancer claims are being denied outright."

Brock watched out of the corner of his eye as Raines approached Adelaide with his briefcase in his hand. He leaned over to whisper near her ear.

Adelaide picked up her purse and briefcase and led the lawyer to the door. Brock edged closer and followed discreetly. Several clients tried to stop them for chitchat, but Adelaide kept walking while calling them each by name. She politely told them that their attorney had a pressing prior commitment and invited them to call her cell the next day. *This woman must have the patience of Job.* No matter how many plaintiffs descended on her, she patiently answered each one as she cut a swath through the crowd for Raines. Using the crowd for cover, Brock quickly made his way to Betty and retrieved Rufus, all the while being certain he was in position to follow when Adelaide and Raines came outside.

When they were successfully clear of the building, he fell in a safe distance behind them. They stopped at Raines's sleek new Range Rover. It was parked on the street, right across from the high school. Brock subtly positioned himself behind a tree and listened. He could make out Adelaide's voice clearly.

"Great parking space."

"Yeah. I got here early to see Case. I wanted to pitch the suit to him before the city council vote next week." Raines checked his watch. "Do you want me to drive you to your car?"

He was clearly in a rush to get wherever he was going. Adelaide must have picked up on that, too. She said, "No, thanks. I'm just down this street. You go on. I'll talk to you tomorrow."

"Thanks." The lawyer slung his briefcase into the passenger seat, climbed in the car, and pulled away.

Brock stayed behind the tree as Adelaide watched the big silver SUV vanish down the main street. Then he followed a block behind as she walked to her car. He was on the clock. He was being paid to find out what Adelaide Reese was up to, and he intended to earn his fees.

But as he watched her graceful form silhouetted against the night by the streetlights, he realized there was more to it tonight than just the job. He didn't like the looks of those rabble-rousers at the high school. The white-haired jerk who had intentionally shoved into Adelaide before the meeting started was one of them...

He increased his pace and shortened the gap between them.

CHAPTER 6

THE NIGHT WAS hot and still. Despite the oppressive heat, Adelaide needed the walk to clear her head. The town hall meetings always made her tense. She found herself thinking about Brock Emerson and his tight T-shirts and snug-fitting jeans. Truth be told, she was thinking more about what was *underneath* the T-shirts and jeans…and how much fun it might be to explore that firsthand. Then she stopped herself—briefly. But she quickly rationalized, what harm could it do to dream? He was a hot guy with strong environmental views and a smart-ass sense of humor. You don't find that every day. A little daydreaming never hurt anyone.

Plus, fantasies of Brock Emerson were a welcome reprieve from thinking about the bastards at the mill. She hated East-Tex's arrogance and atrocious insensitivity. It galled her to sit and listen to them tell bald-faced lies about their misdeeds. How could they not be moved by the lives they were ruining? What about Grace and all those poor folks on the Families in Need list? She knew from her own experience the depth of the damage those chemicals could do to the environment and the people who inhabited it. She'd been one of them. Sometimes all of that seemed like a lifetime ago. But other times—like after listening to the Families in Need list—it seemed like just yesterday.

Tears welled up in her eyes. Adelaide felt their suffering. Their pain was a crushing weight on her heart. She made no effort to avoid feeling it. They were real, live, breathing human beings, and they were suffering for no good reason besides the greed of a corporation that put profits ahead of people.

Sometimes, it made her so mad, she stayed up most of the night thinking of different ways to prove that the mill had done this to the town. She was furious with the thugs in mill uniforms who were so horrid to Arthur Wesley. The big white-blond guy reminded her of the Abominable Snowman. His buddy bore an amazing resemblance to a gorilla. In her mind, she tagged the pair *Yeti* and *Big Foot*.

She turned back and watched people filtering out from the meeting, many of them clients. They made their way to their mostly older-model, worn-out cars. They had the keyed up, exhausted posture of the almost defeated. These were not folks who could wait out the storm at their vacation home in Aspen. She and Addison Raines were their only real hope for a way out.

As she put more physical distance between herself and the meeting, the stress started to ebb away. In no time, she would be back in her room, enjoying a nice bubble bath. As she approached her truck, she was thinking about the chick flick she was planning to watch on the hotel network. Despite her best efforts, images of a certain sexy journalist kept creeping into her thoughts no matter how many times she shooed them away.

To distract her wandering mind from the topic of the handsome Mr. Emerson, she stopped to admire a beautiful antique vase in the window of a consignment shop. She squinted to read the price tag through the glass.

"Lookie here, boys. It's Little Miss Smarty Pants."

As she turned toward the voice, the white-blond guy from the meeting stepped right in front of her. Only this time, instead of waving around his meeting agenda, he was wielding a knife.

His gorilla buddy emerged from the shadows and stepped to her side. Another one of the rowdies came up right behind her. She was surrounded. Her heart raced, and her mouth went dry. A pang of fear shot through the pit of her stomach.

"You and your lawyer pal are going to put us all out of work," Big Foot said as he moved up against her.

The third guy grabbed her from behind, bear-hug style, and lifted her off her feet. He had one hand over her mouth. She gagged from the taste of sweat and grime as he pulled her into a nearby alley. Pure, distilled terror rode an adrenaline luge as it screamed through every fiber of her nervous system. She fought to grasp what was happening, but panic was decimating every rational thought.

Big Foot got right up in her face. She could smell cigarettes and beer on his breath. Yeti, clearly the leader, stepped up and grabbed her hair, pulling her head back and exposing her neck. He put the knife to her throat. Her heart slammed against her chest wall as every detail stood out to her—the glint of the blade, the cold feel of the knife against her throbbing carotid, the tiny droplets of spittle oozing out of the corner of the awful man's fleshy lips. A deep primal rage rose in her chest like molten lava while her pulse roared in her ears. She struggled to stay as calm as possible. *Concentrate on surviving. Panic later.*

Yeti's mouth was next to her ear. She could feel his breath like mustard gas burning her skin when he spoke. "Yeah. You tell him if he knows what's good for him, he better get in his fancy Range Rover and drive himself back to Dallas. And he better take you with him."

Big Foot chimed in. "I need my job just like everyone else in this town does. You get that mill shut down, we're all going to be screwed."

Yeti was wild-eyed and sweating, high on the adrenaline rush. He was big and dumb and crazy and flanked by his pals. A bad combination. He ran the tip of the knife down the front of her throat to her chest and drew it to the top of her left breast. He groped her with his free hand as he whispered in her ear, "Or something real bad might happen to both of you."

Big Foot continued. "You both get out of our town and quit making trouble where you're not welcome. Stick around, and you might just end up having an accident like Mayor Johnson."

The third guy holding her from behind spoke for the first time. She could feel his chest moving against her back as he talked.

"Maybe we should teach her a lesson right now...do something to show Raines how serious we are."

Big Foot looked to Yeti. "Yeah, Raines's going to put us all in the poorhouse while he makes the big bucks. I hate rich assholes. I say we show that hotshot lawyer we mean business."

In that moment, she knew with certainty she was going to be hurt, maybe killed. Surrendering to survive was no longer an option. She was going to have to fight to save herself.

Adelaide went limp. The change in her body posture surprised her captor, causing him to momentarily loosen his grip. When he did, she elbowed him in the ribs. As she heard the sound of the breath leaving his chest, she scraped her shoe down his shin and stomped his instep. He screamed in pain and released her.

But no sooner was she free than Big Foot grabbed her by the throat and dragged her to the ground. Straddling her, he began to choke her. Glowing red dots appeared in her field of vision as the overwhelming, all-encompassing fear of asphyxiation enveloped her. She grabbed one of his fingers as he clutched her throat. Once in her grasp, she began to hyperextend his right index finger toward the back of his hand. He screamed in pain.

Yeti spotted what was happening and grabbed her wrists, prying her hand loose from Big Foot's finger. He grabbed both of her arms and pulled them over her head, pinning her wrists to the concrete. Deprived of air, she couldn't scream.

Adelaide saw more flashes of neon red and blue dots before

her vision tunneled down to nothing but the sight of Big Foot's face, twisted with rage, looking down at her.

Then, a shadowy form emerged from behind Big Foot. It appeared to be flying through the air. She thought she might be hallucinating. She heard a scream and the pressure on her neck released. She greedily gasped the rush of air into her lungs. Then, her arms were free. Still addled from the oxygen debt, she rolled clear of the melee and scrambled to a sitting position, clutching her bruised neck.

As her vision cleared, she saw Rufus with Big Foot's ear clenched between his teeth. The third man appeared to be unconscious on the ground. Brock Emerson had Yeti by the front of his shirt. He slammed the huge man into the wall and swept his legs out from under him. Yeti fell to the ground.

Before Brock could stop him, the blond monster recovered the knife he had been holding to Adelaide's throat and began swinging the blade, stabbing at Brock. Brock kicked him repeatedly in the ribs until Yeti dropped the knife and fell back against the pavement, gasping for air.

Brock grabbed Adelaide's hand and pulled her to her feet. He whistled for Rufus as he scooped up Adelaide's purse and briefcase off the ground and dragged her down the block toward her truck. Regaining her footing, she followed as Brock ran toward the SUV. She looked over her shoulder and saw Yeti scramble to his feet and stagger toward them. Big Foot and the third guy were following close behind. The fob in her purse automatically unlocked the doors when she grabbed the handle. Rufus jumped in and leaped straight into the back of the Explorer. Brock threw himself into the passenger seat and slammed the door, shouting, "Go, go, go!"

Fear crackled through her body like lightning in a bottle. Her hands shook as she pushed the ignition button, and just as Yeti lunged for her door handle, she threw the car into gear and sped away.

CHAPTER 7

ADELAIDE RACED OUT of town and straight onto the interstate. "Call nine-one-one. We'll stop to meet them when we get somewhere I can pull over."

Nine-one-one? Not good. "Let's hold off on the cops right now. First, we've got to concentrate on getting somewhere safe. Just stay on this road while I think it through."

Whimpering, Rufus crawled back over the seat and into Brock's lap. He began licking Brock's shirt and scratching furiously on the seat. The dog became more and more agitated, trying to stick his head between Brock and the seat back. As Brock tried to wrestle Rufus into his lap, he felt something wet on the dog's face. He flipped on the map light.

"Oh, God! He's bleeding. His face is covered in blood. The albino must have cut him."

Brock's heart pounded as he thought of losing his best friend. He was used to the risks of undercover work. He took those chances willingly. But Rufus…he didn't have those choices.

Adelaide tried to keep her eyes on the road. "What do you want me to do?"

He looked around frantically, checking for anyone following them. "Pull over. I've got to get out so I can see how bad it is."

The seconds seemed like hours as Adelaide pulled the car onto the shoulder and turned on the emergency flashers while Rufus squirmed and whimpered. Brock handed her the leash hooked to Rufus's collar. "Stay where you are. Hold this in case he tries to follow me. I'm going to get out. Let's get him in my seat so I can check him over."

Adelaide took the leash. As Brock opened the door and got out of the SUV, the truck's interior lights flashed on. Struggling to control the dog, he saw a large bloodstain on the tan seat back where he had been sitting. He looked down, checking himself and saw an equally large crimson stain on the side of his shirt. Rufus was pulling on the leash, barking and licking at the bloody spot.

Adelaide followed his gaze. "The blood's yours, not Rufus's."

He pulled up his shirt to reveal a cut about four inches long running along his right side, just about even with the base of his rib cage. *Crap.* The adrenaline had masked the pain since the scene in the alley, but now that Brock was aware of it, the cut felt like flaming napalm running down his side.

Adelaide quickly tied Rufus's leash to the steering wheel. She grabbed her flashlight from under the seat, jumped out of the truck, and ran around the hood to Brock. Turning on the Maglite, she examined the wound. He craned his neck to see. It was a fairly deep cut. But it didn't appear to have made it past the rib cage.

"We need to slow down the bleeding. Let me help you out of your T-shirt. We can use it to put pressure on the wound." She helped him peel the shirt over his head. He watched her work. Her hands were rock steady as she folded the shirt and pressed it against the gash. She sure didn't crater in a crunch. On the contrary, she had put up one hell of a fight in that alley, and she was getting the job done here as well.

Forcing himself to take his eyes off Adelaide, he studied the wound. Though it wasn't life-threatening, blood oozed around the

T-shirt. *Crap. This is just going to add fuel to the fire about calling nine-one-one.*

She pulled the front door of the SUV open as far as it would go. "Get in and I'll recline the seat."

His head was swimming, and he was feeling unsteady on his feet. He slid into the seat without argument. Satisfied he was settled, Adelaide ran back to the driver's door and quickly untied Rufus's leash from the steering wheel. The dog stood on the console, licking Brock's face. Weakly, he whistled. "Back seat, Rufus. Back seat." The dog reluctantly jumped off the console. Standing on the floor of the back seat, he rested his paws on the console, staring at Brock.

Back in the driver's seat, Adelaide started the engine and pressed the link button on her console. When the Ford Sync operator answered through her car speakers, Adelaide said, "I need directions to the nearest hospital sent to my GPS."

"Stand by." Momentarily, the GPS dinged and showed that the directions were ready to begin guidance. "Do you want me to dispatch an ambulance to your coordinates?"

Ambulance? Damn, damn, damn. Brock used the armrest to pull himself upright. The pain was remarkable, but he had to put a stop to this ambulance business—and fast. He cleared his throat to steady his voice. "No, thank you, ma'am. Those directions'll do fine. We could just use a little first aid. Have a good evening." With that, he reached up and hit the end button on the control panel. It felt like liquid lightning was pouring down his side, but he had to get control of the situation and he had to do it now. "No hospital."

Bathed in shadow from the yellow interior lights of the truck, Adelaide looked confused. "What do you mean, *no hospital?* You've been stabbed in a knife fight where I was attacked by a gang. We need to get you to an ER and call the cops."

He struggled to keep his voice casual. "Nonsense." He lifted the bloody T-shirt and checked the wound. "I was cut more than I was stabbed. The packing has slowed the bleeding down to a trickle. It looks a lot worse than it is. If you take me to a hospital, I'm part of this story instead of reporting on it."

"This is absurd. Who cares about the story at this point?"

He decided to work the professional responsibility angle. "I do. This is my living we're talking about."

"At the very least, you should have a tetanus shot. Anyway, it's best you get checked out to be sure nothing vital has been damaged. Then we'll call the cops."

He groped for an angle that would work. He recalled her telling Raines about the run-in with Jackson at the fire. *She already thinks the Fairfield County government is colluding with the plant… and she's probably right.* "Do you really think the Fairfield County sheriff's office is going to help us? They're tied up with that plant in more ways than any of us will ever know."

"Fine. We call them anyway. If they don't do anything, we call the Rangers. This is an assault with a deadly weapon. On both of us. We could have been killed."

He had to act fast…do something to derail the cops/ambulance/hospital plan. Any of that would involve ID, and that would blow his cover. The Brock Emerson persona would disappear like a puff of smoke in a tornado. He was in no shape to drive, and he couldn't let her into his hotel room—*there's always a chance some stupid detail you missed will come back to bite you in the ass.*

"Look, I'll make a deal with you. Take me back to your hotel. We'll get me cleaned up and then think it through. Besides, there's a real hospital in Nacogdoches—not like that quack shack in Pine Grove the GPS is trying to take us to."

He lifted the bloody shirt off the wound again. The bleeding had almost stopped.

Adelaide shook her head. "This seems outright crazy to me.

But you're a grown man, and you can make your own decisions. We'll do it your way."

Breathing a silent sigh of relief, he looked at her. Even in mind-bending pain, cut open and bleeding late at night on this damn country road, he couldn't keep from noticing she was beautiful. He smiled a crooked smile as he slumped back on the seat. "Doing it my way… That's the kind of thinking I like."

He spent most of the drive to her hotel trying to formulate a plan. As long as he was with Adelaide, he had to stay out of anywhere that would involve showing ID. He had long suspected that the sheriff in Pine Grove was in cahoots with the mill, though nobody they were dealing with at East-Tex would admit it. What the various players on that side of things knew about his identity was anybody's guess. Any way you sliced it, though, he couldn't count on some yokel deputy not blowing his cover. Beyond that, the ER was out of the question. That meant ID and insurance cards and all kinds of identifying information, and the system had been designed so there was no good way to circumvent that.

He'd have to do some first aid in the hotel and wait until he could get off by himself to get stitched up and dosed with some serious antibiotics…and then he'd hunt those assholes from the alley down and make sure they understood who they were screwing with. But in order to get to that point, he'd just have to play the next few hours by ear—and he absolutely had to make for damn sure he didn't pass out or do anything else to give Adelaide any hint of a reason to start dialing nine-one-one.

Twenty minutes after they sped away from the alley, Adelaide pulled the truck into the parking lot of the Swiss Chateau Inn & Suites.

"I'm pulling up to the side entrance. We can hardly walk through the lobby with a dog and both of us covered in blood."

He straightened up in the seat. "It doesn't look like the place is exactly crawling with guests tonight."

Adelaide parked as close to the door as possible. They sat in the truck for a couple of minutes to check out any movement in the parking lot or around the side entrance to the hotel. When they didn't see so much as another soul, he said, "Let's make a break for it." Adelaide grabbed her purse and briefcase. Brock whistled for Rufus, who jumped over the console and hopped out the door after his master. Adelaide followed them through the glass door into the back hallway of the hotel.

After a few quick, long strides, they were inserting Adelaide's key card into the magnetic lock. A green light blinked as the mechanism clicked and the door opened. Adelaide tossed her purse and briefcase onto the luggage rack.

"Go get in the shower, aim the spray above the injury and let lukewarm water run over the wound. Lather up some of that Dial bath soap. It's antibacterial. I have a first aid kit in the back of the truck. I'll go get it." She snatched up her key card and left the room.

She returned shortly and knocked on the bathroom door.

"I'll be right out. This soap hurts like hell."

In a couple of minutes, Brock opened the door to the bathroom with a towel wrapped around his waist. He was holding a hotel washcloth to the wound.

He found himself studying the look on her face. He was pretty sure she liked what she saw, but he couldn't be certain. *I bet she's a hell of a poker player.*

Adelaide eyed his side. "How's the bleeding?"

"It seems to have slowed down since I got out from under the water."

Pulling on some vinyl gloves from the first aid kit, she bent over to take a closer look. She put her hand on the washcloth, briefly brushing his. The contact was charged, even through the vinyl. He was sure she felt it, too, but she never let on. She carefully peeled the washrag back from the wound.

"The way the injury is positioned, every time you move, you're going to open it up again. You need stitches."

He jockeyed for a better view in the mirror and took another look at the cut. "I'm not so sure about that. I've had some experience with this."

Adelaide cocked a brow. "You been in a lot of knife fights?"

"I was with a crew from my college newspaper that was in New Orleans right after Katrina. We had disaster health-and-safety training before we went in. The whole place was rife with debris—most of it sharp. We were getting cut and scraped up all the time. The rule was, if you can't see muscle, bone, or fat, if the edges of the wound are not ragged, if ten minutes of pressure stops the bleeding, and if it's less than a quarter-inch deep, stitches are probably not necessary." He studiously avoided the part about cuts over an inch and a half long or injuries located where the edges won't stay together requiring medical attention. *Better not to get bogged down in details.*

He moved to study the wound more closely in the dresser mirror. "The pigsticker that redneck used must have been pretty damn sharp. These edges are almost completely straight. And I don't see the rib or any fat."

She rolled her eyes. "It's not like there's an ounce of excess fat on you anywhere, so that doesn't really count."

He smiled. "So you're noticing my body fat percentage... hmmm."

She shook her head, but he could see her cheeks color. "Forget I said anything."

He cleared his throat. "Let's just bandage it up tight and see how I do for a couple of hours. No need to rush into anything that may not be necessary."

She straightened up. "I think that's a really bad idea. But if you insist, there's nothing I can do about it."

Adelaide opened the first aid kit and went to work. She held up a single-use bottle of alcohol. "Okay, tough guy, I've got to sterilize the wound and it's not gonna be pleasant. If you'd let me take you to the hospital, they could give you an anesthetic."

He was trying for casual, but he knew this next part was going to hurt like a sonofagun. "It's not a big deal."

She poured the alcohol onto the wound and then wiped the excess off with a gauze pad. She kept pouring and wiping until the small bottle was empty. The alcohol burned like sulfuric acid every time it hit the cut. Opening a tube of antibiotic ointment, she slathered it on the gash then covered it with large gauze pads and miles of tape. Finished, she stepped back to inspect her work. "It's not great, but it's the best I can do here with what we have to work with. You really should see a doctor and get some antibiotics. I don't even want to think about what was on that knife."

The infection risk was real, but it could be handled in the next twelve hours or so. Sooner was better, but that wasn't his most pressing problem. Right now, he needed to get the bleeding under control so he could get himself mobile. The damn irony of this was killing him—*I've spent weeks trying to find a way into her room, and now I'm here and all I can think of is getting out.*

"If I had one of those elastic back supports, I could use it to help hold the bandage in place and keep me from moving wrong."

She tossed the exam gloves in the waste basket. "There's an all-night Walgreens down the road. I can be back in half an hour."

The walls were turning to liquid and his body was going all rubbery. "I'd go myself, but I'm feeling a little woozy." He thought of Dali's melting pocket watches as he grabbed for the counter to steady himself.

She reached out to him. "We better get you in bed before you fall."

He put his left arm around her shoulder and leaned against her, feeling her taut body pressed along his side. Even with the floor moving under his feet, he wasn't too far gone not to realize how good her body felt next to his. When they reached the bed, he eased himself down, struggling not to engage his obliques.

Reaching for his wrist, she took his pulse. "You've lost a lot of blood. We better get you some fluids."

She pulled a bottle of water out of the little refrigerator and handed it to him. "Here. Drink this. Meanwhile, I'm going to help you elevate your legs."

While he drank the water, Adelaide stacked pillows from the bed and a cushion from the reading chair. When he finished the water, she helped him lie back and lifted his legs onto the pile of pillows.

"Are you still dizzy?"

The world around him was returning to a solid state. "It seems to have passed."

She looked around. "Where's your phone?"

"I think it's in my backpack on the counter in the bathroom. Could you just bring me the whole thing?"

She retrieved the battered canvas bag and set it on the bed. Using a pen from the desk drawer, she scribbled her cell phone number down and handed it to him.

"Here. I'm going to the drugstore. You better stay lying down."

"Can you grab me something to wear? T-shirt, sweatpants… whatever they have. I don't want to put that bloody stuff back on. And Rufus must be hungry. Do you mind getting him a couple of cans of whatever they've got?"

She nodded. "If you get worse, I strongly recommend calling nine-one-one. We're at the end of what I know to do for you." She handed him another bottle of water.

As she headed out the door in her perfectly fitted jeans, he couldn't help thinking Adelaide Reese was a woman who looked good from every angle.

Gingerly, he slid his backpack over from the edge of the bed. He slowly pawed through it until he found the small pillbox with a couple of Vicodin. After he had gutted it out for six days following a back injury while he was working a case, he always made for damn sure he had an emergency stash of pain meds with him when he was undercover. He swallowed one and looked around.

He really wanted to search the room. When he rolled to get out of bed, his side felt like the San Andreas fault splitting wide open. He would have powered through the pain, but the bleeding started again in earnest. Slumping back onto the bed, he put pressure on the cut. He'd have to search later. Rufus inched over to his wounded master and gently rested his triangular head on Brock's left thigh. He rubbed behind the dog's soft, pink ears and said, "Don't worry, pal. I'm gonna be okay." *I hope.* The dog wagged his thick tail, thumping it against the bed.

Brock groped in the backpack for the phone. Retrieving it, he hit speed dial. After the third ring, he heard his partner's voice.

"Hey, buddy! What's new in beautiful Pine Grove? How was the monthly bitch-and-boo-hoo session?"

"We've got a complication."

The teasing camaraderie was immediately gone from Vance Shakleton's tone. "Talk to me."

"Some mill employees got out of hand during the meeting and got tossed about halfway through…"

"So? Those meetings are just venting sessions for pissed-off residents. Raines is using them as infomercials to sign up more plaintiffs and pressure the mayor to drag the city into the suit."

"That's not the problem. I was following her on foot after it broke up. She'd parked to hell and gone from the auditorium. Right by the dry cleaner's, three of the troublemakers jumped her—came out of the alley. They were shit-faced drunk…one of them had a knife. They got her down and were getting ready to take turns on her by the time I got to them."

"Jesus H. What'd you do?"

"What the hell do you think I did, Vance?"

His partner snapped, "I don't know. That's why I asked."

"Rufus took out the one on top of her, and I handled the other two."

"You *intervened*? Are you out of your mind?"

"Out of my mind? What the hell did you want me to do? Stand there and let three thugs gang-rape her so I didn't risk blowing my cover? I told you after the job in Wisconsin…I don't trust these people."

Vance was silent for a few beats before Brock heard him take a deep breath. "Listen…you know how I feel about field decisions. You were the guy on the ground. You did what you thought you needed to. I'll back you up on that. But let's not go off half-cocked blaming this on the mill. What makes you so sure these guys were mill employees?"

"Oh, I don't know, Vance. Being a trained detective and all, I considered every available clue…like the mill uniform shirts they were wearing. One of them was the big guy with the white hair that drives Remy around sometimes."

"Look…East-Tex may not be your favorite client these days. I get that, but you can't hold them responsible for what a gang of drunken yahoos did after work. That's just not reasonable."

Brock thought that through and let out an exasperated sigh. "Hell, I don't know. Maybe you're right. It did look pretty spontaneous…like a bunch of drunk rednecks making bad group decisions. I'll give you that. But I just think we should consider backing off this."

"Backing off this? We pull in over half a million dollars a year plus expenses from the East-Tex account. Backing off this is out of the question."

Brock sighed. "Have you heard anything about the cause of the fire?"

Vance cleared his throat. "Yeah, I talked to Darren a few hours ago. Something about a coffeepot."

Brock laughed out loud. "You can't seriously believe that shit about the paper napkins and the coffeepot. Christ, Vance, there was an explosion that rattled windows damn near to Longview. The freaking sirens went off for fifteen minutes. Coffeepot, my ass."

Vance shifted gears. "Are you and the woman okay?"

Brock shook his head in frustration. "Hey, thanks for getting around to that. No, we're not. She's probably pretty bruised up. Far as I could tell, she put up a pretty good fight before Rufus and I got there. But, overall, I think she's good to go. I didn't make out so well."

"What? You're hurt?"

"The guy with the knife slashed me before I was able to disarm him."

"You got cut by a guy who brought a knife to a gun fight?"

"I wasn't carrying. Since the whole place is on edge, the sheriff set up security outside the meeting—had that thug Jackson and some of his henchmen checking bags and wanding people at the door to the auditorium. I didn't want to get into it with them. I left the Glock locked in the truck."

"How bad?"

"About four inches on top of the last floating rib, right side. Cut, not stab. Bled like a bastard, but I've about got it stopped."

"Where are you? I'll send one of the guys—"

"I'm in her hotel room. She's gone to the drugstore for first aid supplies."

Vance laughed. "Her hotel room? Now that's my boy! Best field operative in Texas. Only you could turn a fiasco like this into a chance to get in the subject's hotel room alone. We've spent weeks trying to figure a way in there. What have you found?"

Brock looked around the room. "Nothing, so far. Every time I move, the bleeding starts again…" Then the magnetic lock clicked. "Okay. I gotta go. I'll call you tomorrow." He heard Vance sputtering as he ended the call.

CHAPTER 8

ADELAIDE COULDN'T STOP replaying the attack in her mind. She could have been raped or killed, and Brock had been hurt trying to protect her. She was worried about his injuries. He needed a damn doctor, and he needed one now. But she kept reminding herself that he was an adult. *His decisions are not your responsibility.* Regardless, she couldn't help imagining what would have happened if he hadn't been there. She hustled into the store, gathered the items she needed as quickly as possible, and headed back to the hotel.

As she drove, she tried to block the details of the attack out of her mind, but they kept creeping into her consciousness like roaches slipping through tiny cracks in the baseboards. She grasped the steering wheel to keep her hands from shaking and bit back tears. Her tough-girl routine was falling apart…

She hit the button to call Ava. "Hey, girl! How was the monthly East-Tex jerk-a-thon?"

"It's been a bad night, Ava."

Her friend was instantly serious. "What happened?"

"Some guys from the mill got out of hand at the meeting. The mayor tossed them out. When I was walking to my car, three of them jumped me, said they wanted me to take a message to Addison to get out of town."

Ava gasped. "Jesus, Ad. Where are you right now? I'm pulling on my clothes this second."

Adelaide shook her head. "That's so sweet, but I'll be okay. But that's not all of it. The hot journalist I told you about… He happened by and busted up the party in the alley. He really put a hurt on the assholes from the mill. But one of them cut him in the process. He's got a nasty gash over one of his ribs."

"Holy shit. Are you at the hospital with him?"

"That's just it…yet one more stubborn man. He won't let me take him to the ER. I patched him up in my hotel room. I'm driving back now with stuff from the all-night Walgreens."

"What about you? How are you?"

Adelaide thought about that a minute. "I'm pretty shaken up. The adrenaline's wearing off, and I'm getting a little wobbly. I'll be sore as hell tomorrow, but nothing's bleeding or broken."

"Ad? Are you sure you don't want me to come down there? I can be there in a little over an hour."

"You're great, but I'm okay. I need to get him fixed up, and then I'll worry about what I'm going to do cop-wise. I probably need to talk to Addison about that first. The politics out here are pretty complicated." Adelaide cleared her throat. "Look, I'm back at the hotel. I'm okay. Really. I'll check in with you tomorrow."

She pulled the truck into a parking spot and shoved the gear-shift into Park. Her blouse had the telltale stench of her attackers' body odor and bad breath laced with stale tobacco smoke and cheap beer. She rubbed her bruised and scraped wrists, damaged when Yeti had pinned them to the rough concrete. The interior light came on as she opened the door and gathered her purse and bag. In the rearview mirror, she caught sight of reddish-purple imprints on her neck—souvenirs of Big Foot's rage.

The sight of the bruises shook her. They were tangible evidence of what had happened. Those bastards could have killed her… choked her to death or broken her neck. She grabbed the steering wheel to steady herself as she started to shake. In her mind, she could feel the desperate desire to breathe and the overwhelming sense of helplessness when they were holding her down…

But, as bad as all of that was, Brock had borne the brunt of their rage in the course of protecting her from harm. Now, he was hurt, and she felt an irresistible—maybe unexplainable—urge to help him. *You barely know this guy, and even if you did, you know how this always ends. Get him cleaned up and be on your way with a clear conscience. Don't set yourself up for any more heartache.*

She took a deep breath, gathered her purse and bags from the seat, and got out of the truck. She squared her shoulders and headed for the hotel. Of course she would help him—it went without saying. But she would take care of herself, too…and not just physically. *Be very, very careful,* she told her heart.

She could only hope it was listening.

CHAPTER 9

OPENING THE HOTEL room door as quietly as possible in case Brock had fallen asleep, Adelaide heard his voice. "Okay. I gotta go. I'll call you tomorrow." He was putting the cell phone down as she came into the room. He looked momentarily confused and surprised to see her. After a short pause, he composed himself and gestured at the phone.

"My agent, Bran Eaton. He called to see how the article's coming. He's sure that tonight's events will make the piece more marketable. He thinks maybe I should consider making it a serial."

He lay shirtless in the bed. Somehow, the towel he had been wearing when he came out of the shower was no longer fully in place and the thin hotel sheet was not concealing much... Adelaide felt a lump in her throat the size of a golf ball. Brock mustered just a hint of a smart-ass grin, and then he winked at her. *Oh, my God...he caught me looking.* She cleared her throat as she tossed the back support onto the bed along with a pair of sweatpants and a navy T-shirt bearing the bobcat logo of the local high school team. "Gotta love a profit motive."

Desperate for some busywork, Adelaide popped the pull tab on an overpriced can of off-brand dog food and scooped the mush onto an old hamburger wrapper the maid had missed. The meaty

smell wafted from the can. Rufus sniffed the air and looked hopefully at Brock. "It's okay, boy." He pointed to the food. "Dinner…
go eat your dinner." Rufus waddled over and gobbled up the food.

Brock held his side and winced as he adjusted himself to sit
up in bed. "In addition to his many other charms, Bran's got
chronic sinus problems. It so happens that he has a refill left on a
prescription for some antibiotics at Walgreens. He said he'd call
in the morning to have it filled here, say he's traveling. I can go
get it, claim I'm picking it up for him."

"That sounds aboveboard. Probably not violating any state or
federal laws with that one." She sat down on the foot of the bed.
She could smell his musky scent mixed with the clean aroma of
the soap. Those damn blue eyes were locked on her. The intimacy
of being so close to him was making her pulse pick up. She did
her best to ignore the sensation. "How are you feeling?"

He shrugged. "Like I've been in a knife fight."

She rolled her eyes. "Very funny. You want some Tylenol?"

"I took a handful while you were gone. They're just starting
to kick in." He adjusted the towel and pulled the covers back, still
shirtless. She couldn't avoid an eyeful of six-pack abs and rock-
hard lats. *Does this guy live in the damn gym?*

He seemed oblivious to her reaction. "The bleeding seems to
have stopped. I'll live."

"You're nuts not to go to a hospital. Meanwhile, we need to
get that back support on you."

He took the clothes and walked slowly into the bathroom
to get dressed. She discreetly turned and busied herself with her
purse, but what she saw out of the corner of her eye did absolutely
nothing to slow down that revving pulse.

When he emerged from the bathroom, he pulled the shirt
up and stood with his arms raised while she extracted the back
support from the plastic clamshell packaging. He gasped as she
wrapped the wide elastic band around his midsection and tight-

ened down the Velcro as gently as she could. As her hands brushed his body, she felt a sizzle. Her mind wandered to touching him in different ways…and different places. *Crap. He feels as good as he looks.*

Adelaide stepped back. She was staring at the bandage and thinking about a time years before. Brock waved his hand in front of her face.

"Hey, Earth to Adelaide."

She started and shook off the daydream.

"You want to tell me where you went just then?"

He was doing the eye contact thing again. Between his drop-dead good looks and almost getting killed saving her life, Brock was making it awfully hard to tell him to get lost. Wincing, he adjusted the back support and lay back on the bed. She sat on the end facing him and folded her legs up. Rufus jumped onto the bed and nuzzled up to his master.

He smiled. "What were you thinking about? From the look on your face, it must have been quite a memory."

She chuckled. "I was just remembering this time when I was a kid. We had a giant fireplace in the family room. One night, we had snow flurries. Dad was an Eagle Scout back in the day, so he can build a fire with the best of them. Only problem was, that night he didn't remember that he had covered the chimney with plywood and bricks two years before to keep the squirrels out. So there we were, at nine o'clock at night, with the house full of smoke. With my mom begging him not to do it, he grabbed the ladder and climbed up on the roof—where he promptly slipped on some ice and broke his arm."

He winced. "Yikes."

"Mom was horrified. She immediately dialed nine-one-one. I remember Dad lying on the roof, yelling down at her. He was demanding that she hang up, swearing that he could climb down the ladder. But Mom, the sensible one in the family, called the paramedics, anyway."

"And was he right? The whole fire department thing was over-kill?" He gingerly adjusted himself in bed. His new position left his calf touching her knee...and he didn't move it. *Yikes is right.*

"Overkill?" She shook her head. "Not so much. It took three firemen and a bucket lift to get him off the roof. He had broken his right forearm clean in two. As if that wasn't enough, he had a concussion and a fractured ankle. He would have probably killed himself trying to come down that ladder."

"Your dad sounds like quite a character. What does he do for work?"

Oh, great. Now we get to the Adelaide is a spoiled, rich girl part. In her experience, women from wealthy families with careers in the hard sciences were practically radioactive to men. She decided to change the subject. Eyeing a silver medallion framed against the navy T-shirt, she said, "What's the significance of the medal?"

He fingered the chain. "It's a St. Christopher medal. My mom gave it to me when I was a kid."

She smiled and leaned in for a closer look. Their eyes met and she caught his scent again. A warm glow mixed with an electric tingle spread throughout her body. She forced herself to study the image of the saint carved into the metal. "It's really an interesting design."

He shook his head. "Thanks. Meanwhile, back at the ranch...I was asking about your father..."

Okay, so he wasn't going to let it drop. It wasn't like a quick Google search wouldn't answer the question. She settled back to her place at the foot of the bed. "Dad started a hedge fund in Dallas back in the eighties. Hess Mountain Capital. He finally retired as CEO last year. Now my brother runs the day-to-day. Dad still sits on the investment committee, and he's chairman of the board. He'll still be at that office watching the ticker when he's a hundred."

"Don't tell me your father's Judson Reese?"

She rolled her eyes. "Don't go making a big deal out of it. We're just a family like everyone else."

"Oh, I see. My bad. I must have missed the part where *everyone else* hangs out at the mayor's house and *everyone else* goes hunting with the vice president."

"The mayor and my dad were college roommates. They were both on scholarship to Penn. Neither of them could have possibly afforded to go there without help. As to the other thing, I've never met the vice president. My father was invited to one hunting event where the vice president was there—briefly. The real story is that my father was introduced to him and the vice president said, 'Nice to meet you, *Jefferson*.'"

"That's not how it looked on the news."

"It was a slow news week. And the PR folks from the company worked it up into a lot bigger deal than it really was to get the press for Hess Mountain."

"I bet you did the whole Idlewild-debutante routine."

She sighed. "Guilty as charged. But it wasn't my idea."

"Why'd you do it if you didn't want to?"

She shrugged. "It wasn't so much that I didn't want to. I just wasn't that into it. But my mom did it. My grandmother did it. Dad thought it would be good for Hess Mountain. The marketing people thought it would be good for Hess Mountain. In the end, the company, the parents, and the grandparents really wanted me to do it. It's hard to fight city hall."

"Spa queen."

"Hey! Watch it. If you weren't on the verge of bleeding to death, I'd punch you for that."

"Okay, I take it back...sort of." He looked puzzled.

"What's that look?"

He shook his head. "I don't get how a Highland Park princess with a blue-ribbon academic pedigree ends up staying in cheap motels in the middle of nowhere duking it out with polluters in dark alleys."

Damn stereotypes. Plus, she wasn't crazy about where this conversation might be heading. She decided to keep it simple. "My senior year in high school, I realized chemistry was my thing. I spent some time with a teacher who talked to me a lot about chemical engineering. He helped with my application to MIT, and I got in." Brock still hadn't moved his leg…and neither had she.

He cocked his head. "Yeah, but chemical engineering is a pretty versatile field. You could have been doing research, developing products for industry, getting patents, earning royalties. Why dig around in the mud and deal with guys like those assholes tonight when you could be in an air-conditioned lab in Dallas making the big bucks?"

It wasn't like she never talked about it, but she didn't exactly advertise it, either. It seemed pretty obvious that he wasn't going to let it drop. Plus, the way he looked at her with those blue eyes…and after what he'd done for her…maybe he was entitled to a real answer. She took a deep breath and let it out while she collected herself.

"My father always believed in the best for his kids. He had grown up poor. He worked hard for his money, and he wanted me and my brother to have every possible luxury, every advantage." She cleared her throat before continuing.

"When I was twelve, the posh summer thing to do for Highland Park kids was to attend out-of-state camps. The thinking was that anyone could send their kid to camp on some muddy man-made lake in Central Texas, where they would be exposed to rattlesnakes and chigger bites. Choices ranged from up north to back east, but certainly far from the rough and tumble atmosphere of Texas. For the truly special kids, the most glamorous places were in Michigan—on the Great Lakes. After studying countless brochures, my parents finally decided on a camp on the White River in Muskegon County. I'll never forget it—Camp Alabaster. I can still see that damn brochure—all the happy kids on the front, canoeing in a beautiful river with water splashing on their laughing faces. Our parents signed me and my brother up for a three-week session. We were both thrilled."

He smiled. "Sounds like the trip of a lifetime for a kid."

She laughed derisively. "Yeah. It was going to be a summer we would remember forever."

She stopped talking for a few beats, seeing her soon-to-be-seventh-grade self hustling off the camp van, racing to her assigned cabin, being so excited to hit the lake...

"Thank God my brother broke his arm at the last minute and couldn't go. After some serious discussion, my parents decided it would be all right for me to go alone. Richard was so disappointed. I remember him being really sad the morning I left. I think he still feels guilty about it to this day."

He cocked his head. "Why would he feel guilty? What happened?"

"What my parents didn't know—what no one could know—was that the entire county was about to become a Superfund site to clean up massive ground and surface water pollution."

Brock swallowed hard. "Crap."

Adelaide shrugged. "Unfortunately, that information was not available until after I had spent three weeks swimming in the White River and waterskiing on Lake Michigan."

Brock looked confused. "Didn't you develop symptoms during the summer...during the exposure?"

She nodded. "The only thing that saved me was that the camp had some plumbing catastrophe right before I got there—some problem with the pumping system for their water wells. Everyone drank bottled water the whole time. But we did all break out with rashes. The camp doctor diagnosed us with poison ivy. Michigan is rife with the stuff, so nobody thought anything about it. We kept right on swimming."

Brock shook his head sadly. "Oh, God."

"Yeah. By the time I got home, I was showing signs of more serious illness. My parents took me to an endless parade of doctors, none of whom had any real idea what was wrong with me. I kept getting sicker and sicker. A year later, we finally ended up at the Mayo Clinic. After days of testing, I remember waiting in the doctor's office for the results. I can still see him walking into that room carrying a big, thick chart.

"Dad asked him right off if they had figured out what was wrong with me. The doctor sat down and folded his hands on his desk. He cleared his throat, slapped on his serious-doctor face, and explained in his most serious-doctor voice that I had experienced a toxic exposure to benzene." Images of her parents' faces that day flashed through her mind. At the time, she didn't really understand the impact of what the doctor was saying, but her parents understood, and they hadn't been able to disguise their terror.

The sound of his voice jogged her back to the present. And this time, it was way more warm honey than whiskey. "Adelaide? Are you all right?"

She cleared her throat. "Yeah. I'm…fine…" She took another deep breath. "The doctor told us, among other unfortunate consequences, the experience had left me sterile. I would never be able to have children."

Brock was quiet for a few beats. He struggled to sit up, flinching as he resituated himself. He reached over and put his hand over hers. Finally, he said, "Jesus, Adelaide. I'm sorry. I didn't mean to bring up…"

She sloughed it off. "Don't be sorry. It's not a secret." She reluctantly freed her hand and busied herself adjusting her hair. "I was actually pretty lucky. Once they knew what it was, the good folks at the Mayo were able to fix everything else but that. Besides being sterile, I'm as healthy as a horse…at least a horse that doesn't live anywhere around here."

Brock smiled sadly, but his gaze never wavered. "I don't know how you can joke about it."

She shrugged. "It's just one of those things you learn to live with. I was so young, I didn't really grasp the full dimension of it then. But when I got older and had to…come to terms with it…"

Images of an engagement ring, boxes of invitations, the look on her mother's face when her father told them the news flashed through her mind. Rufus was watching her with curious eyes. She shook her head to clear it. The dog scooted toward her and rested his egg-shaped muzzle on her leg. She rubbed his smooth coat absently.

"When I graduated from college, I went on a pilgrimage to find a fix. After countless futile visits to dozens of doctors, one day I finally realized this was something I could never change and trying was a waste of time. I needed to move on. And moving on, to me, meant finding a way to make something good out of what had happened to me."

"So you decided to become a crusader."

Crusader? The term irked her. "Call it what you will. I had my mind, my education. I decided that I would cope by using that to help other people facing the same thing that had happened to me—and by stopping these polluting bastards anywhere I could find them."

He eased himself up against the pillows. "The crusader comment…that came out wrong. I didn't mean it the way it sounded."

After a pause that was just a little longer than she intended, she cleared her throat. She dug change out of her wallet, picked up her key card, and headed to the door. "I'm going to get a soda. You want something?"

He winced as he sat fully upright. "Really, I'm sorry. It was a jackass comment."

She smiled a perfectly polite, Highland Park smile. "No problem. Just lie back and relax. You sure you don't want something?"

He shook his head. "No, thanks."

She headed down the hall. This guy was some kind of package—smart, hot, brave. He'd jumped right into the middle of her mess to save her and didn't seem to blame her the least bit for his being hurt. And there was definitely chemistry between them. No doubt about that. She had felt it since she first saw him at the rest stop. But the *crusader* comment, however innocently he meant it and however sorry he was for saying it out loud, told her he didn't have any real idea what she had been through or what it meant to her.

She fed the coins into the machine and made her selection. She pulled the soda out of the slot and headed back down the hall to her room.

Popping the tab on a can of Pepsi, she slung her briefcase onto the hotel desk and took out her laptop. Working to keep a matter-of-fact tone in her voice, she opened the cover of the machine and waited for it to boot up. "I'm going to go to the EPA website…see if anything might have shown up on further analysis of those monitoring station samples that Brett's guys collected the day of the fire."

He was quiet for a few beats then she heard the damn warm honey again. "I was really enjoying getting to know you… Please forgive me for being glib—it was totally inappropriate. I tend to do it when things get too real. It's a shitty character trait. Please come back. Let's pick up where we left off…before the part where I was an asshole. Help me get my mind off the damn pain in my side."

She smiled her socialite smile. *Thank you, Mom, for teaching me how to be a socially appropriate Texas lady.* Most of the time that whole thing seemed like crap to her, but right now, she was glad it was in her skill set. She shut her laptop. "Sure." She sat back down on the foot of the bed cross-legged. An awkward silence was forming. To fill it, she said, "So, what's your story? We've heard all about my tales. Now, it's your turn."

"My story is not nearly as interesting as yours. The only mayor I've ever met is the one you introduced me to tonight."

She shook her head. "Come on. Fair's fair."

He paused for a minute, seeming to collect his thoughts. "All right, here goes. I grew up in Iowa. My parents have a farm there, outside of Cedar Rapids."

"Sibs?"

"I have a brother who's got a degree in agronomy. My sister married one of his roommates. I can't imagine a career comprised of knowing everything there is to know about corn, but they all seem to love it."

"Are your parents still living?"

He grimaced as he adjusted his pillow to make better eye contact with her. "Yeah. They're both still on the farm."

"I Googled you last night. You've published a bunch of articles on environmental issues. I read several of them. Very well written. How'd you end up being a writer?"

He seemed momentarily confused by her question. But when he winced and adjusted himself against the pillows again, she wrote the expression off as related to the pain. "I majored in journalism at Coe College. When I graduated, I got a gig at the *Des Moines Register*. I got interested in environmental issues after the floods in 2008. I've been writing environmental pieces ever since."

"I worked on water quality issues after that flood for my thesis. That was absolutely horrible. Where's your family's farm?"

He paused. "Just west of town."

She brightened. "I was working on water well contamination in the Cedar River basin. I may have actually tested on your parents' place. Where are they from where Highway 30 hits 218? I'll never forget that billboard with the giant ear of corn driving the tractor…"

Brock looked uncomfortable and was staring off into space.

With the exception of the *crusader* thing, she hadn't had such a nice, natural, *real* conversation with a man in a long, long time. She had been feeling a real connection to him. Now, she'd inadvertently said something to break the spell. Why in the hell did relationships have to be so frigging confusing? *Damn it! This is NOT a relationship! I'm helping him out tonight because he helped me…that's all there is to it. Tomorrow, we go our separate ways.* "Uh-oh. Now it's my turn. Did I say something wrong?"

He shook his head and smiled sadly. "No. Not at all. It was just a hard thing. You mind if we talk about something else?"

"I'm sorry to have dredged up bad memories. Subject closed." She thought back to those days in Cedar Rapids…all the people experiencing such terrible losses. And they never whined or complained. They helped each other and cared for each other so stoically it was hard to realize how much they suffered… She felt like a conversational bull in an emotional china shop.

His eyes were drooping. "I'm pretty wiped. I think I need to get back to my hotel. My truck is still over by the high school. Can you drive me over?"

She shook her head. "I'm thinking you shouldn't be moving around, much less driving. We can get your truck in the morning."

He looked too weak and tired to argue. He ruffled the dog's ears. "Rufus needs a walk. I'll sneak him out the back for a quick outing."

So you can rip that cut open and start bleeding all over again? Men! "No deal. I'll take him. I don't want him pulling on you." Adelaide picked up the lead off the dresser. "Hey, Rufus, time for your evening stroll." The dog didn't budge.

Brock nodded his head toward Adelaide. "Time to go outside." He pointed with his left hand. "Outside." The dog reluctantly hopped off the bed and went across the room to Adelaide, looking back at Brock between every step. He sat obediently while she hooked the leash to his collar.

She took her key card and started out the door. Unsure of the hotel's pet policy, she stuck her head out into the hall and looked both ways for other guests or hotel employees. Finding the coast clear, she opened the door and tugged on the lead. Rufus was still reluctant to leave his master. Adelaide pulled again, whispering his name. The dog wouldn't budge until Brock repeated the *outside* instruction in a commanding tone. Rufus dropped his head, and they made their way outside. Momentarily, he took care of his business and immediately pulled her back toward the room.

Brock was sound asleep. Rufus bounded across the room and jumped on the bed. He sat next to Brock and licked his face. Even with all the commotion, Brock didn't move at all. He was down for the count. Adelaide silently watched the scene for several minutes.

She walked into the tiny living area of what the hotel generously called her *suite*. When she'd checked in, the desk clerk had told her the small loveseat folded out. She removed the cushions and pulled out the hide-a-bed. After taking a quick shower, brushing her teeth, and changing into leggings and a T-shirt, she climbed into the small bed and turned out the light. She could hear the rhythm of Brock's breathing from across the room. One part of her found the idea of being alone in a hotel room with a gorgeous man who had just saved her life a romantic fantasy come true. The more reasonable part of her remembered the dull, aching pain of being abandoned. She recalled the agony of loving someone and having them start to fall in love with her...only to decide she was nothing but damaged goods. She fell asleep feeling the presence of a brave, handsome man in her room and wishing that she didn't have to spend the rest of her life alone. As she drifted off, she thought, *Maybe I should get a dog.*

CHAPTER 10

ON A GIANT billboard by the highway, the Swiss Chateau Inn & Suites advertised a "fresh hot breakfast" complete with pictures of fluffy scrambled eggs and golden-brown waffles bathed in syrup. The options they actually offered were considerably less scrumptious than the pictures. Adelaide and Brock sat at a chipped Formica table in the hotel's dingy breakfast area choking down microwaved powdered eggs and sticky instant grits. They chased the goop down with lukewarm coffee and watery frozen orange juice served in tiny foam cups. There were no waffles to be found.

Adelaide wadded up her flimsy paper napkin and tossed it on the cheap foam plate. "That was really tasty."

He nodded. "The eggs tasted like MREs. I think they grocery shop at the army surplus store." He winced as he leaned back in his chair. "So, what's on your agenda today?"

She surveyed the empty eating area and scanned the rest of the small hotel lobby then leaned forward and spoke softly.

"If I tell you something off the record, do you swear it'll stay that way?"

He normally loved this part—lived for it—the part where the subject started to trust him, confide in him… With such a cynical woman, he had expected this to be a lot harder. But somehow, this time—with this woman—it wasn't as much fun. Come to think of it, it really wasn't fun at all.

Instead, it just seemed dishonest and unfair and tawdry. Adelaide was a kind of decent he'd never seen up close before. But work was work. Time to suck it up. He leaned into her conspiratorially. "Absolutely."

"I'm going to take some samples from a pond over by the mill."

He looked around. "Why are we whispering about that? Isn't that what you've been doing in front of God and everybody for the past few months?"

She shook her head. "Well, not exactly. This particular pond happens to technically be on mill property."

"What do you mean *technically?*" He screwed an *Are you crazy?* look on his face. "You're not planning on breaking into the mill compound?" He was torn between keeping the flow of info roaring by and stopping what could be a really bad development before it got legs.

She shook her head. "No. The pond is outside the mill fence. I can get to it easily enough. No *breaking* necessary. It's just the *entering* part that's a little tricky."

Even though he had studied a slew of maps of the mill and the surrounding area before he came to this backwater, he had no idea what she was talking about. He'd learned long ago a key investigative technique for getting information from subjects…*ask them.* "I'm not following you. How do you know it's on mill property?"

"I've suspected all along that there was some kind of boundary problem because of the location of the ridge that forms the southern edge of this particular pond. Yesterday, I went to the county clerk's office and checked the field notes in the title records. Sure enough, the pond is on acreage that the mill has title to. I have no idea why it's outside their fence."

Oh, boy. Got to put a stop to this. "Can't you just get Addison Raines to get a court order for a sample?"

She rolled her eyes. "I don't believe for a second the mill would produce a sample from where I want it taken. For all I know, they'd send me some test tube of water from the North Texas Municipal Water District."

Suddenly, he remembered bits and pieces of conversation he'd overheard between Remy Stone and Darren Blackwood a few weeks before. They were saying something about samples from some irrigation wells outside of Amarillo. Brock reviewed the agency's active case log every morning, and he hadn't heard anything about a case in Amarillo. At first, Vance had seemed surprised when he'd asked him about it, but then he'd told Brock that he'd heard talk that East-Tex was having some trouble with an agricultural co-op near a mill up in the Panhandle and that must have been what they were talking about. *That for damn sure better have been what they were discussing, and not some fake samples... or we'll all be talking about it from our jail cells—right before we go straight to hell.*

Adelaide continued. "I can tell from the microbes and mineral content in the other samples they've supplied that they didn't come from around here."

Uh-oh. Brock fought to keep his expression neutral. It took some effort. Hardball was one thing, but felonies were another. Could Stone and Blackwood have actually been talking about the Pine Grove suit? *That's what...obstruction of justice? Contempt of court? Falsifying evidence?* If East-Tex was committing these crimes, what else could they be up to? If they got caught, InfoGlobal—and every investigator working on an East-Tex case—would undoubtedly be dragged into the fray. There wasn't a corporate client in the world that wouldn't throw the PIs under the bus at the first sign they were about to get busted for some litigation-related shenanigans... *Jesus.*

"I need to take it myself," Adelaide said. "Plus, I don't want them to know what I'm up to."

Brock's heart was pounding so hard, he began to wonder if Adelaide could hear it from the other side of the table. His wound started to throb, but he managed to keep his voice casual and steady.

"And what exactly *would* you be up to?"

She looked around the hotel lobby again, checking for eavesdroppers. "That pond is uphill from a creek that runs right into the recharge zone for the Carrizo-Wilcox Aquifer. I know for a fact the pollutants are coming through that creek into the water wells in Fairfield County. All the flora and fauna in that creek are either dead or dying. I just haven't been able to find the source of the contamination. I suspect that this pond is a key to figuring that out."

He considered that for a while. He could tell by the tone of her voice…there would be no talking her out of this, and he didn't have time to get anyone on the phone about it. His realization about the possibly—no, make that *likely*—bogus water samples was already bad enough…no telling what would come out of today's adventure. To make matters worse, the albino guy and his pals worked at the mill. What if they saw her? God knows what they would do if they caught her out in that pasture alone. Besides, one of the fundamental rules of investigative field work was to improvise and use every opportunity to gather information.

Best he could do was go along. He could sort the rest of it out later—he hoped. "Want someone to ride shotgun?"

CHAPTER 11

AS THEY WALKED down the hall from the lobby, Brock couldn't help but wonder what he had gotten himself into. Why wasn't he scrambling into the nearest men's room to call Vance? Why wasn't he doing something to stop this? He shoved the thoughts aside—something in his gut was propelling him forward, toward the day's investigation…and toward Adelaide Reese.

They found Rufus sitting on the bed panda-bear style, leaning back against the pillows more or less upright, with his stubby, muscular hind legs splayed out in front of him. His front paws rested lazily on his pink belly. The dog cocked his head as Adelaide set down the plate they had brought back from the pitiful buffet. When Brock whistled, Rufus jumped off the bed and ran to his master. Brock snapped his fingers, pointing to the food. "Go on, buddy. Eat your chow." The bull terrier was not nearly so offended by the quality of the "fresh hot breakfast" as Adelaide and Brock had been.

While Rufus greedily slurped down the food, Adelaide called Raines's office and got through to a junior staff attorney. After the usual pleasantries, she got to the point.

"I just stuck a HIPPA form for Grace Hinkle in the Current Problems folder in the Casework Dropbox. Those bastards at Pro-

Kare Health are jerking her around on anti-nausea meds—again. Can you get on that this morning then let her know when you get it lined out? Poor gal's sick as a dog."

Brock watched as she talked to the lawyer. She was tireless in her concern for these people. It was like they and their countless awful problems never left her mind.

"Customer service is useless over there. But I remembered we met a guy from their general counsel's office at the toxic torts conference in Wichita Falls last month. Remember? The guy with the bad toupee? Anyway, I linked his business card with her questionnaire. Probably better to just start there."

He watched her flip through the notes on her legal pad while she listened to the lawyer. She was so much more than just a beautiful woman. She was that for sure…but Adelaide was different—different from any woman he'd ever known. "By the way, did you get the pharmacy to fill Bill Wilkerson's steroids? The idiots at Shermann's Drugs were claiming he wasn't due for another month. He asked me about it at the meeting last night. He'll be out of pills day after tomorrow. I thought we'd gotten that handled."

He observed her as they finalized a few more details before she ended the call. Just hearing her—seeing her—touched him in ways he'd never been touched before.

Adelaide caught him watching her as she stowed her phone in her purse. "What?"

"Oh, nothing. Just you get assaulted in an alley not twelve hours ago, and then you're up at the crack of dawn moving electronic files around so some legal beagle doesn't have to spend time looking for forms they've already got. All this for people you hardly know."

Adelaide gave him a strange look. "I don't *hardly know* Grace Hinkle. Grace was one of our first plaintiffs. She has acute myeloid leukemia and is on her third round of chemo. She's got terrible problems with nausea, and the only meds that will control it are sky-high pricey. The damn insurance company gives her shit about it every time. Shermann's Drugs has a computer system they must have bought at Goodwill. Bill can't miss those steroids. He's recovering from chemo and has to gain weight." She shrugged.

He looked confused. "I just didn't realize that chemical engineers were social workers."

While Rufus pushed the empty plate around the room, licking off every last morsel, Adelaide collected two white hand towels and a box of tissues from the bathroom.

"I'm not a social worker... Look. We're here to help these people. Lawyers can get results from insurance companies that subscribers never can." She pulled a laundry bag from the hotel closet. "Addison doesn't have time to deal with all of that. The guy I just talked to is a staff attorney on the case, but his main task is to function as a caseworker of sorts for the plaintiffs."

From her suitcase, she extracted a clean T-shirt and pair of jeans. He watched the passion inside her light up her face and color her cheeks as she talked about her clients' suffering. She stuffed the lot in the bag. "These people are *really* sick. By our latest estimate, up to twenty-five percent of them will die before we get this case to trial. If they don't have the meds and treatment they need because they are too sick and too weak to fight insurance companies that don't care one wit about them, they'll spend the rest of what time they have left in unnecessary misery. I'd do anything to help them. That's what this whole thing is about."

Jesus. He wondered how in the hell he had sat not a foot from her last night and told her that bs story about his "family" in Iowa, hanging tough on his cover—basically just lying through his teeth—when this stunning, genuine, benevolent woman had just bared her soul about the life-changing impact polluters had had on her. And how much of this tidal wave of morality was about the *stunning* part? After all these years in the field, could he actually be thinking with his dick? He doubted it, but he guessed anything was possible.

Visions of sitting in that bowling alley in Milwaukee, chowing cheese-curd fries and knocking back Schlitz while he hustled Dudley O'Doole flashed through his mind. First, he worked that poor bastard until he tried to off himself. Now, he was scamming the Texas version of Mother frigging Teresa. Sometimes this job could really suck. He was starting to hear the faint wails of an alarm going off deep in his conscience... But now was not the time to get religion. He was in the field in the middle of a job that was just about to come off the rails. He nodded noncommittally.

She pressed her point. "You didn't hesitate to wade into the mess in that alley last night, and you got cut for your trouble. You could have been killed. But you didn't think, *Well, this is just some gal I met at a barbecue joint. I think I'll just keep walking. She isn't my responsibility.* You're no different from me."

Yeah. I'm no different from you the same way hell is no different than heaven. A montage of images flooded his mind. The explosion at the plant, Blackwood's ridiculous fiction about the paper napkins, Grace Hinkle in her turban and the look of relief on her face when Adelaide gently squeezed her shoulder and promised to help her, Dudley O'Doole... Struggling to clear those thoughts and seem nonchalant, he smiled and dipped his head toward the laundry bag. "What's that stuff for?"

She slung the bag over her shoulder. "Sample collection can get a little messy. I need something to clean up with. Speaking of messy..." She tossed him another plastic laundry bag. "Best pack up everything with blood on it. I don't want housekeeping to think I murdered someone in here last night."

Man, this gal thinks of everything. He was beginning to wonder if she had actually done undercover work. He took the sack and collected the bloodstained towels and clothes. Pulling the drawstring on the plastic laundry bag, he caught the metallic scent of damp blood. He tightened the knot and tossed the sack next to his backpack. His side was already throbbing, and this little field trip hadn't even started yet.

After Adelaide stuck her head into the hallway and gave the all clear, they snuck out the side door and loaded Rufus into her SUV. Before heading toward the mill, she pulled through the Walgreens drive-through where they picked up Bran Eaton's donated antibiotics. Adelaide reached into the floor of the back seat and produced a bottle of water.

"Here. Use this to take one of those pills. The sooner you get started with that, the better."

He swallowed the pill and took a long pull on the water bottle. *What I need is a penicillin shot, some major pain drugs, and a few days in bed.* But he was deep into this case now, and he was just going to have to gut it out.

"I was thinking...if you're coming along, maybe you could be my surveyor's helper—and my overall lookout."

Why the hell not? I am so far past the part where I should have called the client, what harm can a little aiding and abetting do? Truth was, Brock was surprised to realize he probably wouldn't have called the client, even if he'd had a chance. He was getting a strong feeling that something was going on here that he didn't understand. All clients lied to you. Every PI who'd been licensed since lunch knew that. But this felt different somehow. He needed to go along to get along until he could get a better handle on the situation. Field work was all about improvising and going with the flow. He shrugged. "Okay, Bonnie. If I'm going to be your Clyde, then I need to know what I'm looking out for."

"Well, I can't exactly just drive up to the pond. I'll have to leave the truck on the road and walk in. I really only need my level and tripod, my phone, and some sample jars."

"So where do I come in?" He knew he should be thinking of ways he could "spill" the samples. *God only knows what those idiots have dumped in that damn pond. Just once, it would be nice to have a client that wasn't a complete pig.* But perfect angels rarely needed private investigators specializing in corporate espionage. Yet he couldn't help wondering where he should draw the line… Hopefully somewhere south of Immoral Boulevard and north of Broke and Homeless Street. *Christ…things used to be so clear.* He forced himself to focus on the conversation.

"I'm going to need you to stand by the creek and hold the staff while I shoot the level from the pond. Then, I'll need you to walk on up to the pond and keep an eye out while I concentrate on recording the coordinates of each test location and collecting the samples. I don't want anybody sneaking up on me."

"Sounds easy enough."

"That would probably be true if you hadn't been in a knife fight about twelve hours ago. Do you feel like you can walk the distance?"

Hope to hell so. He shrugged casually. "No problem. How far are we talking?"

"The creek runs right by the road. After I get the elevation, you can stow the staff in the truck before you head up to the hill. It's about a hundred yards uphill from the road to the pond. I'll carry all the equipment. I just need you to hold the staff and look out for mill employees while I collect the samples."

Brock smiled. "Hey, I'm a tough guy. I'll make it."

CHAPTER 12

ADELAIDE PULLED THE truck into a scenic overlook. Popping the hatchback, she started arranging her equipment. Brock carefully made his way out of the passenger's seat and around to the rear of the Explorer.

"Do you have a remote start on this truck?"

"Sure. We can use it to keep the engine running so Rufus stays cool while we work."

"My thoughts exactly. Now, show me what you need me to do."

Adelaide took the surveyor's staff out of the cargo area. She extended it and showed Brock how to hold it for her.

"Be sure you have your phone. We'll need to be communicating while I shoot the level. When I tell you I'm done, just collapse the staff and put it back in the truck and walk on up to where I am. I don't think there's much chance of getting caught at that stage. The ridge that forms the southern end of the pond should shield us from view. The only real risk I run of being seen from the mill is when I collect a sample from the northern edge of the pond."

He looked toward the plant. "That northern thing is going to be pretty tricky. You'll have to be in front of the ridge. If anyone happens to be looking this way from the back of the mill property, you'll be seen." Since he hadn't called anyone about this spontaneous little side trip, he was just a tiny bit concerned he might be seen, too. *Then it'll really hit the fan.*

She pulled camo coveralls from the cargo area and stepped into them. "These will help." She held up a camouflage-painted telescoping pole with a bottle on the end. "So will this. It's a subsurface grab sampler. I can reach twelve feet with it. I'll belly-crawl out from behind the ridge and use this to sneak a sample from close to that north bank."

She stuffed several sample jars into the outside pockets of her coveralls. Pulling out her phone, she silenced the ringer. "Set your phone to vibrate. Better we don't make any noise we don't have to."

He adjusted his phone.

"Now, call me so I have you at the top of my Recents list." She rattled off her number.

The tripod was stored in a camo bag with a strap. Slinging the strap over her shoulder, she picked up the case containing the automatic level and turned to Brock.

"Here's the fob for the car. The remote start will run for fifteen minutes. You can set it when Rufus is settled. Then, go on down to the creek. That's public land, so there's no reason to worry about being there. Just don't set up the staff until I call you. That'll give me a chance to get ready before we start waving surveying equipment around. No need to attract any more attention than is absolutely necessary. I'll call you when I'm ready." She pulled a camo net over her face.

"What's with all the camo gear? MIT training commandos now?"

She rolled her eyes. "A West Nile outbreak creamed the hunting business in West Texas a couple of years ago. I was working out there on groundwater contamination from fracking. At the end of hunting season, outdoor gear was on sale for practically nothing, so I stocked up." She adjusted the strap over her shoulder and started up the hill.

The pain in his side was getting worse, but coming here with her was too big an opportunity to pass up. She had probably been right about going to the ER. He just couldn't deal with filling out forms and showing identification right now. He greedily downed another one of the painkillers. He stashed the last one from the pillbox in his pants pocket so he could get to it without his backpack. That would get him through until he could figure something else out. He turned to Rufus and stroked his head. "I'll be back soon, pal." He used the remote to lock the doors and start the engine and then carefully made his way to the creek.

As he waited, he watched Adelaide hiking up the hill. He was always careful not to get emotionally involved in his work. It clouded your judgment and affected your decisions. Doing it never ended well.

Yet there was something irresistible about this woman. From the time he had first talked to her at the rest area, he had felt an intense personal connection with her. On one hand, she was daring—almost fearless. She'd been a formidable presence when she'd busted him under her car—not rude, but certainly not a pushover. On the other hand, she could seem so vulnerable and feminine. She was incredibly patient and kind with all of the sick plaintiffs. She never seemed to tire of their almost unending requests for help.

Just thinking about her made him feel things he knew he should never be feeling in this situation. How could he keep deceiving her? Where was this going to end up when she found out the truth about him? Speaking of which, he needed to be on the damn phone calling the mill, calling the office, calling someone and telling them what the hell was happening out here.

He reached for his phone to make the call, but something

stopped him. As he watched Adelaide making her way to the pond, he thought about what courage it must have taken to face what happened to her and then turn that into a lifelong battle to help others. He thought of his own hard work, his own decisions that had gotten him to where he was—part owner in an agency, living in a beautiful loft apartment, driving a Porsche. He and Vance, fighting their way to the top, covering each other's backs…

The phone vibrated in his hand. He answered, and the sound of her voice evoked something deep within him. Adelaide spoke with authority, no doubt about that, but there was a soft and feminine quality to her speech, something…sexy. Silently, he wished she sounded more like a drill sergeant and less like Kathleen Turner. Her instructions pulled him from his reverie.

"Okay. I'm ready. Extend the staff and move it slowly forward and back like I showed you. My level will tell me when you have it perfectly vertical."

It didn't take long to find the vertical position. He heard her whisper over his phone's speaker.

"Got it. Now stow the staff in the truck and head this way. I'm going to start collecting my samples."

Brock used the remote to open the hatchback of the SUV. Rufus leaped over the back seat and greeted him. He put the staff back in the Explorer, told Rufus goodbye, and reset the engine before making his way up the hill.

He could feel the pain pill he had swallowed a few minutes earlier starting to kick in. Pill or no pill, the hike was much harder than he had thought it would be. Making matters worse, his progress slowed considerably as he approached the pond. The water had saturated the black clay soil, turning the ground around the pool into a sticky mud-gumbo bordering on quicksand. Every time he pulled his right foot free of the muck, pain shot through his side like a buzz saw. He put on his game face and slogged ahead, putting one foot miserably in front of the other.

Some guys whined about difficult field conditions, made excuses. Not Brock. He and Vance hadn't gotten from where they'd started to where they were in this life by quitting when things got tough or complicated.

When he finished his climb, Adelaide already had the grab sampler out. She disconnected the telescope from the automatic level. Her hand glanced his as she traded him the scope for her car remote. Every single time he touched her—however innocently or accidentally it happened—a tiny thrill ricocheted through his body. Since when had the daring Brock Emerson turned into such a sap for a beautiful woman? What on earth was happening to him?

"You keep a lookout for anyone coming out of the buildings into this back area behind the mill. I'll start collecting my samples."

He rested the telescope on the berm, concealing himself behind the ridge as Adelaide began scooping water from the pond by extending the camouflaged pole from behind the embankment. After pouring the last bottleful into a sample jar and labeling it, she hunched down next to Brock.

"I'm done with everything but the sample from that north edge of the pond. Let me see the telescope. I want to pick my spot before I start over there."

He handed her the scope. Adelaide held it up to her eye and surveyed the territory. Suddenly, she ducked below the ridgeline.

Brock whispered, "What?"

"Some guys just came out of the mill." She snatched her cell phone from the outside pocket of her coveralls. In a fluid motion, she used a special adaptor to clip the camera lens of the phone over the eyepiece of the telescope. She carefully edged back up to rest the device on the ridge and whispered, "I'm going to take some video."

Brock slowly peeked over the berm. He didn't need a telescope to tell what was happening. Two men in mill uniforms were dragging a third man in business clothes along the back fence of the facility. The third man was struggling to get free. *What the hell?* Things were happening too fast and he was too banged up to intervene. His first instinct was to make a spectacle of himself...get the attackers' attention, stop whatever the two thugs were doing to the third man, but that would put him and Adelaide both in danger. Was he healthy enough to protect her if the thugs came after them? He looked over at her. *Whatever it is, the damn expert witness for the people suing my client is recording it. Damn. Damn. Damn. How did I let this happen? And what the hell are they doing?*

Before Brock could improvise a plan, the two men dragged their victim behind the southern-most building on the mill property, where they would have been safely out of sight—if Adelaide and Brock hadn't been hiding behind the ridge. In an instant, one of the attackers pulled a pistol from his waistband and shot the struggling man in the back of the head. The victim immediately went limp.

Adelaide gasped. Brock, looking on without benefit of the telescope, could still tell what had just happened. He was too stunned to speak. Both stared gape-mouthed at the scene unfolding behind the mill's sheet metal buildings.

Brock's mouth went dry. The pain in his side ratcheted up with his rising blood pressure. This surely wasn't the first time an undercover gig had gone off the rails...but murder? *Playing fast and loose with the EPA is one thing, but killing someone in cold blood? I knew not to trust these crooks. What have we gotten ourselves into?* Brock hunkered down but kept an eye on the action from behind the berm. One of the attackers pushed a button on the outside of the metal building. A large garage door rolled up, revealing a white Suburban. Using a remote control, the shooter clicked open the rear hatch. Working together, the two killers lifted the unmoving victim into the cargo area of the white SUV.

The accomplice ran to the front of the truck and jumped into the driver's seat. After shutting the back door, the gunman took one last look around before heading to the passenger's door. Just as he looked to the south, a gust of wind blew, causing the telescope Adelaide had resting on the ridge to wobble.

The momentary movement allowed the telescope lens to pick up a ray of sunlight. Brock reflexively shut his eyes to the bright flash. His heart raced when he realized the burst must have looked like a supernova to the killer. The gunman stared directly at Adelaide and Brock's position. Without hesitation, Adelaide ducked down below the ridge and yanked Brock along with her.

"He's looking straight at us. I think he may have seen us," she whispered.

"Oh, we're made, all right. But I don't think he can identify us. Maybe he's not even sure what he saw."

Adelaide whispered, "I'm going to take a little look over the ridge. With this camo net on, if I move slowly, I shouldn't be that obvious."

As Adelaide peeked back over the berm, Brock rose up enough to see the killer slapping the back of the Suburban and yelling something. He jumped out of the way as the driver threw the big truck into Reverse and shot out of the garage. The Suburban lurched into Drive and sped through the east gate of the property. Meanwhile, the shooter ran into the empty bay. Momentarily, another metal door rolled up. The gunman emerged driving a white Crown Victoria—straight toward Adelaide and Brock. The back gate to the mill property opened automatically, and the big car shot through.

"He's coming for us. Run for the truck. Run!!!"

Adelaide scooped up her equipment and started running downhill. Brock grabbed his side and followed as fast as he could. Adrenaline shot through his body. The pain in his side subsided, and he picked up speed, almost catching up to Adelaide.

It didn't matter how fast he ran, though. He was never going to be able to outrun the Crown Vic with its V8 engine. The car was gaining on him by the second.

Having had a head start, Adelaide reached the truck first. The fob in her pocket unlocked the doors automatically as she approached. She threw her equipment in the front seat and dove in after it. With the door still ajar, she threw the car into gear and headed for Brock just as he was clearing the creek and stepping onto the road.

He looked over his shoulder. The killer had reached the pond. It was all downhill from there. Soon, the massive car would be upon them. Brock grabbed his side and made one last push toward Adelaide and the Explorer.

Powerful though it was, the Crown Vic had not been designed for off-road driving. The car began to lose traction as it hit the soggy, clay-rich soil around the pond. Not prepared for the conditions, the driver stepped on the gas to overcome the loss of speed. The back tires began to spin, and the car threw up a fountain of mud.

Adelaide skidded the Explorer to a rolling stop on the two-lane road as Brock stepped onto the shoulder. He grabbed the passenger door handle and lunged into the front seat, landing hard on Adelaide's surveying equipment. They sped away as he muscled the passenger door shut. Rufus lapped his face when he turned to see the Crown Vic stuck up to its axles in the black muck.

CHAPTER 13

AS ADELAIDE STEERED the SUV back onto the highway, she kept checking the rearview mirror. She could hear her pulse pounding in her ears like it was blasting out of a subwoofer. She clenched the wheel to steady her hands. "No sign of the Crown Vic. I think the mud saved us."

Brock was wedged up against the passenger's door, trying to wrangle the surveying equipment into the back of the SUV. As he wrestled the tripod around so that he could actually sit in the seat, he checked the side-view mirror. "Don't get your hopes up. There's a pickup with mill markings coming up fast."

She stole another glance in the rearview. The pickup was almost airborne as it crested the hill not far behind them. It must have been going at least ninety. "The guy in the mud must have called for help."

Brock was still looking in the side mirror. "He's gaining on us." A pause. Then in a louder voice, "Gun! Driver has a gun!" She felt him yank her down in the seat as she struggled to keep control of the truck.

She heard shattering glass as a star pattern appeared in the rear windshield. A bullet whizzed between them, punching a hole in the front glass.

Brock ducked down in the seat. "You okay?"

A flood of adrenaline raced through her veins. It brought her an ultraclear, hyperfocused mindset. She was too terrified to even feel the fear. "Yep. You?"

"I'm all right. They're coming up fast. They'll be on us in a few seconds."

Adelaide steered to the far right of her lane. She crossed her left hand over her right, grabbing the far side of the steering wheel. She yelled, "Hold on!" as she slammed on the brakes and yanked the steering wheel to the left. The car slid into a hundred-and-eighty-degree spin, ending up in the opposing lane. She straightened the wheel and hit the gas just as the pickup was coming up on her bumper. She sped past it in the opposite direction. In an effort to follow her, the truck's driver hit his brakes and attempted the same maneuver. Lacking Adelaide's skill, though, he failed in his timing, and the pickup skidded off into a bar ditch and rolled onto its side.

In their mirrors, they both looked at the overturned vehicle, its tires spinning lazily in the air in a cloud of steam escaping from beneath the hood. Rufus barked triumphantly.

The force of the turn had pinned Brock up against the surveying equipment as he clutched his shoulder belt in one hand and his backpack in the other. He steadied himself as she sped away from the wrecked pickup.

Her eyes were locked on the road. "Call nine-one-one."

"Not so fast. We need to think this through before we go calling the cops."

She couldn't believe what she was hearing. "What do you mean *think it through*? We just watched a couple of goons kill a guy by shooting him in the head. Then, those same goons just chased us halfway across Fairfield County while they shot out my windshield. That bullet missed us by inches. I don't see what we need to *think through*." She had worked herself into a state. Her heart rate was up, and her voice had risen to a crescendo.

"Listen. If your interpretation of what happened with that deputy and the other folks at the fire scene is right, then the Fairfield County sheriff's office is in on the deal somehow. We're still in Fairfield County, so that's what nine-one-one gets you here."

She looked around. "We've got to get off this road...and the hell out of this county." Without looking, she grabbed a road map off the seat and slapped it into his chest. "Find a cutoff going east. Fast. And nothing that goes anywhere near the plant."

"Why east?"

"Just do it. I have a plan."

CHAPTER 14

BROCK KEPT AN eye on the mirrors. As far as he could tell, they had lost the killers. *Thank God for small favors.* Not that he thought the bad guys were gone for good, but he'd take any reprieve he could get.

He was still amazed by that driving stunt Adelaide had pulled during the chase. What a woman! Where do you find a gal who is beautiful, brilliant, funny, and drives like a cross between Danica Patrick and 007? Adelaide Reese kept surprising him—and that didn't happen very often.

Adelaide drove east for half an hour. She followed FM 2109 until it hit 69 just outside the town of Zavalla. There, she merged onto 69 and followed the road on out to the northwest until it merged with 59. Despite the green highway signs advising of exits for Wells and Woden, the only habitations in sight were a few lonely farmhouses guarded by some skinny, anemic-looking cows.

Brock had spent most of the drive trying to figure out what the hell was going on and what to do about it, but he was coming up with way too many questions and not nearly enough answers. While the standard field response to any crisis is first, don't blow your cover and, second, keep the operation going, that gets a little weird when it seems like your own client might be trying to kill you. Despite stalling Adelaide about calling the cops, he was damn sure that he had just seen two guys in mill uniforms kill a guy in a suit. And the guy who had looked him in the eye when Adelaide flipped the one-eighty was the same burly guy who had led the attack on Adelaide in the alley. Brock would have recognized him anywhere. *I need to just contain the situation until I can get Vance on the phone...*

Eventually, they began to see signs for Lake Naconiche. Adelaide cut off the pavement onto a caliche road and headed to the northwest. She dropped her speed to keep the dust down as she weaved her way through a maze of narrow, unpaved roads, finally ending up on something that was really no more than a rut. At the end of the rocky trail, the lights of the Explorer shined on an enormous log-cabin-style lodge that seemingly materialized out of the ether.

Brock breathed a tiny sigh of relief. He stared, amazed at the structure's sudden appearance. "Is that a hotel?"

"Not exactly. It belongs to Grace Hinkle now. She inherited it from her mother. It was her parents' getaway."

Adelaide reached into her console and retrieved a garage door opener. An overhead door rolled open into a detached garage adjoining what appeared to be a boat house several yards from the main building. She drove in and parked.

"Jeez." His eyes swept across the interior of the building and rested on a custom Champion bass boat that had been hot stuff once upon a time but now looked like it had seen better days. Adelaide got out of the truck and came around to Brock's door. For a moment they both stopped, and their eyes met. He smiled. "I think I love Grace."

Adelaide helped him out of the car and took Rufus by the lead. "That makes two of us." She hit the button to shut the garage door behind them.

He watched the door clatter on its tracks. "I'm feeling safer already."

"Don't get too frisky, sport. We're not in the clear yet."

Rufus jumped and whimpered with excitement. Brock moved gingerly, trying not to start his wound bleeding again. He looked around. "This place is huge."

"Yeah. About seven thousand square feet."

"Grace owns a seven-thousand-square-foot lodge for a 'get-away' and she can't afford her nausea medicine?"

"Grace's mother just passed away. This is all that was left in the estate."

He shook his head. "If she's so broke, why hasn't she sold it already?"

Adelaide shrugged. "Because there are about a zillion liens against it. Her father was a big-time Tri-Cities cardiologist—with an even bigger-time gambling problem. Ran up insurmountable debts. While Grace was still in college, he got the bright idea to pay the loan sharks off with some poorly devised Medicare fraud scheme. He was sentenced to ten years in the Federal Prison Camp in Bryan. He died a couple of years ago, before he finished his sentence. Her mom started drinking after the legal trouble started. She just passed away last June. The stress and the alcohol killed her."

"What are you doing with the garage door opener?"

"I've been out here several times with the Realtor. One of Addison's partners, a guy named Simpson from their real estate section, is trying to get the title straightened out so she can sell it. She wanted to Airbnb it, but it's not in good enough condition, and there's no money for the fix up."

They walked slowly up the ten steps leading to the covered porch that wrapped all the way around the giant glass picture windows of the lodge.

"Who was her father?"

"His name was Jack Westminster."

Brock held tightly to the banister and climbed slowly. The

Westminster name definitely rang a bell. "Jesus. I remember reading something about that not long ago." His side was throbbing, and he was afraid he had done some real damage during the race to evade the killers.

"Yeah. It made the papers again when he died year before last. He got killed by some prison gang over drugs being smuggled into the facility. The guy was just bad news. Poor Grace is as good as she can be, but her family has been a cross to bear all her adult life."

Adelaide got out her key ring and held it up in the last vestiges of daylight.

"Grace says before the fall they had great parties out here."

He eyed twelve faded wicker chairs surrounding a long firepit table and let out a soft whistle. "I bet they did."

As they crossed the giant porch to the front door, Brock leaned against the cedar railing while Adelaide struggled to fit the key into the lock. Noticing her hand was trembling, he pushed himself forward as carefully as he could and stepped over to her. When she didn't move away, he edged in close and took the key. Wordlessly, he fitted it in the lock and turned it.

The mechanism clicked, and the door opened into a vast living area. Adelaide cleared her throat, retrieved her key ring, and flipped a switch that illuminated a giant elk horn chandelier suspended from a sixteen-foot ceiling. The cobwebs woven between the horn prongs gave the room a dilapidated, almost spooky feel. Tossing her keys on a console table in the entryway, she said, "We need to get you out of those clothes and see about redressing that wound." She hung her purse on a hook by the door into the kitchen and turned to him. "Then, we have to figure out what we're going to do about the folks who are trying to kill us."

Brock nodded as he stared at the immense living space. "I like the undress part." As he struggled to keep up his game face and control the pain, he thought she was so brave, so determined... and so pure in her resolve. She wasn't doing any of this to get rich. Hell, she was already rich. She was involved in this mess out of moral conviction. What would she think of him if she knew about his connection to the men who had almost killed them… and to the company that might actually be killing Grace and all those plaintiffs like her by poisoning their water, just like Raines was claiming it was? Hell, *he* was beginning to question what he thought of himself…

CHAPTER 15

ADELAIDE LED BROCK down a long terrazzo hall toward the large master suite on the first floor of the lodge. Rufus took every step they did, absolutely refusing to let Brock out of his sight. Adelaide thought about Brock and Rufus…how connected they were. How alarmed Brock had been in the car the previous night, thinking Rufus was bleeding. How lying there on her hotel bed about to pass out from blood loss, he had worried about Rufus having dinner. She found a tiny part of herself wondering if Brock—or any man for that matter—could ever worry that way about her. *Great. Now you're jealous of a terrier.*

She was still reeling from the charge that had passed between them as he'd helped her unlock the door. Despite her best efforts, she was having trouble concentrating on anything else. Finally, her rational mind kicked in. *This is no time to be falling for some guy you hardly know. You need to get him patched up, cut him loose, and call the cops before you get hurt…or worse.* She was an engineer, not a commando. She stopped and opened the door to a hall closet, extracted a pair of men's shorts and a T-shirt, and passed them to him.

"I promised Grace I'd have someone pack up the personal effects before the house is listed, but we're nowhere near that yet."

The opulent bedroom opened into a marble-clad bathroom. The once-glamorous feel was overshadowed by the water stains on the ceiling and the desilvered edges around the vanity mirror.

"Get out of those bloody duds. When you're cleaned up, I'll throw everything in the wash."

He raised an eyebrow. "Remember what Robert Benchley said?"

Adelaide smirked and threw a towel at him. "What would that be?"

"I've got to get out of these wet clothes and into a dry martini."

She couldn't help but notice his well-developed biceps as he grabbed for the towel. She caught herself. *Stop acting like he's here to pick you up for the prom and get him some help.* "You don't need a martini, you need a blood transfusion."

While Brock took a shower, Adelaide called Grace.

"Adelaide! I'm glad you called. Whatever you guys said to that insurance company sure got them moving. I got my meds this afternoon."

"That's great. It's good to see those lawyers making themselves useful. Are you feeling better?"

"Thank God. I actually had Cream of Wheat for lunch, and it all stayed down."

The sound of Grace's husky voice soothed her anxiety and calmed her jangled nerves. "I just wanted you to know I'm at the lodge."

"Is there progress on selling it?"

Grace didn't miss Adelaide's pause—she was a woman well accustomed to hearing bad news.

"What's wrong?"

Adelaide let out a deep sigh. "I don't want to go into detail. I mean, telling you might drag you into something you don't want any part of."

"Ooh. Sounds juicy. Is there a man involved?"

Adelaide paused again. She needed to formulate her answer carefully. "Well, there is…just not how you'd think. And I've got a bit of a problem. This man has been injured…he has a gash on one of his lower ribs, and he doesn't feel like he should go to the authorities."

"Now that sounds *really* juicy. Just stay put. This is one thing I can help you with." Grace laughed. "I don't know anything about personal injury litigation or real estate land titles or fighting with insurance companies, but when it comes to crooked doctors, you're talking to the right girl. Tell your Prince Charming to hang tough. Help is on the way."

"He's *not* my Prince Charming. He's a pigheaded man who refuses to go to the ER. We had gotten the bleeding stopped, but we had a little setback this afternoon that has thrown him right back to ground zero."

Grace groaned. "Men can be so difficult. By the way, is this one a looker?"

Adelaide smiled. It was good to hear Grace feeling well enough to girl-gossip. She listened to the shower and pictured Brock behind the steamy glass and sighed. "I'm not getting into that."

"Oh, I bet he's dashing."

He had been pretty damn dashing when he'd jumped into the fray in that alley…never mind when he was strutting around in nothing but a towel. Just the thought got her pulse pounding…

Adelaide cleared her throat. "I've got way more important things to worry about right now than how dashing he is."

"No need to worry about this. I'll handle it from here. Stay by the phone. Since you're being so mysterious, maybe you should lock the place down and set the alarm. We dropped the monitoring, but the sirens still work. Don't open the door for anyone unless they tell you my name."

"Grace…"

"Don't *Grace* me. Go have yourself a stiff drink…and pour

one for lover boy. I think there's probably still part of an old bottle of single malt in the liquor cabinet." Before she could respond, Adelaide heard a dial tone.

Brock called to her from the bathroom, and she hurried to the master suite. She found him shirtless and wearing the borrowed shorts—giving her an eyeful of legs that could belong to a rider from the Tour de France. He had bound his side up with a towel. A small bloodstain was showing through the terry cloth. Her chest tightened when she saw two bloody towels resting on the floor.

"We're putting a pretty good dent in the East Texas towel supply. I'll be happy to replace these for Grace."

He got into this mess saving me, and now he's worried about towels... "We've got worse problems than towels." She looked around. "Where's the back support?"

Brock pointed to the pile of bloody clothes.

"I'm going to put the whole lot in the laundry. Meanwhile, I'll see if there are any elastic wraps around here." Adelaide rifled through bathroom cabinets and came up with an old roll of ACE bandage. She held it up for him to see. "Voilà."

He raised his arms. His lats formed a perfect, muscular V as they led her eyes to his six-pack abs. *Oh. My. God.* She forced herself to focus on the task at hand, wrapping the bandage tightly around the hand towel, securing it in place. He winced but didn't make a sound.

When she finished, he gently brushed her hair from her face then softly placed his index finger under her chin and tilted her face up toward his. As he stared down at her, his gaze reached straight into her chest and revved her heart rate like a jet engine lining up for takeoff. The moment seemed to last a lifetime. She felt her face flush with the heat of excitement. His body was strong and powerful, while his touch was tender and intimate. She wanted him in a way that could only lead to other things—things that were bound to end in pain and disappointment.

She swallowed hard and forced herself to take a step back. He looked disappointed but didn't complain as she gathered the length of the T-shirt she had retrieved for him earlier. *Of all the toxic sites in all the polluted towns in the world, he walks into mine.*

She cleared her throat and stammered, "Um, if you'll hold your arm out, I can…I'll help you get this over your head." While he did as she asked, Brock never broke his gaze. She felt her knees weakening. Maybe a little Rick and Ilsa wouldn't be such a bad thing… Then she remembered the end of the movie. *It never works out in the end.*

Finished with the first aid, she pulled herself together and spun abruptly toward the door. Heading to the kitchen, she stopped in the laundry room and put the bloody clothes and towels in the washer, stripped off her now-filthy camo coveralls, and dumped in the last of an aging box of detergent. He followed languidly. She imagined she could feel his gaze on the back pockets of her jeans. The moment ended when Rufus began circling the two of them like an Aussie with his flock, emitting sharp barks between verses of what sounded like off-key singing.

Brock looked down at him. "You hungry, pal? I get it. I bet this nice lady here can hustle up something for you to eat." He winked at Adelaide. "*Can* this nice lady hustle him up something to eat?"

Again with the winking. Damned if it doesn't get me in spite of myself. "This nice lady will see what she can do."

Adelaide opened and closed cabinet doors until she hit pay dirt. She looked down at Rufus. "Well, sir, tonight's off-the-menu specials feature tuna or sardines served on a chipped dish with a side of tap water."

Brock laughed and took the cans from her. The brush of his hand against hers sent tingles up her arm. She swallowed hard.

He perused the labels. "Better do the tuna. I worry about the bones in the sardines." He handed her the can. This time, the brush of his hand lasted way longer than it had to. She didn't want to move. She wanted him to take her in his arms and hold her and tell her everything would be all right...

Rufus yapped a sharp bark. Adelaide started and took the tuna can. "We hear you, bud. The chef is working as fast as she can." Adelaide peeled back the lid and took a plate from the drainboard. She poured the tuna onto the dish and set it down for the dog. "Dinner is served." When she looked up, Brock was still watching her intently. Their eyes locked for a moment before she looked away. She could feel herself sliding down a slippery emotional slope. *This is like one of those twisting water park slides, only this one dumps you into quicksand.*

Searching for busywork, she fussed around the kitchen. Opening the refrigerator, she said, "You hungry?"

He eased onto a barstool. "I could use a stiff drink."

"Well, Grace just recommended one for both of us." Opening the liquor cabinet, she extracted a dusty bottle of Macallan and two crystal old-fashioned glasses.

He settled carefully on the stool, leaning on the large granite island positioned in the middle of the kitchen while she poured two fingers of the Scotch into the glasses and slid one in front of him.

He took a healthy drink and swirled the amber liquid in the glass. "That's damn good whiskey." Setting the glass down, he said, "Come to think of it, I am starving. I guess there's nothing like some assholes trying to off you with machine guns, capped off with a good car chase, to work up an appetite."

She sipped the single malt, savoring the smoky aftertaste. "There's more canned stuff in that cabinet where I found Rufus's tuna. Meanwhile..." She rooted around in the pantry and emerged holding up a bag of chips and a jar of salsa. She set her find on the counter. "I better check the dates."

He shook his head. "Best not to get bogged down in details."

He tore open the bag while she popped the lid on the jar of salsa. His arm touched hers as he reached to swipe a chip through the tangy mixture of tomatoes and onions. She looked into his eyes and knew good and well it wasn't an accident. She could literally feel the heat between them. Despite the homicidal maniacs and bleeding knife wound, her mind wandered to the thought that this evening in a safe house might have some real potential. Just as her reasonable engineer mind chimed in reminding her to dial 1-800-Reality, the doorbell rang.

CHAPTER 16

ADELAIDE STARTED WHEN she heard the chimes. Then she remembered Grace promising help for Brock's injury. But how could Grace have arranged a house call this fast? Barking, Rufus ran to the foyer.

Adelaide peeked through one of the sidelights running beside the massive front door. A middle-aged man in jeans and a Grateful Dead T-shirt was standing on the front porch. His salt-and-pepper hair was woven into a braid that was draped down his back past his heavily tattooed neck. He was wheeling a jumbo Zero Halliburton aluminum spinner suitcase. She pressed a button for the intercom.

"Yes?"

"Grace Hinkle sent me. I'm looking for Adelaide Reese."

Brock looked at her with confusion as she turned the bolt. "What are you—"

"Grace was worried about your injury. She didn't tell me anything except not to let anyone in unless they used her name."

She opened the door and the visitor walked into the house and hefted his case onto the coffee table in the living room.

He pulled out a red-and-white kitchen timer and twisted the chunky dial a quarter turn. The contraption began to tick. "You have fifteen minutes. Where's the patient?"

Brock hesitated for a couple of beats before he shrugged and walked up to the stranger, carefully extending his hand. "I'm Brock."

The man didn't respond. He didn't even look up as he opened his case and extracted exam gloves. "May I see the wound?"

Brock carefully pulled his shirt off over his head and gingerly removed the bandage and the towel. The man probed the wound with his gloved hand, seemingly unconcerned with Brock's involuntary gasp. "Early signs of infection."

Through clenched teeth, Brock said, "I got some antibiotics from a friend this morning."

The man held out his hand. "Show me."

Brock dug the pills out of the pocket of his borrowed shorts. "You have a real interesting bedside manner."

"And you have eleven minutes left."

The visitor glanced at the orange bottle and handed it back. "Better than nothing, but not by much. Are you allergic to penicillin?"

Brock shook his head. "No."

The man meticulously cleaned the wound while Adelaide stood listening to the annoying timer wondering if he would finish before the bell rang. He injected a topical anesthetic and neatly installed ten dissolving stitches then slathered the area with ointment and bandaged the wound.

Adelaide peeked at the timer. Three minutes left.

A tetanus shot followed by a whopping hypodermic of penicillin made up the finale. After stripping off his gloves, the man handed Brock a large zipper sandwich bag of pills and bandages. He rattled off instructions on wound care and drugs.

When the kitchen timer dinged, the man silenced it and plopped it into his bag. He gathered his materials into his case and headed to the door.

Adelaide put her hands on her hips. "Grace was great to call you. I really appreciate you coming."

He wheeled his case out the door, turned, and said, "Anything for Grace. Sorry about the clock, but she understands why I'm on a schedule." He closed the door and headed down the driveway. No vehicle was in sight when he disappeared around the bend, pulling his suitcase behind him.

As Adelaide locked the front door, Brock shook his head and said, "If this day gets any weirder…"

Just then, Adelaide's phone rang. Seeing Grace's number, she hit the speaker button.

"Your friend all taken care of?"

"Yes, thanks. Who was that masked man?"

"Don't ask. Suffice it to say, he's a very smart guy who's had a very…interesting life. He knows what he's doing. Better yet, he knows how to keep his mouth shut. How long did he give you?"

Adelaide laughed. "Fifteen minutes."

Grace snorted. "I'm surprised you got more than ten. But then again, he's a sucker for beautiful brunettes."

Brock silently mouthed, "Me, too."

Adelaide caught herself perusing his shirtless form as Grace continued. "Is there anything else I can get you? I'm sorry the place is such a dump…" Adelaide could hear the sadness in her voice.

She thought of Grace's bravery. "It's beautiful, and you're very generous to share it with me. You've done more than enough. I'll call you when we clear out. It won't be long."

Grace paused a moment before continuing. "I trust your judgment. But you don't always have to be the hero. I'll be here. Let me know what you need."

After signing off with Grace, Adelaide headed into the kitchen. She dug a couple of cans of ravioli out of the cabinet, perused the labels, and looked up at Brock. "Only a few months out of date."

He rolled his eyes. "After what we've been through in the past twenty-four hours, call me silly, but I'm not all that worried about out-of-date ravioli."

She opened the cans and dumped the contents into bowls.

Brock dug in with gusto. "This is great! I'm starving."

Adelaide eyed him. "You're easy to please."

In between bites, he said, "Grace Hinkle seems like a real character."

Adelaide smiled. "She's amazing. Sick out of her mind with chemo and still worried about me."

He nodded. "What's her story?"

"After the scandal with her father made her more or less toxic waste in Dallas high society, she wisely decided to move somewhere everyone in town didn't know about her dirty laundry. She came down to Pine Grove and got a job with a water well company. She ended up marrying Dan Hinkle. He's a great guy who is one of their drillers. Then she got sick. It's been a hard three years for her. She's a real trouper, though. I'm proud to know her."

Brock stared at Adelaide, fork in midair. "I really like the way you talk."

She felt her face flush. "Stop it." But even as she said it, she peeked again at his chest, then bit her lip and gulped the last bite of the sticky ravioli. "It's what I love about my job…connections with such great people. Over all the years I've been doing this, I've met wonderful, kind, decent folks who are in the middle of what is probably the worst thing that will ever happen to them, and they still rally around each other with Families in Need lists and the like. I can't tell you how many cookies have been baked for me by people who were so sick they could barely stand, thanking me for helping them. It breaks my heart and reminds me I'm the luckiest person alive."

They finished eating, and Adelaide cleared the table. As she washed the dishes, Brock picked up a towel and dried. He was standing so close, she wondered if he could feel the heat rising off her. She imagined it was visible like the shimmering waves rising off of a Texas highway in August. She drew a breath and, despite the Betadine, she could still smell his musky scent.

She caught herself. No matter how hot, how strong, how tender Brock could be, they had real problems, and it was time for serious decisions.

CHAPTER 17

THE ANESTHETIC GRACE'S pal had injected was wearing off, and Brock's side felt like he'd been hit with a bat. While she was cleaning up, he had downed one of the pain pills Dr. Dead-head had left him. It was taking effect, ratcheting the pain down from brain-splitting to just a dull roar.

Adelaide hit the button on the Keurig. "You want coffee?"

There were a few grocery-store brand pods left in the rack by the machine. He shrugged. "Sure."

The machine whirred and gurgled, then spewed out two cups of coffee. She handed one to him. As he savored the aroma, she nodded toward the massive great room.

"Let's go in the living room. That couch is a lot more comfortable than these barstools."

He took one end of the couch, and she took the other. Rufus hopped up in between them and assumed the panda position. She looked at the dog. "That's so damn cute. Did you teach him to do that?"

Brock shook his head. "He's done it since he was a puppy. I actually considered naming him Bear because of it, but I didn't want to create any interspecies identity problems." He rubbed the dog's exposed belly.

Adelaide reached over and scratched Rufus's ears. "How long have you had him?"

He thought back to the day he'd found the beast. "I was taking the garbage to the dumpster at my apartment complex. I heard this faint whimpering sound. I looked around and found Rufus hiding between the dumpster and the wall, not quite three pounds, cold and wet and almost dead. I stuck him inside my coat, and we headed straight to the vet's. I bottle-fed him for weeks until he was strong enough to eat. We've been together ever since."

Adelaide petted the dog's belly. "You're a lucky dog. Do you know that?"

Rufus licked her hand.

They sat in an awkward silence for a time. Finally, Adelaide set her coffee cup down and said, "We need to talk."

Oh, boy. Here it comes. Stalling for time, Brock adjusted his position on the couch so he could see her better.

He had established three immediate goals until he could get a better handle on things. First, keep them both alive. Second, no cops and no hospital. Third, figure out what the hell was going on and line up an exit strategy.

Corporate espionage, litigation support—that was one thing. Murder—that was just off the hook. He for damn sure didn't sign up to have anything to do with killing anyone. For all of Vance's talk about clients and their contributions to the bottom line, he would never have anything to do with this, either. Vance had saved Brock's life when they were kids—more than once. Brock had no intention of flushing their careers down the toilet, never mind landing them in prison, by getting caught up in some hornets' nest they had nothing to do with. He'd have to hear her out and wing it from there. He slowly put his feet up on an ottoman and said, "Okay. Let's talk."

She spoke carefully. "I know you have objections, but we have to call the police, and I think we need to do it now. We witnessed a serious crime. Very bad men are after us. We could have been killed."

He rubbed his chin as he considered his response. Any way he looked at it, calling the cops was a bad choice. The sheriff and that jerk Jackson played a lot of poker with Stone and Blackwood. They were too tight socially not to be in bed together on whatever crooked shit was happening at the mill. Vance swore he was wrong about that, but Vance wasn't in the field with these guys. And God only knew what clandestine crap East-Tex was doing that he and Vance could have unwittingly stepped into. "I was almost half a mile away looking with my naked eye, peeking over a dirt ridge. Then, I was looking over my shoulder while I was running hell-bent for leather to get to you before that Crown Vic mowed me down. Never mind that my side was splitting open while all that was going on. I don't think any cop would consider me a credible witness. Hell, I wouldn't consider me a credible witness."

He could see it in her eyes, even before she spoke. *She's not buying it.* He hated being less than frank with her, but he had an inviolable obligation to client confidentiality, and unless one of the agency's lawyers told him otherwise, he couldn't just blab out unsubstantiated hunches and supposition about a client—especially to the expert witness for the plaintiffs suing them. He could lose his license and be done for in the business. Jesus…talk about a rock and a hard place. He longed for the days when the world was clearer…the days before Milwaukee—and before knowing Adelaide—had blurred all the lines.

"Well, I *know* what I saw. I saw two mill employees drag a man out of the building and shoot him in the head before they threw his lifeless body into a company Suburban. The accomplice burned rubber out the east gate of the plant before the killer chased us like dogs while he tried to shoot us dead. That's what I saw."

Only one word reverberated in Brock's mind—*de-escalate.* "I didn't hear a shot. At the pond, I mean. Did you?"

She seemed to consider it then shook her head. "Not while we were at the pond, no. But, as you said, we were a half a mile away. But I know damn well they shot at us while they were chasing us. You're the one who yelled about the gun right before those holes appeared in my windows."

He shrugged. "But we can't prove where those holes came from or who put them there."

Adelaide was visibly exasperated. "Why are you being so pig-headed about calling the cops?"

He kept his voice steady. "I told you. Involving the cops won't be good for my story."

"Your story?"

Uh-oh. He could see her anger rising like a rocket at Cape Canaveral.

"Your story? Are you insane?" She was starting to shout now. "Do you think I give a damn about your story? In less than twenty-four hours, I've been assaulted, you've been stabbed, we've watched a man get killed, and we've outrun gangs of men trying to murder us—twice." She was shrieking now. "And you're worried about your story? I should have my head examined." She got up and started pacing. Rufus watched her, his head swiveling like a spectator at Wimbledon. "I should have called the cops the minute we got out of that alley. This ends right now." She headed for the phone in the kitchen.

He struggled to maintain his unflappable façade as he quickly changed tack. "I'm also thinking about you." The strength of the tone in his voice apparently stopped her.

She spun around. "Me? You're thinking about me while you tell me not to call the cops and get help before these maniacs finish me off?"

He crossed over to her. He was so close, he could feel her breath.

"Yes, I'm thinking about you. What's going to happen when you call that high-dollar law firm you work for and tell them their star witness is tied up with a police investigation? That she's involved in that investigation because she was trespassing on mill property, illegally collecting water samples? When you're hip-deep in some criminal investigation, maybe being investigated yourself, what's that going to do to all those poor folks in Pine Grove and their chances of getting compensation for their injuries?"

For a moment, he was silently shocked at himself—at how quickly he had manufactured that manipulative tactic, how true he could make it ring. It certainly wasn't the first time he'd come up with some rationalization like that, but it was the first time he'd ever noticed himself doing it. And it was sure as hell the first time he'd ever felt anything but delighted when it played. This time it felt just a little bit…shameful. Truth of the matter was he *was* worried about her calling the good old boys at the Fairfield County sheriff's office. With each passing hour, he was more and more convinced that East-Tex, the sheriff's office…hell, the whole lousy bunch of them, were a big nest of copperheads. And he didn't want to go stirring that up until he was good and damn ready to handle whatever viper raised its ugly head. Until then—for now, at least—years of experience propped up his game face and kept him in character.

She turned away. "I'm not the only expert who can handle this. I can turn my information over to another engineer, and he or she can pick up where I left off."

The strategy was working. She was still talking about calling Raines and the cops, but her tone was losing some of its steam. A shadow of doubt was creeping into her voice. As crappy as he felt about it, now was the time to keep pushing the point…just not too hard.

"But your problems will taint the whole plaintiff group." He reached out for her shoulder, and she turned to him. "Are you willing to do that to all those people on the Families in Need list? All of those people are relying on you and Raines to help them."

She shook her head. "Okay. I have always been mindful of what you're saying, but I admit maybe I need to think it through some more." She looked away, then reached down and picked up her empty cup. "I'm going to get a refill. I need to pull myself together."

He watched as she turned and stalked into the kitchen. She had a point…he must be out of his mind not to call law enforcement. Granted, every instinct in his field-operative brain told him to avoid the cops, figure it out on his own, protect his client's confidentiality. But sure as God made little green apples, some really bad shit was going down, and he was out here in the middle of nowhere with a knife wound and no gun—and the expert witness for the plaintiffs. Jesus.

If the mill had anything to do with the murder, that made them the enemy, plain and simple. If they didn't, then there was probably nothing to fear from the cops. But years of investigative work had taught him it was never that simple. Never. Investigations were like mapping fields of icebergs. You knew damn well that, no matter how good you were, you were only seeing a fraction of what was happening below the surface.

Seeming more collected, Adelaide returned carrying two steaming cups. She set one down on the coffee table in front of him. "Peace offering."

He smiled. "Thanks."

She looked into his eyes. "I'm sorry I was angry. This isn't your fight. You got dragged into this mess saving me from those thugs. Maniacs are shooting at you because you're helping me. It was inexcusable of me to shout at you."

He reached out and touched her hand as she released the mug. The moment overflowed with what? Connectedness? Intimacy? Whatever it was, he'd never felt it before, so he couldn't say for sure. Brock had spent time with some of the most beautiful women in Dallas. He'd even dated one of the Cowboys cheerleaders for a while. He knew quite well what carnal attraction was. But this was different. He felt something profound when he touched Adelaide, something...real.

When she slowly removed her hand but sat down on the sofa near him, the magnetism continued. She met his eyes, and their gazes held for a moment before she looked away almost shyly. She was beautiful, compassionate, decent, altruistic...and she was apologizing to him for her frustration with what was nothing more than his undercover manipulation of her.

His carefully constructed pretend-world began to spin out of control in his head, forced into a whirling vortex by his feelings for Adelaide...and some strange new fixation with the truth, whatever that was. He was *in this mess*, as she put it, not because he'd self-lessly intervened to stop an attack against her, but because he was being paid a grand a day to spy on her—paid by the very folks she despised the most in the world. He thought about his earlier concern that being so hot for her was clouding his judgment. This was way beyond anything like trying to get her in the sack. He was in the deep weeds now.

Realizing he'd been silent for too long, he smiled and settled in, turning toward her, letting his leg brush hers. "Nothing to apologize for."

"You may be right about one thing. Our memories are probably faulty about what we saw from a distance under all that stress." She paused. Then she whipped around. "Oh, my God! I almost forgot! I have that video I shot with my phone."

He nodded. He was certain he'd eventually be answering a lot of questions about how the hell that came to be, so he may as well see it now. More importantly, maybe he could learn something from the recording that he could use to keep her out of harm's way. Though he couldn't put his finger on the moment it had happened, somewhere along the line, keeping Adelaide Reese safe had become the most important thing to him. "Fair enough."

CHAPTER 18

BROCK FOLLOWED, WATCHING Adelaide as she dug her phone out of her purse while she led him through the lodge down a long hallway. She moved with grace and purpose, her posture erect and strong. Her body was lithe and muscular under her jeans. He imagined himself exploring the mysteries hiding under the denim. She stopped when they came to a library with a twelve-foot coffered ceiling. The walls were covered in dark mahogany paneling. Faded spots marked the places where paintings must have once hung. He imagined those had been sold off during what Adelaide referred to as "the fall." Shelves of faded leather-bound books surrounded an antique mahogany library table with an ornately carved trestle base. An out-of-date computer workstation with a decent-sized flat-screen monitor was perched on the massive desk. Adorned by dark-red velvet balloon shades, high privacy windows lined the top two feet of the exterior wall. The room had the musty smell of broken dreams.

Brock looked around in awe. "Wow. This is straight out of some Victorian novel." Rufus sat down at Adelaide's feet. He looked up at her and cocked his head with inquisitive eyes. Brock pointed to an antique sofa with intricately carved mahogany framing upholstered in red brocade fabric. "Chair, Rufus." Without hesitation, the terrier hopped onto the couch, which burped up a cloud of dust around him. He sneezed and shook his head before curling into a circle and resting his chin on his front paws. Adelaide scratched his ears.

"Grace calls this the Bat Cave. The grade of the lot is such that this is essentially a basement. From the outside, this place doesn't exist."

He eyed the windows. "Aren't those skinny windows visible from the yard?"

She shook her head. "Not anymore. Overgrown shrubs completely hide them from view. That's one reason it's so dark in here." She pulled the brass chain on a green-shaded banker's lamp sitting on the desk.

Brock walked along the rows of books, perusing the volumes, running his finger through the thick dust on the shelves.

"This was her father's study—whatever that meant. God knows what crooked deals he cooked up in here." She nodded toward the faded spots on the wall. "Two Alfred Jacob Miller hunting scenes got sold off to feed the lawyers. There was an Alexander Pope over the fireplace that would have gone a long way to fixing everything, but the creditors snatched it before we could get it sold."

Adelaide plugged her phone into the computer and downloaded the file.

"We'll be able to see better on this monitor." In moments, the video appeared. She paused it.

"Pull up a chair. Let's take a look."

Gingerly, Brock pivoted an oxblood wingback chair so he could see the workstation clearly and eased carefully down into it. The chair was very close to hers. He could feel her presence and her breath. Again, he caught the faint scent of her shampoo. His shoulder was touching hers as he leaned in for a better view. He longed for the feel of his arms around her, his mouth on hers, the heat of her body. He struggled to pull himself together. *Cool your jets, buddy, before you get yourself in trouble you can't get out of.*

Adelaide adjusted herself in the wheeled task chair, breaking the spell. She hit a key and the video began to run. The scene played out just as Brock remembered it. In the end, the killer turned around and looked straight into the lens of Adelaide's camera. Brock felt like the man was looking directly at them sitting there in the run-down library. Even at that distance, Brock could make out the killer's white-blond hair.

She stopped the video and turned to him, raising her eyebrows. "Now would you like to tell me that I don't remember what I saw?"

His mind was reeling. He shook his head sadly. "No."

She turned back to the monitor. "I want to see if I can get a good shot of the victim."

Despite her repeated efforts, they were never able to get a view of the dead man's face.

"Let me see what I can do with the attackers." After some jockeying back and forth, Adelaide turned the monitor for Brock to get a clearer view. There, staring back at them, was the dark, hairy guy with the long black beard, holding the victim from behind. And beside him was the pale, white-blond giant, holding the gun. The enlarged faces filled the oversized monitor. Both men bore the unmistakable signs of the punishing retribution they had received from Brock and Rufus in the alley. Their rage and hatred oozed through the pixels.

Adelaide stared at the screen. She started to shiver like she was naked in the Arctic. Brock took her into his arms and held her against him.

"They were going to kill me. I know it. I can still feel his hands around my neck, still smell them—the beer and cigarettes and sweat. I was so scared…"

He held her tight, gently rocking her back and forth while

he stroked her hair. He whispered to her softly, "You're safe now. Nothing is going to happen to you here."

She clung to him. "How do you know that? You can't know that. I'll never be safe. You're right. The cops won't help. They're probably in on it. Nothing can help. They're going to kill me. They killed that man, and they're going to kill me."

Brock wanted to comfort her, take away her fears. He felt a tightness in his chest, heat rising through his heart as he held her close. "You're going to be just fine. I'll make sure of it." He held her back at arm's length and put his face down even with hers. "I promise you. I will not let anyone hurt you. You're safe with me." He felt for her in a way he had never before felt about a woman—or anyone else, for that matter. God help the bastard that tried to hurt her again.

He took her hand. "Come on." He led her back through the lodge to the huge master suite. He discreetly busied himself turning down the bed while she peeled off her clothes. He caught her reflection in the dresser mirror as she slipped into bed. He was mesmerized by her ivory skin and the enticing curves of her body. He covered her up and brushed her hair back from her face.

"The alarm is set. No one is going to get in."

The stress had exhausted her. She was falling asleep despite her fear. "Can you stay until I go to sleep?"

"Absolutely." He settled in, sitting on the side of the bed. "I'll be right here." Rufus jumped onto the bed and lay down next to her on the opposite side from his master, resting his head on her thigh.

In minutes, her breathing changed from ragged gasps to the rhythmic breathing of sleep. But every time he shifted his weight, she would moan and reach for him.

He looked around in the dim light. *What the hell have I done?* Here he was in the middle of nowhere, essentially in bed with a subject who had no idea who or what he was. He had broken his cardinal rule of never becoming emotionally involved with a case—and never, ever getting romantically involved with a subject. His calm detachment was gone, just when he needed it the most.

Worse, he knew that he and Vance had gotten themselves into way more than they had ever bargained for with this job. Vance was doing what Vance did best—keeping the agency healthy and growing. But what about him? His part in this deal was to get in the field and get the information their clients were paying for. Instead, the expert witness for the plaintiffs suing their client had video footage of a murder being committed by mill employees on mill property. And what about those water samples? They were still in the back of the SUV. And why wasn't he out there right now engineering a "leak" in those vials? He knew Vance would say his number one priority should be getting rid of evidence that had been illegally collected during a trespass on mill property... But what if East-Tex really *was* killing the town? What if they were knowingly dumping poison into that pond and polluting the Pine Grove water supply? How could he and Vance be defending that? Was it true that the mill had been providing fake evidence in response to discovery orders? Every time he tried to parse it out, the whole situation devolved into a kaleidoscope of swirling images.

Adelaide shifted in her sleep and snuggled up closer to him. He looked down at her and stroked her hair. To make matters worse, he could only imagine the emotional train wreck that would befall both of them when she found out the truth about him—which she no doubt would—eventually. It was inevitable now. With all the craziness in this operation, just fading away into the shadows was obviously off the list of possible outcomes. How much she would ultimately know might be debatable. But, without a doubt, she would learn enough that she would never trust him again.

One thing he knew was, no matter how this whole mess

played out, he was not about to let anything happen to her, no matter where the threat came from—no matter what that meant for his career. He was past the point of no return on that score. When she was finally settled, he rose quietly from the bed and left the room, leaving Adelaide under Rufus's watchful eye. He had a call to make.

∽

Adelaide woke up in the darkened room alone. Struggling to orient herself, she felt a weight next to her. When she ran her hand across Rufus's long, soft muzzle, he scooted in closer to her and grunted. Feeling the dog next to her reminded her of where she was. Then, it all came rushing back to her: the alley, the murder, the chase—all of it. How could this be happening? She forced herself to think it through.

She had no idea about the identity of the murder victim or why he would have been killed. As the questions raced through her head, a terrible realization hit her. Shortly after Addison had filed the lawsuit the previous spring, Adelaide had gotten three anonymous, untraceable emails from someone inside East-Tex Consolidated. The information they contained was disguised to look like it came from a layman. But, in her opinion, there was a professional understanding behind it.

The leads she got from those early emails had all proved to be true. She and Addison had always worried about the mole getting outed and them getting caught up in some whistleblower-versus-trade-secrets mess. They'd never answered the correspondence—never let on to anyone that she had received it or that it had even existed. All of her follow-up on the anonymous leads had been done in such a way that the information she developed appeared to be linked to other sources of information—like maybe she got the idea from published studies or from a government record. She scoured her memory for any mistake she could have made, any way she could have accidentally done something that led to her email friend being killed…but she couldn't come up with a single thing.

This whole mess was not what she bargained for in her life. Using science to beat corporate polluters—great. Being jumped in alleys and chased by gun-wielding killers—not so much.

And then there was the question of Brock. She had been fine on her own. It had been two years since the broken engagement. She didn't notice men anymore—not even extremely attractive ones. She had her work, her friends… She didn't need a man. Or at least she didn't think she did…until she'd stopped into Babe's that night. But she remembered her promise to herself from the start—to help him through the injury but nothing more. She scolded herself. *This isn't real. This is just the emotional result of being thrust into a high-stress situation with a handsome stranger. Wait until you get to know him and find yourself right back with a broken heart…*

She couldn't hold back the tears. As she cried quietly, she told herself it was just a tension-release from all the stress, all the fear of what was going to happen next, the worry about the suit and the clients. But deep down, she knew it was more. Deep down, she wanted Brock in a way she had never wanted her jackass ex-fiancé—or any other man.

But she wouldn't be able have him. Men wanted families—and she could never give him that. There was no need to pretend things would ever be different.

She wiped her eyes as Rufus licked her face. She snuggled up to the dog and forced herself back to sleep.

CHAPTER 19

BROCK MADE HIS way to the far end of the house, went upstairs, and closed himself up in one of the multitude of bedrooms in that wing of the lodge. Satisfied he was isolated, he tapped the keys on his phone. Vance answered on the first ring.

"Where are you, buddy? The hotel didn't know where you were, and your cell kept going straight to voice mail..."

"We've got honest-to-god deep-shit trouble, Vance."

Vance's tone was instantly serious. "Go."

"This morning, Adelaide confided in me that she was going to pull water samples from that pond just outside the mill fence behind the metal buildings. She invited me to go along and help her. I didn't have an opportunity to call in, so I rolled with it."

"You helped her take samples from that pond?"

Brock couldn't decide if Vance sounded more wary or astounded. "Yeah. There wasn't a work-around. Even if I'd managed to slip off and call you, anybody busting us would have probably blown the operation. I was the only one who knew she was going. This woman is smart—really smart. She would have connected the dots."

"Jesus."

"That's just the start of it." He ran Vance through the details of the shooting.

"Shit."

"It gets worse. The killers made us."

Vance's voice was rock steady. "How'd you get away from them?"

"She outran them. She drives like freaking James Bond. And it's a damn good thing she does since I still don't have a piece and couldn't return fire."

"She outran them?" He sounded incredulous.

"No shit. And get this—she used her iPhone and a surveying telescope to make a video of the murder."

"She did *what?*"

"Listen. You need to get the damn lawyers together as soon as the sun comes up and find a way to get us clear of this."

Vance cleared his throat. "Where are you now?"

Brock looked out the window and saw nothing but stars and the dark shadows of the woods. "Beats the hell out of me. An hour or so east of Pine Grove out in the middle of nowhere. I couldn't find it again if I had to, so I don't think anyone's going to get to us. I was checking for tails the whole way here."

Vance seemed to be thinking. After a few beats, he said, "What about the water samples? Did this happen before or after she pulled them?"

"Screw the damn water samples, Vance. Focus, for Chrissakes. I am not going to prison for some shit these East-Tex assholes did. I'd give my left nut for my Glock, but even without it I'm pretty sure I can keep us alive until the lawyers get a plan put together. We pay those bastards enough—call 'em tonight. Wake 'em up if you have to…"

"No cops. I repeat. No cops. Do you understand me?"

Brock took a deep breath and let it out. "I've gotten Adelaide to hold off on that, but that's not going to last long."

Vance's voice was almost a whisper. "When I tell you no cops,

I mean *no cops*. Meanwhile, you find those water samples and get rid of them. I don't care how you do it. Just do it."

In that moment, Brock detected something different in his partner's voice. In all these many years, he'd never heard his old friend panic, but he could have sworn that was what he was hearing. "Vance? What in the hell is going on? What aren't you telling me?"

Vance seemed to sense that maybe he had gone too far. His voice softened. "I'm sorry, buddy. I'm just tired. You know something? I don't think I've ever heard you call a subject by their first name… Oh, God, are you screwing this woman? Not that I disagree with the tactic, but you've always been iron-assed about not doing it."

Brock was an inch away from shouting. He closed his eyes and struggled to maintain his composure. "No, I'm not in bed with her. We're hunkered down hiding out from a bunch of maniacs who are trying to kill us…not drinking mai tais at a Sandals resort. What in the hell are you thinking?" Just saying the words, it hit him how attractive the Sandals thing—and the idea of being in bed with her—sounded. He pushed the thoughts aside. Now was *so* not the time.

"Sorry. You're right."

"Don't jack around with this, Vance. We're tap-dancing in a minefield with this damn case."

Vance laughed sadly. "Buddy, we've been tap-dancing in one minefield or another all our lives. Remember that night in Texarkana…you were what, eight? When we were hiding in the ditch behind that motel? You were so cold and scared, I was afraid you were going to wake the whole damn place up if I didn't get you to stop crying…"

Brock swallowed hard. "Yeah…I remember." He could see Vance peering over the edge of the ditch, waiting for the men in room twelve of the run-down Hilltop Inn to leave for their predawn hunt. He could feel the squeeze as Vance boosted him up and pushed him through the tiny frosted bathroom window into the bathtub of the dingy motel room.

They feasted on everything those hunters had left in their ice chests—a banquet of jerky and pimento cheese sandwiches and chips and cookies. Then Vance folded up the blankets off the beds, stuffed all the warm clothes the hunters had left into pillow cases, and shoved all of it back through the window before they snuck away...

Vance went on. "Just leave this to me. You say you're not screwing her, fine. But I know you're into her...I can hear it in your voice. I don't give a damn how hot she is, though. I talked to Remy tonight, and there's a mole in the mill. Some sonofabitch is leaking info to Raines. They don't know who it is yet, but they're working on it. So you better figure out if she's the one hustling information out of that plant. This is hardball, buddy. And you can bet your ass Adelaide Reese is playing it, too. Hell, for all we know, she's hip to who you are and is working you as hard as you're working her."

Before Brock could answer, the line went dead.

Getting caught up in a client's crap was every investigator's nightmare. Yet it happened all the time, and he could handle it. But the thought of Adelaide getting chewed up in a mess like that—maybe hurt...or worse—he couldn't stand even the possibility of it.

He headed back downstairs. He'd be spending the night as close to her room as he could get.

CHAPTER 20

BROCK SLEPT FITFULLY. Every time he went to roll over, his damn side felt like it was going to rip open again.

After he got off the phone with Vance, he had chosen the bedroom next to the master suite in case Adelaide called to him in the night. Yet it seemed that she had managed to sleep through. She'd looked so exhausted when she'd crawled under the covers, she could have probably slept with a brass band playing at the foot of the bed.

He finally gave up trying to sleep just before the sun rose. He made his way to the laundry room and took his own clothes out of the dryer. He tossed the borrowed shorts and T-shirt in the washer and pulled the laundry room door shut to keep the noise from waking Adelaide. Then, he made a cup of coffee and took it to the living room.

He surveyed the stunning view of the lake afforded by the dirty picture windows on both sides of the room. He sat on the large brown-leather sofa facing east and sipped his steaming coffee as the sun broke over the horizon in subtle shades of pink that gradually gave way to flaming rays of red light.

He considered his situation. While he had been so adamant in his denials to Vance that anything was happening between him and Adelaide, his partner's instinct hadn't been far off. What had started as such a strong connection with her, a crackling electricity arcing between them, was morphing into a powerful magnetic attraction. He could feel it so strongly, there was no way she could be oblivious to it.

But whatever it was, it had to end. He could not get involved with a woman—especially this kind, decent, brilliant woman—under completely false pretenses. It was morally unacceptable, never mind professional suicide. In all the years he'd worked this job, he had never let this happen—until now.

Maybe Vance was right. Maybe Adelaide was working him the way he was working her, or was supposed to be, anyway. To him, it seemed impossible that the person hugging the frail chemo patient and demanding steroids for some guy she hardly knew could be running a con on him. But Vance hadn't gotten as far as he had in this business without a pretty keen investigative sense. Brock couldn't write Vance's intuition off out of hand.

He considered a million ways to tell her the truth. But in every scenario he could imagine, she was livid and ended up hating him. Not that he could blame her. Worse, coming clean with her could be the end of his career. Breaking client confidentiality by revealing his real identity could cost him his license…and drag the whole agency through a world of hurt at the same time. Vance would never get over it, never forgive him. When it came down to it, neither would the licensing board. He *and* Vance would both be screwed for good, never mind the liability they'd incur to East-Tex for violating their confidentiality. No. The only thing to do was to stop whatever was happening between them in its tracks.

This is a job, he thought. *Nothing more, nothing less.* He was a professional, and it was high time he went back to acting like one. He remembered the first time he had worked undercover and unwittingly found evidence that their client wasn't entirely on the up-and-up. Vance looked him straight in the eye and said,

"Whoever promised you these people would be angels? They may be assholes, but they are *our* assholes. We took their money, and we keep their secrets. That's how it works. If you don't like that, go work at Walmart."

He thought about how hard he had fought to get this far— about where he had come from and how determined he was to make something of himself. The idea of throwing all of that away over a tryst with a subject was absurd.

But Adelaide was different, and this was way more than a tryst. She wasn't just another designer-clad package of arm candy he could squire around the hipster night spots of Dallas. He'd never known a woman like her. The way she cared for those plaintiffs, worried about their prescriptions and insurance claims…she was smart and kind and driven. Where had she been all his life? And why in the hell did she have to show up here now?

His thoughts were interrupted as Adelaide emerged fully dressed from the bedroom wing of the first floor, Rufus trotting behind her. Her eyes were puffy. Maybe she had been crying after he left her to call Vance. Otherwise, she seemed back to her regular self.

Puffy eyes or not, she was a beautiful woman. He felt a strong desire to ask her if she was all right—to comfort her…reassure her. But that, he remembered, was not on the agenda anymore. This was just business. He stood up to greet her.

"Morning."

She looked startled. Apparently, she hadn't seen him sitting on the couch. "Good morning." Rufus toddled over to his master and grunted. Brock leaned down and scratched his ears. "Hey, pal…how'd you sleep? Were you a good guard dog? Did you keep a close eye on Adelaide?"

She nodded groggily. "He was a very good boy. He's a bed hog, though. Every time I moved, he scooched over and got right up against me."

Lucky him... Brock stopped himself. *No more of that!* He held up his coffee cup. "I hope it's all right. I helped myself."

She shrugged. "Feel free."

Awkwardly, she turned and headed toward the kitchen. She took a mug from the cabinet and popped one of the few remaining pods in the coffee maker. She stood at the counter and seemed to be composing her thoughts. Finally, she looked directly at him and spoke.

"I'd like to apologize for my behavior last night. I don't know what came over me. I think it was just a culmination of everything that's been going on. You were very chivalrous, and I'm thankful. But I just wanted to assure you that I'll handle myself better in the future."

He knew he should be relieved, but he couldn't deny the part of him that was disappointed that she wouldn't be coming to him for solace anymore. Disappointed or not, though, he had a job to do. He forced a casual smile and said, "No apology necessary. It's been a crazy couple of days. Let's just call it even."

She gave a curt nod. "Very well. I'd like to talk, if you don't mind." She took her coffee to the long oak dining table and sat down. Rufus hopped up into one of the dining chairs and assumed the panda position. Brock brought his cup and joined them.

Adelaide took a deep breath and let it out. "I've thought this through. I did what I did. Right or wrong, I need to level with my client about it. When the office opens at eight, I'm going to call Addison and come clean. He can fire me or not—that's his choice. In any case, I'm fessing up. Then, depending on how he wants to do it, he can call the police or I will. I'm perfectly willing to leave you out of this. I'll take you and Rufus back to your hotel before I talk to the cops. I won't mention you in any of this. You can do what you want."

He mulled that over for a moment. "Well, if you've decided, then that's your deal. I just want to remind you of one thing."

She set her cup down carefully and looked him square in the eye. "What would that be?"

"When you tell Addison Raines that you illegally entered mill property, he becomes part of that act. You're his consultant, under his umbrella. What you do, in effect, he does. He's innocent now. He can swear on a stack of bibles that he didn't have any knowledge of what you were up to. But once you tell him, he's in the soup, too. Do what you think is best, but you may be dragging your guy into something that he's relatively unsullied by thus far."

She nodded. "Thanks for pointing that out. I've considered it, of course, but I'll give it some more thought before his office opens."

Awkward pause. She pushed back from the table. As she did, the morning light streaming through the kitchen windows cast her in a warm glow. The sight made his breath catch. *Puffy eyes and day-old clothes...and she's still just beautiful.* He struggled to keep a neutral expression, hoping she hadn't caught him staring. She didn't seem to have noticed.

"Well, then...I'm hungry," she said. "It's likely going to be a long day, so I need to eat. How about I hustle us up some breakfast?"

He nodded. "Sure. That sounds great."

Adelaide laughed. "Don't be so sure. It's probably more ravioli and stale chips." She turned to Rufus, who was still lounging in the dining chair, and rubbed his belly. "What about you, buddy? You hungry?"

The dog opened his mouth, yawned, then yapped. Brock got up and walked into the kitchen. "I think that's a yes. Didn't you say there was some more tuna around here?"

She nodded and pointed to a cabinet. "Over there. How's your side feeling this morning?"

"It's a lot better, thanks. Dr. Deadhead fixed me up." He opened the tuna can and poured the contents into a bowl. Rufus folded himself off the dining chair and made his way to the kitchen. Brock shook his head. "That dog can hear the sound of a can opening a mile away."

Before he could bend over, Adelaide took the bowl from his hand and set it on the floor. "We don't need you splitting your side open again." Their eyes caught as her hand brushed his in the exchange. He felt the warmth of her touch spread up his arm, straight to his chest. *Keep it together.*

He looked around, desperately trying to fill the now-very-awkward silence. "While you get breakfast going, I'm going to take Rufus outside. Do you mind if I take your keys and get my backpack out of your truck? In all the commotion yesterday, I never brought it in. I wanted to look through my notes to see if there's anything in there that might give us a clue as to what's going on around here."

She shrugged. "Can't hurt." As she pulled her purse off of a hook in the entry hall, he picked up a remote and turned on a TV mounted on the kitchen wall. He looked at her. "You mind?" She shook her head.

The air between them was thick with emotion and things better left unsaid. He figured the blather of early morning television would be much better than the glaring silence they were experiencing. She dug around in her purse, produced the fob, and slid it across the granite counter to him. As he picked it up, the picture on the television resolved and the sound came up, blaring the end of a jingle for a used car dealer. As he headed out the door, the anchor for the Lufkin early morning news program came into view. She shuffled the papers on her desk then looked at the camera intently.

"And now, we go to Jason Ellsworth on the scene at the East-Tex Consolidated mill in Pine Grove. Jason, what more can you tell us about the missing engineer?"

A young reporter in an ill-fitting suit spoke from outside the mill. "Well, Jackie, this is what we know so far. Around midnight last night, the Pine Grove police received a phone call from Beth Wesley, the wife of Arthur Wesley, the chief safety and compliance officer here at the plant. That's when she reported her husband missing."

Brock stopped in his tracks as Adelaide did a double take. She grabbed the remote and turned up the volume. The young reporter continued.

"According to Mrs. Wesley, her husband called her yesterday morning and said he would be working late at the plant. When Mr. Wesley hadn't come home or responded to any of her calls by 10:00 p.m. last night, Mrs. Wesley drove to the mill where she found her husband's car in the employee parking lot. The plant reports that a thorough search of the facility was conducted, but Mr. Wesley was not located. His briefcase was still in his office, as was his uneaten bag lunch."

The anchor fixed her face in a questioning look. "Well, Jason, that certainly sounds perplexing. Has the plant issued a statement?"

The young reporter nodded solemnly. "I just spoke with Darren Blackwood, the plant manager, by phone a few minutes ago. He declined to be interviewed and referred me to Remy Stone, local counsel for the mill, who emailed me this written statement: 'We regret that Mr. Wesley has failed to contact his family. East-Tex has no knowledge of Mr. Wesley's current whereabouts. Mr. Wesley is a valued member of the East-Tex team and a well-respected part of the Pine Grove community. Management regrets these unfortunate events and hopes that Mr. Wesley returns home safely.'"

The camera cut back to the anchor, who asked, "Have you learned anything else, Jason?"

The young reporter looked solemn. "Well, Jackie, I've spoken with a source knowledgeable about the situation who tells me that Mr. Wesley has been on probation status at East-Tex for the past three months in relation to his substance abuse issues.

My source tells me Mr. Wesley was advised yesterday morning by plant management that he was being terminated. Mr. Wesley reportedly stated at that time he was checking into an alcohol treatment program today."

Adelaide and Brock stared at the set. The anchor was describing a traffic accident on the interstate when Adelaide muted the television.

"That's hogwash. I've known Arthur Wesley professionally for years. He's never been a drinker. He's diabetic. Anyway, he's the quintessential family man. He would never go off and leave his wife without letting her know…" Her voice trailed off. She and Brock looked at each other and seemingly shared the terrible realization at the same time.

"Oh, God. Oh, God." She started running down the hall to the library. Brock followed her with Rufus tight on their heels.

Adelaide perched on the edge of the task chair and activated her hotspot. She called up the video she had downloaded to her Dropbox the night before. Brock sat back down in the wingback chair and stared at the monitor.

"It can't be him…it just can't be." Her voice was shaky. He could tell she was fighting back tears as she ran the video in slow motion. She advanced the images frame by frame. At one point, something fell out of the shooting victim's shirt pocket. Adelaide enlarged the image and stared at what she saw.

Her voice was as tight as a piano wire. "It's him."

Brock stared at the screen. The victim's face was entirely blocked from view. "How can you tell?"

Without a word, Adelaide placed the crosshairs on a blurry rectangle in the lower right-hand corner of the screen. She ran the video forward and back until Brock could make out the object tumbling from the victim's shirt pocket as he struggled to free himself.

Then, Adelaide enlarged the image. As the pixels resolved on the screen, Brock saw an old-fashioned leather appointment book. It was burgundy.

Adelaide slumped in the chair. "Arthur always used that. I asked him about it at a conference once. A bunch of us were teasing him about being in the Stone Age, not getting with modern technology. He said his dad gave it to him for his graduation."

She looked so sad. Despite his earlier promises to himself, he couldn't control his urge to comfort her. He rubbed his hand on her back. "You must have known him pretty well."

She shrugged. "We were at lots of the same conferences and meetings. He was in management at the Dallas office of the EPA's OSC for several years before he went to Washington. Our paths crossed on a bunch of cases. He is…*was* a good guy. Everyone knew that."

He sat next to her and tucked her hair behind her ear and stroked her cheek as she fought not to cry. Her brown eyes were flecked with gold that shimmered when the light hit her brimming tears. Brock was mesmerized by her beauty and absorbed by his overwhelming desire to comfort her—to keep her safe—when Adelaide sat up ramrod straight.

"Wait a minute. At the town hall meeting, I overheard a conversation Arthur had with Blackwood's assistant. She came up to Arthur and said that Blackwood had called her and said something about his child being moved to ICU and told her to go find Arthur and get him to cover the staff meeting the next morning—which would have been yesterday. She asked if he could do it, like she was going to have to figure something else out if he wasn't available. He took that appointment book out and looked at it." She closed her eyes as she recounted the conversation. "He said, yes, he could cover the meeting in the morning…that he didn't have anything scheduled until yesterday afternoon when he was meeting with…" She bit her lip. "Oh, who did he say he was meeting with?" She scrunched up her face then she snapped her fingers. "Contractors. He had to meet with contractors about repairing the fire damage."

An image of the assistant taking Wesley aside flashed through Brock's mind. He sat forward. "I'd forgotten about that, but now that you mention it, I remember it, too. I heard the conversation from where I was standing. If that's the case, then the claim that he had been fired and had told Darren Blackwood that he was going into rehab yesterday can't be true."

"Yep. Complete and total fiction."

Their exchange was interrupted when Rufus let out a guttural growl. His ears perked up and the hair on the back of his neck stood straight up a second before he started barking ferociously. In a flash, he sprang off the sofa and made a beeline out the door. Brock grabbed Adelaide by the hand. He didn't want to put her in danger, but with an unknown threat somewhere around them, he couldn't bear to leave her alone. He forced her behind him as they scrambled back down the hallway. A sharp crack followed by the sound of shattering glass shot through the lodge. As they turned the corner, the large picture window on the front side of the living room fractured into a million pieces and the spider-webbed glass collapsed.

Heavy rounds came sailing past their heads, exploding against the cedar paneling in sequence, a chorus of ear-splitting blasts raining wood shards down on the living room.

"Shit. That's an AR-15." Brock's heart was pounding like a drum solo at a Rush concert when he grabbed Adelaide and ducked back into the hall, throwing her to the ground and shielding her and Rufus with his body as a hail of machine gun fire began. In an instant, the drapes were shredded. The cedar wall looked like a cheese grater as the room was engulfed in a curtain of lead. The wind whipping through the broken windows carried the deafening sound of the guns.

The roar of the fusillade washed over them like a tidal wave. Adelaide was coughing from the dust and debris. The gunfire was quickly destroying the entire front end of the log building, eliminating any possibility of an exit through that part of the house.

Brock stood bent over, putting himself between Adelaide and the attackers. He yanked her to her feet and pushed her hard. Frightened by the sound of the gunfire, Rufus bolted ahead of them. They all raced back down the hall.

Brock shouted over the din. "Is there a door in this part of the house?"

Adelaide shook her head. "Only windows."

By the time the trio reached the library, bullets were coming through the windows of the bedrooms across the hall.

"They're coming across the front of the house."

Adelaide looked up at the red balloon shades. "It'll be tight, but we can fit through those transom windows."

His heart raced as he bounded to the workstation and knocked the monitor onto the ground. He mustered all his strength to drag the huge mahogany desk to the exterior wall, then climbed up on top of the table and peered out the narrow privacy windows. He twisted one of the balloon shades over the curtain rod.

The bullets had shredded the walls of the rooms across the hallway and were now coming straight into the library, splintering the wood paneling and ripping through the faded fabric of the once-beautiful furnishings. He opened the window and motioned for Adelaide.

"Get up here. Now!"

She climbed up beside him. Biting back the pain from his wound, he grabbed her around the waist and hefted her up to the window. "Grab on to the frame."

She did as he said and pulled herself through the opening. The coffered ceiling tiles began to splinter.

Adelaide's eyes darted around. "Jesus. They must be on the roof now, firing down at us."

Rufus leaped onto the desk. Brock felt a hot poker stabbing

into his side now. He set his jaw and lifted Rufus through the window. Adrenaline surged through his blood as he grabbed the bottom of the window frame and lifted himself up, giving him strength to overcome the agony ripping through his body as he struggled through the opening. He pulled the shade down and shoved the window back into place just as a hail of bullets stitched a line across the beautiful coffered ceiling of the library, ripping through the carved wood like a deadly buzz saw.

CHAPTER 21

BROCK PUSHED ADELAIDE down behind an overgrown huckleberry bush while he shielded her crouching form with his body. Rufus wedged himself between them.

Out of the corner of her eye, Adelaide caught a flash of movement before she heard a male voice saying something she couldn't make out. The sound was coming from the far side of the property, probably the front porch. She pointed toward the sound and Brock nodded.

"They're moving all the time. But I think right now the lodge is between us and the bad guys." He looked around frantically. "How far to civilization if we take off through the woods?"

She shook her head. "Not an option. A bunch of it's swamp crawling with alligators."

He looked toward the garage. "Is there a way for me to get into the car without opening that overhead door?"

She was panting and shaking. She nodded as she tried to catch her breath.

"How?" He took her by the shoulders and looked straight into her eyes. "Tell me how to get to the car so I can get us the hell out of here."

His stern tone snapped her out of her near state of shock. She shook her head to clear it. "There's a window into the boathouse on the other side, facing the lake."

"Is it locked?"

"I don't think so."

She could hear the men's voices growing louder. They were firing their guns again. One of them clearly had an automatic weapon of some sort. The shots were coming too fast...

"What good is that going to do us? How are we going to start my car? The fob is in my purse in the kitchen."

"No, it's not." He dug into his pocket and held up the device.

One of the transom windows twenty feet from where they were huddled blew out, sending shards of glass all the way into the driveway. A cold fear raced through her veins.

"That's the back bedroom, right next door to the library."

Brock took her face in his hands and turned it to his. "Here's the deal. If I make it to the other side, when I get the overhead door open, you run to me like the hounds of hell are on your heels."

"The hounds of hell *are* on my heels."

"If I don't make it, you crawl through these bushes until you can get in the woods and find the best hiding place you can."

Before she could argue, he was sprinting across the open space toward the garage. She was terrified to see him running in the open. She felt incredibly vulnerable without him—and she couldn't bear the idea of him being hurt. Somehow, Brock Emerson had become something to her no one had ever been before...

He reached the building, seemingly undetected. Another second and he had slipped around the corner and out of her sight. She watched the garage door like she was waiting for the Second Coming.

More of the transom windows were shattering, each one like a nasty little bomb, spewing shards of glass as bullets flew through the openings. The attackers would be in the library any second. She had to move. Then she heard the rattle as the boathouse door began to rise. The relief that momentarily washed over her was overshadowed by terror as one of the library's narrow windows exploded. She sprinted to the outbuilding, ducking under the still-opening door. Rufus was not a step behind. She yanked open the passenger door and threw herself into the SUV, then turned and grabbed Rufus's collar, hauling him in behind her. Brock cranked the engine and threw the truck into gear.

"Buckle your belt and hold on!" he yelled.

As he maneuvered the truck down the driveway, two men in ski masks jumped into a white Suburban parked next to the house. The big tires spun and burned rubber as the attackers chased the fleeing Explorer.

As Brock sped toward what was no more than a path on their left, Adelaide pointed and yelled, "Turn into that lane."

Brock squinted through the windshield. "Is that really a road?"

She shouted, "Do it now!"

Brock cut the wheel just as they were about to miss the turn. The Explorer fishtailed and swerved as they hit a deep pothole. The truck bounced hard, then landed on all four tires, keeping its forward momentum. The jolt was so powerful, Adelaide felt the air leave her lungs as she slammed against the shoulder belt. Rufus struggled to keep his balance on the floorboard beneath her feet.

The driver of the Suburban didn't react in time and missed the cutoff. Adelaide gasped for breath as she turned in her seat and watched the driver throw the white truck into Reverse and then cut down the lane. In fifty yards, the road was going to hit a T-intersection.

Brock shouted, "Which way?"

"Right! Go right!"

As Brock made the turn, what looked like a large overgrown grape arbor came into view. "Pull under the arbor. Go forward as far as you can."

Brock did as she directed. With the Explorer stopped deep

within the tunnel of greenery, Brock scanned the mirrors. "Did they see us?"

She stared out what was left of the back windshield. "I'm not sure, but I don't think so. We'll know soon enough."

Out the back window, they both watched as the Suburban paused at the T before taking a right. In a few seconds, the truck sped past them. They breathed a collective sigh of relief.

"Give it three minutes. If they don't come back by then, they'll have hit a paved fire lane that will take them to the interstate."

Brock looked into the thick, leafy vines engulfing the tunnel. "If they come back and find us, we're screwed because we're nose-in to a dead end."

She shook her head. "If they come back and find us, floor it straight through here for another fifty yards. We'll come out on a rut that leads to that fire lane, and then it'll just be a race. The good news is that the Explorer will fit, but the Suburban is going to have a hard time squeezing through."

As he squinted through what was left of the windshield, she said, "I know. It looks like we're going nowhere, but it's passable. These vines are just hanging down. The Explorer will push right through."

"What is this place?"

"Grace showed it to me when we first came out here. This was an old covered bridge that was moved here and used as a movie set back when she was a kid. They left it here, and it's been swallowed up by kudzu, but it's still passable."

The seconds passed like hours. Adelaide shook her head. "How in the world did they find us? Why would anyone think that either you or I would end up at Grace Hinkle's lake house?"

He shook his head. "I have no idea."

"I would have seen someone following us through all those back roads. I didn't see a soul, and heaven knows I was looking."

"Have you contacted anyone and let them know where you were since we were at the pond?"

She shook her head. "Nobody except Grace."

They waited as they watched the digital clock on the dash turn over three more minutes. No Suburban.

"Okay. I want you to back out of here and go back in the other direction. Like you turned left at the T. That will lead us away from them, whichever way they go on the interstate. That way, we don't have to worry about passing them in either direction."

Brock put the SUV into Reverse and followed her instructions. Rufus crawled up from the floor, scaled the console, and sat on the back seat, his ears up and his triangular eyes darting from side to side, ever wary of more threats. Brock kept checking the rearview. In short order, they approached a paved FM road. He looked around and said, "I know this road. It'll take us to a little town called Martinsville. There, I'm going to cut north on County Road 7. Eight miles past the turn there's a place for us to stay."

As the Ford bounced along the last few yards of the caliche road, a terrible clanging sound began emanating from the undercarriage. Adelaide looked around desperately for evidence they were dragging something.

"I think there's something stuck in the chassis. Pull over so I can take a look."

Brock shook his head. "I don't think that's such a great idea. What about those alligators you were talking about? Besides, we don't really know where the bad guys are. I sure don't want to be parked by the side of the road and have them drive up."

"Alligators? We're on a state highway. If the axle breaks in two or the transmission craters because of something lodged in the drivetrain while we're out here in the middle of nowhere, we're really in trouble. I think that's worse."

"Worse than being caught like sitting ducks when a Suburban full of killers happens to drive by? I'm going to have to disagree with you there."

She was getting angry. This was her car, after all. Why did

men get so damn stubborn whenever it came to machines? Brock Emerson was handsome and kind and brave, but here he was being a know-it-all about *her* vehicle. *Maybe it's in their DNA...*

"I'm an engineer, damn it. And this is my truck...a truck that was never designed for serious off-roading, especially at high speeds. Where were you when we went airborne back there when we hit that pothole? I'm telling you we need to see what's wrong with the truck before we drive it to death."

"Just hang on a minute..."

He turned the Explorer onto the paved roadway of FM 95. The sound was even louder during the turn but subsided when they straightened out on the relatively smooth blacktop. Adelaide turned her head sharply to listen. Nothing.

Brock looked relieved at the silence and turned to her with a see-I-told-you-so look. "I think we had picked up a branch or something. We must have dropped it when we made that last turn."

She looked out through the remnants of the back windshield. It was impossible to tell if anything that could have been stuck in the undercarriage had been knocked free and deposited behind them. She stared out the window in annoyed silence.

After several miles, they saw a sign welcoming them to Martinsville. Brock turned left without comment. As the car rounded the corner, the rattling began again, only now it was a full-fledged banging. Adelaide glared at him. "What? Are you afraid you'll get kicked out of the boys' club if anyone ever finds out you listened to a woman about car trouble?"

No sooner had she spoken than the sound faded away. He produced one of those high-wattage smiles. "What car trouble?"

She shook her head. *Jesus...just because he's gorgeous doesn't automatically make him right...* But he had just risked his life to save her at the lake house...and in the alley...and at the mill pond. So, upon further consideration, it probably wasn't such a big deal if he was being a bit Neanderthal about the rattle. She'd check it when they got wherever they were going.

Eight miles past the turn, they saw a sign for the Caddo Inn. The Caddo was an old-time motel—a U-shaped single-story cinder block structure with a low-pitch gravel roof and a covered parking space next to every room. A small, kidney-shaped swimming pool sat in one corner of the U, surrounded by a faded beige aluminum fence. The missing tiles around the top edge of the pool reminded Adelaide of broken teeth. A pair of rusty, fifties-style metal lawn chairs straddled each of the thirty guest room doors. The office was up front near the road with one leg of the typical A-line roof providing a porte cochere for arriving travelers. The faded Motel sign perched on top of the building was listing along with the sagging ridgeline. The neon lighting in the typical mid-century roadside sign had long since given up the ghost. Brock pulled under the covered driveway in front of the office and stopped.

Adelaide surveyed the scene. "This place looks like the Bates Motel."

He let go of the door handle and turned to her. "Exactly what would you have me do? Whip out a black card and have the Amex concierge make us a reservation at a local five-star? Sorry, but this is the best I can do while I'm being chased by lunatics who just turned a solid log house into a block of Swiss cheese while they were trying to kill us. It's a motel away from the interstate with individual garages where we can hide this truck and where they don't ask questions. I'm going to get us a room until we can figure out a plan."

With that, he got out of the truck and jogged into the motel office. Her cheeks stung as she watched the glass door close behind him. She hated being scolded; it always embarrassed her, especially if she thought she might have had it coming. She hadn't meant anything by the Bates Motel comment, but she could see his point. It wasn't like she had a better idea…and it sure wasn't like the place she'd picked had worked out so well. Her stint as chief crisis-travel-guide had gotten them hosed down by automatic weapons fire. Plus, men who worked for a living were always, to some degree, put off by her family name and her father's prominence. They could never accept the idea that she just didn't care about the money—theirs or hers—so comments like the Bates thing were always taken in that context. Truth was, Brock Emerson was some version of a man she'd never imagined could exist. He was daring and chivalrous and compassionate, never mind drop-dead handsome, and she felt things for him she'd never felt before. She didn't know what any of that meant for her, but she was pretty sure it meant something. No matter what it was, though, in the end, it always came down to the issue of having a family, and she just couldn't face that again. Before she could think that through, he emerged with a key and got back in the SUV. His voice was more even. "Room number seven. In the back corner."

Brock backed the truck into the covered slot between the shabby rooms. He looked over at Adelaide as he maneuvered the Explorer into the corrugated metal shed. "Just in case we need to get out of here in a hurry." He grabbed his backpack and whistled for Rufus. As Adelaide headed into the room, he locked the doors with the remote and followed.

Once inside, Adelaide pulled the faded curtains and went straight to the phone. She had to call Grace to tell her the terrible news about the lodge. Grace answered on the first ring.

"Oh, my God, Adelaide…are you all right? I've tried and tried your cell, but I get no answer. I was scared to death you were trapped in the lodge."

"How did you know about the lodge?"

"Bob next door called me. He heard the gunfire. He couldn't find you or your friend. I felt a little better when he couldn't find your car, but I was still worried out of my mind. It sounds crazy, but he said somebody shot up the place. He says it looks like some scene out of *Die Hard*."

Adelaide gave her the broad strokes of the attack and the vehicle that chased them. "It was pretty intense, but we're both fine. I am so sorry about the lodge. It's my fault. I should have never gone there."

"Oh, stop it. Stuff doesn't matter. People matter. You're okay. The rest is noise. It was about to fall in on itself, anyway. I've been thinking about it since Bob called. It's probably a good thing. Maybe this'll convince those creeps with the liens to work with us. Anyway, if anyone's going to be sorry, it should be the insurance company. Hell, Dan said maybe we can just take the insurance money and let the lien holders have the place. They can sort it out."

Adelaide marveled at Grace. She was so kind, so practical. "You can be sure Addison will make those insurance people pay every cent they owe. You have my promise of that. And I'll make up anything that's not covered."

"I am sure of all of that. It'll be fine. Bob's already got the sheriff there. I'll tell them about the white Suburban. I'm not worried about it. I've got really important news."

Adelaide smiled. "And what would that be?"

She could hear Grace beaming through the phone line. "I actually had a pork chop and spinach for lunch and didn't throw it up. That's what I'm concentrating on."

After Adelaide finished her conversation with Grace and hung up the phone, she collapsed on one of the sagging double beds. Visions of Grace and her husband, Dan, swam through her mind. Dan knew all about Grace's family's fall from the lofty heights of Dallas society—and he couldn't have cared less about any of it, except that it had been painful for his wife. He just loved Grace and wanted her well and healthy and happy. Anyone who felt inclined toward any nasty commentary about her parental woes might find themselves on the wrong end of his pipe wrench. As long as Adelaide had known Grace and Dan, she had found herself secretly wishing she could find a man somewhere who could love her as unconditionally as Dan loved Grace. A part of her wondered if maybe… She stopped herself. *That's not how it works—not for me, at least.*

Brock was surfing the five channels he could find on the old tube television for any news that might mention the lodge. Finding nothing, he turned the set off, came over to her, and sat on the edge of the bed.

"So, you know the person who owns this place?"

He sighed. "I'm in a group that hunts here every year. Edna and her husband owned this place when they first got married. He got killed in Vietnam. She's never gotten over it."

"How does she live? This place looks deserted."

"She owns the three hundred acres the motel sits on. She leases that out for hunting and lets the hunters stay here. There's no hunting season now, so I knew the place would be empty—and the fact that Edna keeps a small arsenal in her apartment and knows how to use it was a plus. She's not much for strangers. It seemed like a good idea."

"I'm sorry about what I said. I think you're amazingly… resourceful. I didn't mean to be critical about this place. I was just feeling the stress."

"I know. I'm so sorry about Grace's house."

She smacked her hand on the faded print bedspread. "I feel so responsible." Rufus hopped up onto the bed, waddled over to Adelaide, and lapped her face. She nuzzled him briefly before he settled in next to her. "If I hadn't gone there, the place would still be untouched. Her house—her only real asset—is torn to ribbons because of me." She got up and started to pace. Brock stood and moved closer to her.

"I'm sure she doesn't hold it against you." He reached out to comfort her, but she pulled away.

"That's not the point. I went there and dragged a perfectly

innocent person into my mess. And it ended up costing Grace. The last thing she needs now is something else to worry about."

Brock wrapped his arms around her and held her tight. She relented. She felt her resistance ebbing away as she buried her face in his shoulder. The dam broke, and the fear and exhaustion and sadness and anger washed away as she relaxed into his strong embrace.

She could smell his musky, male scent. His chest was strong and muscular. His arms enveloped her in a kind of safety that she was not accustomed to experiencing. However mad she was at him, at the faceless, nameless forces hunting her, at East-Tex and all the other paper mills of the world, right now, she wanted him. She wanted to feel his skin against hers, feel his mouth on hers, feel him inside her.

She kissed his neck and moved up to his face. He took her head in his hands and held her face in front of his, looking into her eyes. Neither spoke as he lowered his mouth to hers and they kissed. A deep, probing, passionate kiss. His mouth was hot, and his lips were soft. He pulled her T-shirt over her head and deftly unhooked her bra. She tore at his clothes with passion and heat and desperation. They both wiggled out of their pants.

As soon as they were both naked, he grabbed her and pulled her body close to his. It was as if they couldn't hold each other tight enough. He kissed her and probed her mouth with his tongue, then held her in his arms as he gently lowered her to the bed. She could feel the strength of his muscles against her back. He stretched out beside her, kissing her breasts and her neck and her ears. Excitement and arousal screamed from every place he touched her, building by the second. It was as though he knew what she wanted, what she needed, even before she knew herself. The lovemaking was just an extension of the holding. It was a way to be closer, more connected, safer.

He whispered, "Just let go. Let me take care of you."

And she did…let go of the fear, the loneliness, the past… all of it. She let him take her, consume her. He made love to her for what seemed like hours, taking her places no man ever had. She moaned, cried out in ecstasy. Over and over he brought her to the edge, then backed off only to bring her back again. In the end, a wave of passion crested inside her and permeated every fiber of her being. He kept kissing her and holding her until the wave passed and a calm overtook her. He rolled onto his back, and she settled onto his shoulder. He kissed the top of her head as he stroked her hair.

"We're going to be okay. I'm not sure how, but we're going to be okay."

She didn't argue as sleep overcame her, and she drifted off in the safety of his arms. She heard Rufus snoring quietly on the next bed. Her last waking thought was, *Dear God, let this time be different.*

❧

Brock looked down at Adelaide as she slept. Thoughts of his earlier pledge to keep his distance from her swam through his head. He caught Rufus eyeing him from the next bed. Brock imagined the dog shaking his head in canine disappointment. *You swore you weren't going to do this…*

If he could just keep it together until Vance got the lawyers to figure out a way to call the cops without jeopardizing their license, he would tell her everything. The op would be over and their relationship with East-Tex would be out in the open. No more secrets. Right now, she needed him…and he needed her. Maybe for the first time in his life, he needed a woman—and not just any woman…*this* woman. Here in this run-down motel in the middle of the Piney Woods of East Texas, he needed her.

Then he thought of the rattling coming from under the Explorer. He'd known what it was the minute he heard it. He'd hoped against hope that he was wrong, but every time he turned or hit a bump it got worse.

He stroked Adelaide's hair and she snuggled against him. He could tell by her rhythmic breathing that she was fast asleep. He gently caressed her cheek, and she rolled over on her other side, pulling the frayed sheet up over her shoulders.

He knew what he had to do. He had no idea how all of this would ultimately play out, but he knew for damn sure that he didn't want her finding a GPS tracking device under her car tonight. But first, he had to call Vance.

Brock moved slowly and quietly. Adelaide was so exhausted, she hardly stirred. He pulled on his sweatpants and shoes and grabbed his phone. Rufus watched his master for a few moments, then yawned, rested his head on his front paws, and closed his eyes. Carefully opening the creaky old motel door, Brock slipped into the parking lot and dialed Vance.

His partner came up on the first ring, sounding disoriented. "What's going on?"

Brock was thrown for a second. What kind of way was that to answer the damn phone? He struggled to keep his voice down. "What's going on is a bunch of assholes with automatic weapons just shot up the place we were staying. Somebody found me, Vance, and tried to kill me. The freaking lodge looked like a sieve by the time I got Adelaide and the dog into the truck. Then the bastards chased us halfway across Trinity County. That's what's going on."

"Where are you now?" Vance still didn't sound right, but he seemed to be coming around.

"Not over the phone. We're safe—for the moment, anyway."

"Are you hurt?"

"Hard to believe it, but we got out of there without any damage to either of us. I'm telling you, Vance, it had to be some of those goons from the sheriff's office. Who the hell else would have freaking machine guns?"

Vance sounded incredulous. "You think the Fairfield County sheriff's deputies found you and your subject in some lake house two counties away and brought a bunch of machine guns to shoot the place up? Buddy, you must be cracking under the stress. Why the hell would they want to do that?"

"Beats the crap out of me, but somebody sure as hell found us and tried to kill us. I'm telling you, it was a frigging AR-15 on full auto."

"Buddy, you're in East Texas for God's sakes. Every redneck with a minimum-wage job's got an AR-15."

Brock wasn't going to have this argument. "What do the lawyers say?"

Vance hesitated just a second, then cleared his throat. "They're still looking at options. There are all kinds of considerations about liability, confidentiality, the contracts with East-Tex...it's a lot to evaluate."

Brock couldn't believe what he was hearing. How could Vance not be moving heaven and earth to get this straight? Office guys never fully understood what their field people were telling them, but he had reached his limit.

"Well, partner, evaluate this. If those overpaid legal assholes don't get us lined out with a plan by the time the sun comes up, I'm going to the cops myself, and they can sort it out then." He hung up without waiting for a reply.

He thought about the conversation as he headed toward the sagging garage. He loved Vance like a brother. Hell, he was the closest thing to family Brock had ever had. But this damn case was turning into a bag of rattlers, and he was not about to let Adelaide get bitten.

CHAPTER 22

A SLICE OF moonlight was cutting through the crack in the cheap drapes covering the dirty motel window. Adelaide woke, not sure where she was. She took a moment to get oriented and realized that Brock was not in the bed with her. As her eyes adjusted to the faint light, she saw Rufus. He was curled up on the other bed, but his eyes were wide open, and he was watching her intently. "Hey, pal. You awake, too?" At the sound of her voice, he jumped over to her bed, and she petted his silky-soft head.

She heard muffled sounds coming from outside the room. Disappointed at Brock's absence, she walked to the closed door out to the parking lot. From there, she could hear Brock's whispered voice, but she couldn't make out what he was saying. Just hearing him through the door, she found herself longing for him.

Despite her desire to be close to him, to feel him next to her, something primal told her not to open the door or turn on the lamp. Staying clear of the light coming through the curtains, she put her back to the window and peeked through the slit in the drapes.

She saw Brock walk to the garage and crawl under her truck. Her heart was racing as Adelaide grabbed her clothes and dressed quickly in the dark. She eased through the door and walked silently to the front bumper of the Explorer where she stood and waited for him to emerge.

Shortly, Brock pulled himself out from under the car. In the yellow glow of the streetlight by the highway, she watched as he emerged from underneath her truck holding a small, battered black box. It was square, about the size of an old-fashioned transistor radio. He froze when he saw her.

Wide awake now and hyperalert, Adelaide struggled to make sense of what she was seeing. Nothing was adding up. She kept flashing back to the scene in the rest area. Something was terribly wrong. Along the way, she had missed some critical piece of information about her environment—about this man. Her heart slammed against her chest wall, and she felt her palms go clammy, but her voice was level and deadly calm.

"What are you doing?"

He opened his mouth, but no sound came out. She stood stock-still and stared at him. He finally stammered, "I can explain."

Without a word, she turned and stalked back into the room. He followed and closed the door behind him. Once inside, she walked to the bathroom and flipped the wall switch as she pulled the door almost shut so only a sliver of light showed into the dilapidated room. There was no need to advertise to cars on the road that anyone was staying in the seemingly abandoned motel. He sat on the edge of one of the beds. She stood ramrod straight and held out her hand.

"Give it to me."

Brock reluctantly handed her the black box. It was badly banged up. The hard-plastic case was scratched and cracked, and the remnants of a clamp dangled off the back of the device. Frayed and tattered wires hung from each end. She moved toward the bathroom to see better and turned the device over in her hands. The thin ray of fluorescent light escaping around the bathroom door illuminated what was left of the gold-embossed lettering: EyeSpy GPS Tracker. She turned back to him.

She struggled to keep her voice level. "Who are you?"

He looked down and bit his lip. "Please…sit down."

She shook her head. "I'm standing right here until you tell me what the hell is really happening here and why you put a tracking device on my truck."

"It was never activated."

Adelaide raised her eyebrows. *How the hell could I not know better?* "I may have behaved like an idiot thus far, but you can rest assured those days are behind us. Don't jerk me around. Whether or not it's been activated is so far beside the point that it doesn't merit discussion."

"No, really. I swear it. I can prove it to you." He removed his phone from his pocket. "Come look."

Grudgingly, she moved to where she could see the screen, being careful to avoid any more of their previously "accidental" brushes. Those encounters were over.

"This is the app that reports the data from the GPS unit. I have to activate the tracker before the app and the device can communicate. I never did that. Let me show you." He pulled up the app, and a password screen appeared. "When it comes up, the app will show the serial number of the device you have there in your hand and ask if I want to activate it." He typed in a password and the app came up. It showed a map of the area and an icon of a car with the serial number in a balloon above it. "Signal Lost. Vehicle last sited at Exit 224 FM 355, Trinity County, Texas."

Brock gaped at the screen. Adelaide moved away from him. She was incredulous and humiliated. But mostly, she was enraged. Her face flushed and her blood roared in her ears. *Thank God I'm so mad.* It was all that was keeping her from feeling her heart break right in two. *I knew better…*

She forced those thoughts from her mind and spoke in a

barely controlled whisper. "You're such a horrid liar that you can't even get your scams straight. You come clean this instant, or I'm going to call the Trinity County sheriff and let them sort this out. I am way past my limit."

Brock stared at the phone's screen and then looked up at her. He started talking, his tone hurried and almost desperate. "Listen. You're right. I'm a liar. You have every right to be as mad as you want. But right now, we have a worse problem. I did *not* activate that tracking signal. Think about it. I didn't need to. I followed you from where you were collecting samples to that rest stop. After I put the device on your car, I kept following you—all the way to the fire. The tracking service starts charging from when you turn it on, so we don't routinely activate them unless we actually need them. Since then, I've always known where you were. I never needed the GPS. I'm telling you, someone has hacked this signal. We don't have to wonder anymore how they found us at the lodge. I have no idea what that means or who's doing it, but it is sure as hell not good for us. The last information whoever they are got was when we pulled off at the exit to this motel. Whoever is tracking us is going to find us. We have to get out of here *now*."

Jesus in the morning! Her mind raced to analyze the situation. She couldn't even begin to sort out what she was feeling. Broken-hearted? Furious with him? Furious with herself? Scared out of her mind?

But this was no time to fall apart. What Brock was saying about someone hacking the tracker made some kind of crazy sense. He might be a liar and a cad, but he was a proven operator in crisis situations.

She nodded. They had to move and move fast. She'd figure out the rest later…assuming there was a later.

CHAPTER 23

THEY WOKE EDNA to tell her that bad guys might be in the neighborhood. The old woman just laughed and pulled out the sawed-off shotgun she kept under the check-in desk. With a loud crack, she slid the forestock and cocked the action, smiling at the distinctive sound. "Let 'em come."

Adelaide used the motel's phone and made a brief call. Brock thanked the old woman, whistled for Rufus, and they jumped into the Explorer and pulled away.

Rufus settled into the back seat as they drove through the night. Brock watched the road silently unfurl ahead of them. He could feel Adelaide's anger at his betrayal. He didn't blame her. For the first time in a long time, he felt disoriented, lost in a mélange of emotions he couldn't sort out.

Finally, he spoke. "Where are we going?"

She shrugged. "I called some people I know. They're on vacation. They're letting me use their place."

More silence. She would probably never forgive him. Explaining would likely just make her angrier. Hell, he couldn't understand what was happening himself—how could he expect her to? But he had to try. He had never felt this way about someone before and feared he might never again. His mouth was dry. He found himself clenching his jaw. He forced himself to take a deep breath. Even if she was done with him for good, he wanted…hell, he *needed* her to see him as something besides a monster.

"I'd like to explain."

She snorted. "You know, the curious part of me thinks that would be just grand. But the more reasonable part of me thinks that, since you are obviously a sociopathic liar with the moral compunction of the Russian mob, there seems very little reason to listen to the next round of deceptive nonsense you're going to try to run on me. So I'd suggest you just save it for the next bimbo gullible enough to believe your bullshit and let you into her bed."

He sat in silence for several miles. A pervasive sadness settled over him like an acrid miasma tinged with desperation. Could he have irretrievably screwed up the best thing that had ever happened to him?

He had dreaded this moment, done everything in his power to keep it from coming, but here it was. Deep down, he'd known the jig was up when he heard that first clanging sound as they escaped the lodge. What the hell had happened to his vow to himself to keep this strictly professional? Jesus, what had he gotten himself—and Vance—into? How much damage had he done to Adelaide with his lies?

He thought about the feelings he'd had back at the Caddo Inn. His uncontrollable, almost primal, urge to protect her, to comfort her. Then they were in bed, and he was lost in her. He'd never known anyone like Adelaide, and he'd never been in a situation anywhere near like this before. He had no idea what to do next.

Sometimes the truth was the only path. He took another deep breath. His heart was hammering in his chest, and his stomach was writhing like a fish flailing on a pier. He was about to turn a corner from which there would be no going back. "I'm a private investigator. Our firm is InfoGlobal."

She looked over at him. "Bully for you. What? Remy Stone hired you to spy on me?"

He shook his head. "No. The mill is the client, not their lawyers."

She shrugged. "Lead counsel for East-Tex is a national law firm. I guess taking the risk of getting caught running an under- cover operation against opposing counsel's expert witness was a bridge too far for them. It makes perfect sense the greedy pigs running East-Tex Consolidated would think up a scheme like this one all on their own."

"I have a partner in the agency. His name is Vance Shakle- ton. Actually, I'm Vance's minority partner. Anyway, Vance used to be head of security for a large chemical company. They made chemical components for pharmaceutical and paper manufactur- ing. When he went out on his own several years ago, he brought a lot of chemical and manufacturing business with him. East-Tex is one of our big accounts from those days."

"Well, you certainly are giving them their money's worth. And carving out a little bonus for yourself while you're at it. Will you be including the details of our little tryst in your report? I don't know how much Edna charged for the room, but I'm sure you don't want to miss that deduction."

Her anger was like a razor, slicing open a part of him he had hardly ever been aware of. "Adelaide, don't," he said quietly.

Her voice was rising like a Saturn V rocket. "*Adelaide, don't?* Did I hear you right? Who do you think you are? The only thing you could have done to make me feel worse about this whole thing was to leave money on the dresser with a note telling me to buy myself something nice. I guess we bugged out before you had a chance. Good for you. You got to save your cash."

Was it just an expression or was it actually possible for a per- son's heart to break? It must be possible, he thought, because it sure as hell felt like his was shattering. For the second time in his career, he was feeling shame over working undercover. *How will I ever make her believe I didn't go to bed with her as part of the operation?* The idea that Adelaide would never forgive him washed over him like a burning Santa Ana wind. "Nobody told me to get involved with you. Nothing that has happened between us that way has had anything to do with the case."

She laughed out loud. "Do I look stupid? I must look stupid. Come to think of it, I must *be* stupid. After all, I let a perfect stranger worm his way into my job and my bed when all the while, he was only there to spy on me for a company that is only slightly less malevolent than the antichrist. Had nothing to do with the case? Save it."

"It's not like these folks are my best pals. They're just clients. They pay me to do a job, and I do it."

"What? The Nuremberg Trials are your role model for career justification? Spare me."

All these years, he'd never given much thought to whether the people and companies InfoGlobal worked for were good guys or bad guys. They were just clients who hired him to do a job—a job he was very good at and for which he was well paid. And what about the subjects? What did his work do to them? He'd never really thought about that, either—until Milwaukee. Since then, that was pretty much *all* he could think about. He knew now that lack of consideration had been a terrible mistake—maybe the worst mistake of his life. And despite all that reflection, the harm his work could do was staring him right in the eye again. His face flushed and shame and guilt engulfed him like lava oozing down the side of a mountain. He could taste bile. "I understand why you're angry. But I've never had anything to do with violence. When I saw the murder, I knew that something was going on way beyond what Vance and I understood. It's not like we thought that East-Tex was some troop of Boy Scouts. But we sure never for a second thought they were killing people. I called Vance from the lodge and told him to get our lawyers to call the cops. Remember, these people, whoever they are, seem to be trying to kill me as well as you."

She was quiet for a minute. "We are assuming that the people after us are from East-Tex. That they know we saw the murder and are trying to tie up loose ends. But we're not really sure of that, are we? Think about it. Who hacked into the tracking signal? It had to be someone who knew you were attaching it to my truck. Who knew about that?"

He thought for a few beats. "Actually, no one besides Vance. There's no formal inventory of the tracking devices. The agency has a bunch of them, and all the investigators use them when we need them. We just keep the one we use in our office when it's not in the field. It's a pain to pair the phone to the device, so our phones are each configured to the unit we usually use so we don't have to go through that over and over."

"What about staff at the agency?"

"Vance isn't big on staff knowing much about anything besides payables, ordering office supplies, and such. We all handle our own reports and time sheets. Vance does the billing. He doesn't want a bunch of hired help knowing who's paying us for what. The other investigators are all ex-cops, ex-military, and the like. None of them is going to have anything to do with murder."

"Did you tell Vance where we were when we were at the lodge?"

Vance? The idea that Vance would do anything to hurt him was incomprehensible. Yet…he hated to admit to himself a niggling voice in the back of his subconscious kept pointing him toward someone at InfoGlobal. But that was ridiculous. Every time that thought crossed his mind, he could feel the earth shifting under his feet and reality would go all Salvador-Dalí-Pablo-Picasso on him. Stress could do crazy things to your thinking…

Brock shook his head. "No. Actually, I really didn't know where, exactly, we were besides to say somewhere in the woods a couple of hours east of Pine Grove. I just told him we were at a place belonging to some friend of yours. That's all I knew. Hell, that's still all I know. I couldn't find my way back there if you held a gun to my head. And before you ask... Why would Vance have asked me where we were when I called him from the lodge if he had access to the GPS? He's clearly not the one who hacked it."

"Why did you remove the tracking device?"

Visions of her standing in the Caddo parking lot staring down at him, fear and disbelief etched on her face, sent pangs of regret echoing through his gut in a series of sick waves. "Because I knew that's what was rattling. We knocked it loose when we hit that pothole. I kept thinking it would just drop off, but every time we turned, I would hear it again. I knew you were either going to crawl under the car yourself or insist on taking it somewhere first thing tomorrow." He checked his watch. "Make that today. I wanted to get it off the truck before you found it. I was hoping that you wouldn't have to find out about me this way."

She drove on in silence. He left well enough alone for fear anything else he said might make it worse. Yet resigning himself to her never forgiving him was just not an option. Somehow, he had to make this up to her...make it right.

Adelaide wound around country roads until she hit 96. When the highway came into Jasper, she turned northwest on 287. An hour and fifteen minutes later, Brock saw the sign for Groveton. When Adelaide pulled over into the parking lot of a Holiday Inn Express, Brock turned and looked at her.

She stared straight ahead and spoke without emotion. "This is the end of the line for us. I'm going on alone. You can call whoever you want to come get you." She nodded to the hotel. "You'll have a place to stay until they get here."

He looked out into the night. This was it...one of those points in your life when, afterward, nothing's ever the same. Right here in the freaking parking lot of a Holiday Inn. On one side of this was

Vance, the agency, the undercover work, the quarter mill a year regularly edging its way up, the hipster loft, the hot arm candy, the glamorous nightlife, the clean detachment of a once-simple view of the world…that's what was outside of the SUV. Inside was the almost certain ruin of his career followed by an uncertain future, the suffering of all the Graces out there, a world full of murky questions of right and wrong, humanity…and Adelaide. A life of unknowns, of things he didn't understand and couldn't predict. He had no idea what demons awaited her…and he had no intention of finding out that they finally got her by reading about it in the paper. He didn't know what was going on, but he did know Adelaide was in danger—and there was no way he'd leave her on her own. He was past the point where that would have even been possible. Once he acknowledged that, he felt the peace that came with certainty as his heart rate slowed and his jaw relaxed. He turned to her.

"No. I'm not leaving you."

For several beats, she continued to stare out into the darkness. Then she placed her finger on the SYNC button above her dash and turned in her seat to face him. "Get out of my car, or I'm calling for help." She looked him straight in the eye. "Do it now."

He gazed at her for what seemed to him like an eternity. "Adelaide…"

She pushed the red button and an operator answered, the voice tinny through the car speakers. "Sync Operator. Do you have an emergency?" Reluctantly, Brock climbed out of the SUV. He opened the back door and hooked Rufus's lead to his collar. The dog jumped out of the truck, looking back at Adelaide as if he was beckoning her to come with them. Sadness gripped Brock as a terrible heaviness settled in his chest. He felt like a part of him was being torn away. As he closed the door, he heard Adelaide say, "Sorry. Hit the wrong button," before she drove off without looking back.

∽

Adelaide's head was spinning as she pulled out of the hotel parking lot. What in the hell had she gotten herself into? Her thoughts were interrupted by the sound of the low-fuel warning tone. She glanced at the dash then scanned the horizon for a gas station. Seeing one just opposite the hotel, she crossed the road and pulled up to the pump. Flipping the switch to open the gas tank, she reached for her purse... Damn. No purse. Damn. Damn. Damn. No credit cards, no money, no phone, no nothing. Crap. A moment of panic zipped through her brain. She drew a breath and exhaled slowly, calming her jangling nerves.

She pulled away from the pump and parked alongside the store, killing the engine. She crossed her arms over the steering wheel and dropped her head as she tried to puzzle out a strategy.

The sound of the truck door opening startled her. She looked up as Rufus bounded through the passenger door and trundled over the seat into the back. She was so angry with Brock, felt so betrayed, was so humiliated by the whole experience...why in the hell was she relieved to see him standing there?

When she didn't say anything, he climbed in. Smiling, he held up a credit card. "Premium or regular?"

She was still furious with him, but she needed gas and there was nothing to gain by being unreasonable. She pulled back up to the pump and watched silently as he filled the tank.

CHAPTER 24

BROCK CLIMBED BACK into the SUV and closed the door. The atmosphere in the truck was so cold he half expected to see ice forming on the windows. The fear of being estranged from Adelaide forever sucked the air right out of his lungs. When she didn't say anything after a full minute—didn't even acknowledge his presence—he finally decided he had to say something. He took a deep breath and dove in.

"You want to be angry. Be angry. You don't want to talk to me. Fine. Don't talk to me. You want to believe I'm the worst scum of the earth, believe it. But I'm not leaving you on your own like this with no resources. When we get to wherever you're headed and I'm convinced that you're relatively safe, then I'll leave, and you never have to see me again." Just saying the words sent pangs of profound regret through him. A heaviness settled in his chest as waves of nausea rolled through his gut, but he fought to keep his voice steady. "Not as long as you live, if that's your choice. But right now, whether you want to admit it or not, you need me, and I'm not leaving you."

She sat motionless for almost another minute. He could practically see the wheels turning in her head...her beautiful, analytical head. Logically, she had to know he was right. *Engineers love logic.*

He waited until Adelaide put the truck in gear and pulled out onto the highway.

She turned north onto 94. They drove on through the night. She wasn't talking, and Brock had enough sense to leave it alone. As the sky began to turn a dark pink, he saw a sign marking the exit to Apple Springs. Adelaide drove on about ten miles past the outskirts of town before she turned off on an unmarked gravel road. They wound around through low scrub brush and towering pine trees for several miles. As dawn broke, they pulled up to a small clearing with something like a large Quonset hut in its center, and Adelaide got out.

"We're here. If you're coming, get the dog and follow me." Her midnight-black hair fluttered in the breeze. He could see her working her jaw muscles beneath her porcelain skin. The sight of her caused a warmth to spread through his chest. But the thought she might be lost to him forever—that he might never be able to have her—jarred him back to reality.

He eyed a battered old pickup parked haphazardly next to the building. "Are you sure nobody's home?"

She shook her head. "They're fixing that up as a hunting truck. I don't even know if it runs." She strode to a metal door where she opened a square plastic cover exposing a dial combination safe lock. After spinning the knob several times, she entered a complex series of turns and stops before rotating the handle and opening a solid steel door reminiscent of a bank vault. As she stepped back, a motion-sensing light illuminated a small square closet with nothing inside but a steep set of spiral stairs disappearing deep into the ground.

"You and Rufus go first. I have to close the door."

Rufus hated stairs, and Brock was afraid he might just freeze. The dog looked at his master with imploring eyes. Brock squatted down and rubbed his chin. "It's okay, buddy. I can't carry you without ripping my side open…I would if I could, but I can't. You've got to man up here. Can you do that for me?"

Rufus looked at Brock for a couple of beats and turned, looking down the long spiral. Seeming to steel his courage, he started down the triangular steps, one tentative step at a time.

"That's a good boy!" Brock followed.

As Brock and Rufus picked their way down the stairs, Adelaide locked the heavy door and followed them. Forty feet of vertical distance down, the spiral terminated at an ornate front door with a combination keypad. Adelaide squeezed ahead of Brock and Rufus and worked the mechanism. The feel of her body next to his as she edged up to the lock reminded him of their time the night before—the heat of her lips, the sensation of her touch, the scent of her shampoo… The door opened, triggering the interior lights to come up and catapulting him back to the present.

Brock looked over Adelaide's shoulder into a huge open space decorated with the finest marble, the most opulent fabrics, and the most elegant furniture he had ever seen—all laid out in a giant circular room. He gazed around in wonderment. "I feel like I just walked into an edition of *Architectural Digest*."

She shrugged. "That's probably because you just did." She pointed to framed magazine pages on one of the curving walls. "I think it was last May's edition."

While Rufus busied himself sniffing around the massive room, Brock walked over and studied the photos. "We're in a missile silo?"

"Yep. The government sold a bunch of these off after the Cold War was over. They let them go for almost nothing. I figured I couldn't get any safer than this."

He continued to study the photos. "How do you know these folks?"

"They're a big deal in the Park Cities. I went to high school with the wife's sister. They knew who I was, so they called me when they first bought this place three years ago. I worked on the environmental assessment to be sure there was no radioactive contamination and that the water supply was clean."

He ran his hand along the glossy key lid of a shiny jet-black Steinway. "Getting all of these furnishings and building products down those stairs was no small feat."

"There's a missile door, remember. It weighs several tons, but it can be opened. They had to have some way to the get missiles in the silo and then to launch them, if it ever came to that. Now there's landscaping over it, but there wasn't during construction. Everything came down on a block and tackle system. It was really something."

He shook his head in amazement. "The rich really are different."

She rolled her eyes. "Not as much as you might think." She walked into the giant chef's kitchen. "We need to eat and come up with a plan." Opening a wide four-door commercial refrigerator, she extracted two Tupperware containers and stuck them in the microwave oven mounted over the eight-burner gas range. She dug around in a cabinet and found a tiny plastic tin of dog food, studied the label, and passed it to Brock for his inspection.

He read the label. "Filet mignon with bacon and potato. You're shitting me."

She shook her head. "Sir Binky the Yorkie is being boarded at his breeder's."

Brock laughed. "We're going to need about five of those."

She perused the cabinet's contents. "Then he'll have to settle for the filet mixed with prime rib and sirloin flavored."

Brock shrugged. "Life's a bitch. He's tough…he'll survive."

Adelaide served the food up into a bowl, set it on the floor, and whistled. "Rufus…dinner is served." Rufus trotted over, sniffed the bowl, and began to suck down the gourmet dog food in huge gulps.

Brock shook his head. "You better not get used to that, pal. When we get home, it's back to Purina for you."

The microwave beeped, and Adelaide removed the containers and poured the contents into bowls. Setting them on a modern teak dining table, she motioned for him to join her.

He pulled out a chair and sat. Looking down the length of the table, he said, "Good to have enough seating in case the Cowboys come over for dinner."

Adelaide dug into her meal. "Only the starters get to sit in here. They have a kiddie table for the second stringers."

It was good to see her being a smart-ass. He loved that part of her personality. The idea that she was lightening up brightened his spirits. He decided to work on small talk. "This place is huge."

"This is only the first level. There are four more bedrooms and a billiard table upstairs." She nodded toward an ornate, winding wooden staircase at the opposite end of the room.

He smiled, but she didn't respond. Back to awkward silence. She seemed lost in thought. Finally, she cleared her throat.

"I've thought a lot about this on the drive up. There's one thing I know. That's science. It never lies. It's never too emotionally involved in the problem to think straight. Science is about the truth, and if you will just listen to it, it will absolutely make you free."

Brock shrugged. He wasn't at all sure where she was going with this. "Okay…"

"I've still got the water samples in the truck. The ones that I collected at the pond."

Mention of the water samples sent a little jolt through him. He was totally burned out on East-Tex Consolidated, but out of reflex, he thought about how Vance had been so adamant that he get rid of those samples. What was Vance not telling him? Something, that was for sure. "The ones you got right before we saw the murder?"

"Yeah, but that's not what matters. What matters is that I collected those samples about forty-eight hours after the fire. That pond is downwind of the mill. Forty-eight hours is long enough for traces of the toxins in the airborne plume to have settled into the soil and water below. Maybe I can find some chemical evidence of what they were so interested in hiding from everyone about the fire."

He took another bite and chewed slowly, considering what she was saying. East-Tex was definitely covering something up about the fire. Their explanation was patently absurd. "I'm with you, but how are you going to do that in a missile silo?"

She shook her head. "I'm not. I'm going to do it in a chemistry lab."

He looked around. "I don't suppose there's one of those on another level here?"

She carried her empty plate to the sink. "Nope. But one of my best pals happens to be a chemistry professor at Travis State University, just up the road. When I finish eating, I'm going up to the surface and calling her to see if I can use her lab tonight. If she agrees, I'll come back down here and hit the rack. I desperately need some sleep. With the exception of a few minutes I slept at the Caddo, I've been up for more than—" she checked her watch "—twenty-four hours. I'll sleep until around six. The university will have cleared out by then, and I'll head that way."

He yawned and stretched. "Works for me." He looked around. "It's not like you can tell the difference between day and night down here." He waited for her to give him some sign that he could follow her to the bedroom, but none was forthcoming. As she went through a door in the curved wall, she said, "Help yourself to one of those bedrooms upstairs. See you around six." With that, she closed the door behind her, and he heard a lock click.

He headed to the spiral staircase. At least she wasn't making him sleep in her truck…

CHAPTER 25

THE SUN SET as Adelaide steered the Explorer through the country roads toward Huntsville. Brock had insisted on coming along. Adelaide was still furious about the GPS and the lying and…all of it. Worse, no matter how mad she was, she still felt a strong attraction to him. Just the thought of their time at the Caddo Inn caused little ripples of excitement to run through her body. No matter. She had vowed to put all of that out of her mind until they could get to safety. She could only juggle so much lit dynamite at one time. Since Rufus couldn't come inside, they opted to leave him happily asleep on one of the king-size beds in the silo after taking him for a short constitutional.

Brock adjusted his seat belt. "What exactly are you going to do tonight?"

"Ava's lab happens to have one Thermo Scientific Antaris II FT-NIR Analyzer."

He rolled his eyes. "I'm sure her parents are really proud."

Adelaide didn't take the bait. She had never been fond of Ava's parents and disliked their lack of support for her friend's work. "Her parents are the worst variety of self-involved Cincinnati socialites. They think her life goals should include marrying a lawyer from her father's firm, throwing a litter of little socialites, and developing a wicked backhand at the club. Foolishly, they don't care one iota about her NIR Analyzer. And don't be a smart aleck. I'm better at it than you are."

He smiled as he looked out the window. "I'm beginning to agree with you on that count."

That warm-honey voice was working its magic. She felt her anger receding. But she reminded herself that this man had lied to her and was aligned with everything she despised. This was a mortal struggle against evil forces, not the Sadie Hawkins dance in junior high. When she didn't reply, he went on.

"So what are you going to do with this analyzer?"

"I'm going to run the samples through it and see what chemical compounds are in each one."

"Don't you have to have a white lab coat and a bunch of funny-shaped beakers to do that?"

She shook her head. "Not with the analyzer. Pour in the sample, push the button, and voilà, answers appear out of the ether. Otherwise, you're right—it's hours and hours in Funny-Shaped-Beaker Land."

Adelaide pulled the car into the campus of Travis State University. She found a visitors' lot and parked. Gathering her briefcase and all of the samples from their fateful pond adventure, she headed to the chemistry building with Brock in tow.

Ava Lawson was in her office grading papers. She was dowdy in an academic sort of way. Her light-brown hair was straight and parted in the middle before it haphazardly fell over her shoulders. She wore a white V-necked T-shirt with black capri-length jeans and gray suede Birkenstock sandals. She wore no makeup and absently adjusted the gold-rimmed glasses perched on her nose as she slashed a red pen across test answers that must not have pleased her. Adelaide knocked on the doorframe and stuck her head in.

"Knock, knock. Anybody home?"

Ava got up from the desk and came to the door to greet them. Adelaide reached out for her friend. Ava's hug triggered a warm sense of comfort that washed over Adelaide and settled her rattled nerves. She introduced Brock, and he shook hands with Ava, who then grabbed a ring of keys from the cluttered desk and led them down the hall.

"I'm taking you to my lab. My team is the only one that uses it. I have four grad students, but they've all packed it in for the day. They were ecstatic when I told them they could leave at six."

Stopping when they reached the end of the hall, she used one of the keys to open the door. She flipped on the light and extended her arm. "The place is all yours. I keep an extra lab coat and safety goggles in that closet."

Adelaide looked around. "This is great. I think the NIR will probably be all I need." She turned and looked directly at Ava. Travis was a state university. Letting outsiders use state property probably violated countless rules. Adelaide didn't want to drag any other innocent bystanders into harm's way. She was still heartbroken over the damage done to the lodge. Guilt and worry over her part in decimating Grace's sole remaining asset felt like a lead weight lodged in her chest, and she was determined to be more careful about whom she dragged into her quagmire. "I really appreciate you helping me out like this. But I'm worried about getting you in some kind of trouble."

Ava laughed. "I publish more than anyone in this department—by a long shot. Without my grant money, this place would be sucking wind. Nobody would dare to complain, even if they knew or cared. Have at it. If anyone were to happen by, just tell them you're helping me with something and send them to my office. I'll be in there grading more papers."

Adelaide made a *yuck* face. "That's gotta be torture."

"Sometimes I look at that stack of exams, and it feels like I'm trying to empty the ocean with a teaspoon. I need to be absolutely sure I have done everything possible to bore myself completely to death before I give up and go home, so I'll be around all evening. Come get me when you're done, and I'll lock up. Meanwhile, let me know if you need anything."

With that, she turned and headed back down the hall like she was slogging through a swamp.

"That is one woman who does not seem like a happy camper."

Adelaide hefted her gear onto one of the scarred black lab benches. "All she cares about is polymers. If she could just sit in this lab and research polymers all day, she'd be in heaven. The admin and teaching load really drag her down. Nothing's perfect."

Adelaide worked the combination lock on her metal case and lifted the lid. She carefully removed her sample jars and placed them neatly beside the analyzer. The machine resembled an old-fashioned boxy laser printer with a screen and keyboard attached. She felt exhilaration race through her veins. Her fingers tingled and her breath picked up. She was in her domain now. She might be vulnerable—maybe even helpless—out in the world being pursued by bad guys trying to kill her. Guns, car chases, crime—those things were foreign to her, and she didn't understand how to defend herself… But here in the lab with the tools of her science, she had a way to tease out the mysteries hidden in those samples and unmask the secrets the mill was trying so hard to keep from her. She felt strong and powerful, and for the first time in days, she sensed the fear fading from her body and being replaced with hope and a new determination.

Adelaide went to the closet and retrieved the safety goggles, a plastic rack of test tubes, a roll of tape, and a Sharpie pen. She put the goggles on and carefully transferred a small portion of the liquid from each sample jar into a test tube before resealing the jar and replacing it in the case. She carefully marked each tube as she went.

Brock eyed the test tubes. "That machine can tell you what's in those samples with no more fluid than that?"

She nodded. "That's the great thing about an NIR for forensic work. It takes such a small amount of fluid for the test, you can generally save some of the sample. Used to be, it was this huge thing to decide if you could risk using up all your evidence for the old-fashioned tests."

Once all the tubes were filled and labeled, she pressed a blinking button on the analyzer and a compartment door on the front of the machine opened. One by one, Adelaide placed each test tube inside the machine and carefully pressed the same button, closing the compartment door. Typing a series of commands on the keyboard caused a graph to appear on the screen and then emerge through the output tray of a color laser printer on the other side of the lab.

Satisfied with the printouts, Adelaide removed the taped markings, emptied and washed the test tubes, and returned them and the other supplies to the cabinet. Giving the lab a last once-over, she locked the lid on her sample case, hefted her equipment off the counter, and flipped off the light. The whole process had taken less than half an hour.

❧

Brock leaned against the doorframe as Adelaide walked into Ava's office and plopped down in a chair.

Ava looked up from her grading. "Anything interesting?"

"You tell me." Adelaide handed the printouts to her pal.

Ava pushed her glasses up on her nose and took the sheaf of pages. "These are from the pond you were telling me about?"

Adelaide nodded. "One and the same."

Ava studied the sheets for a time, flipping the pages back and forth. She cocked her head from side to side, as if looking at the graphs from a different angle would change their content.

"Well, you've obviously got organic toxins in the pond. You've got enough organochlorines and benzene here to kill an elephant.

The samples are pretty uniform in their contamination, so the whole pond is just one big toxic stew. God help those poor souls in Pine Grove if they've been drinking runoff from this pond. I know that's what you've suspected all along."

Adelaide nodded. "Now we can get a court order from the judge to send an independent lab out there to take samples from that pond, and we'll have them dead to rights. I'm thrilled with that."

Brock couldn't really believe he was listening to this conversation. Here he was, aiding and abetting his client's adversary's expert witness, who was now gloating about how she had that same client nailed on the very charges he was supposed to help defend them against. This was exactly the kind of information he was being paid to develop. Yet the very idea of reporting what was happening in this room to East-Tex was as alien to him as joining a traveling circus.

Worse, how could East-Tex be doing something this evil? Stone and Blackwell had sworn to him on more than one occasion that the plaintiffs' claims were all nothing but fiction, the runoff from the plant was harmless, and a bunch of ambulance-chasing lawyers were posing as tree huggers trying to save the world just to make a buck. But Adelaide wasn't a tree hugger…she was a scientist, and Ava Lawson sure didn't have a dog in this fight.

It seemed pretty clear now that East-Tex was poisoning Pine Grove.

For the first time in his life, the ground under Brock's feet had turned to quicksand. He didn't know where he stood or which way was up. Investigative clients were rarely angels, and all of them bent the truth to some degree when they told you their stories. They did it to paint themselves in the best possible light…all of that went with the territory. But shortcutting around a few arcane and overly burdensome EPA regulations was a hell of a lot different than outright killing people—with bullets *or* chemicals.

As he stood there in Ava's office, it seemed so absurd that he had ever believed East-Tex was anywhere near the side of right. It terrified him that he'd gone along with their explanation of what was going on in Pine Grove even when it didn't completely ring true. Had he ignored his better judgment because of the big bucks that came with being the company's field magician? Had he essentially helped them kill people in return for a fat paycheck? He felt like he had swallowed a rock, and he was starting to sweat. What the hell had he done? He forced himself to focus on the conversation.

Adelaide leaned forward in the chair, resting her elbows on her knees and running her hands through her hair. "It's the rest that's got me confused."

The chemist flipped through the pages one last time before she handed them back to Adelaide. Pushing her glasses on top of her head, Ava leaned back in her chair. "Same for me. I have no idea what single process yields hydrochloric acid, iodine, sodium hydroxide, acetone, and toluene. It's definitely not paper manufacturing. That's not the suite of toxins you get there at all. That's organochlorines and benzene and a bunch of volatile organic compounds in the air. I have no idea where the rest of that stuff is coming from."

Adelaide fanned the sheets. "Neither do I. But I'm going to have to find out."

Ava shook her head. "Whatever it is, it's definitely not trace from the airborne plume you were talking about. The concentrations you see there mean those agents were dumped outright into that pond."

"Curiouser and curiouser," Adelaide said as she tucked the pages into her briefcase.

Ava said, "One thing's for sure. Regardless of where it's coming from, you don't want to have anything to do with acetone and toluene in your water supply—not any more than you want benzene and organochlorines."

Adelaide shook her head. "You can say that again. Those samples are like a deadly cocktail of laundry bleach, lacquer thinner, pool acid, paint, and nail polish remover." They both looked at the periodic table on Ava's wall as if it were a crystal ball. Finally, Adelaide spoke. "Is your library still open?"

"Sure. It's open until 2:00 a.m. You need chemical journals?"

Adelaide shrugged. "It's the only place I know to start."

Ava nodded. "I agree." Grabbing a sheet of paper off her desk, she scribbled on it with her red pen. "We have guest log-ins for visiting professors." She passed the page to Adelaide. "That'll get you into the databases."

Adelaide hefted her briefcase. Slinging the strap from the sample case over her shoulder, she thanked her friend and they hugged goodbye. Ava and Brock shook hands, and he followed Adelaide down the darkened hallway of the empty chemistry building.

A deep foreboding came over him. No doubt now—there was a bad moon rising. It seemed clear to him now that everything he had been told about the mill was a lie and that the fire was the result of some other, clandestine toxic operation. He and Vance were in more trouble than he could have ever imagined.

Images of Grace Hinkle and all the other plaintiffs gathered around Adelaide flashed through his mind. The thugs attacking her in the alley…the blatant lie about the cause of the fire… Then he saw an image of Dudley O'Doole lying in that hospital bed, and he knew with complete clarity that his soul was hanging in the balance. Who he would be, how he would live the rest of his life— all of that would be determined in the coming hours and days.

Watching Adelaide's determined stride, he marveled at her courage, her sense of right and wrong, her sacrifice for her principles. He couldn't bear the thought that he had found this beautiful, decent woman who had brought him to a place in his life he had never imagined being, only to lose her because he hadn't woken up to the reality around him soon enough. Every time he thought about the possibility of losing her for good, panic would hijack his gut and knead it like dough. All he could do was keep on putting one foot in front of the other. *One step at a time, buddy. One step at a time.*

He opened the door for her as they headed out into the night in search of answers.

CHAPTER 26

ADELAIDE LUGGED HER sample case back to the truck. She adjusted her grip on her briefcase before locking the Explorer. She thought of the printouts she was carrying, and they made her feel strong. She was on her turf now. It was just her and the data. This is what she was trained for, what she did best. No matter how confusing the world could be, science had never failed her—not in her professional life, anyway.

Following signs along the walkways, she and Brock made their way to the library. Even in the darkness, she felt Brock's presence next to her. She was still strongly attracted to him—even now, knowing what she did about who and what he was. She felt a tightness in her chest, a fear that gripped her. How was it that she could discover secrets in a sample jar down to the atomic level, but she couldn't tell what was going on in her own life…hell, in her own bed. Science didn't help her there; it never had. There was no equation to balance, no reaction to study. And that left her feeling confused and afraid, like she was surrounded by snakes hiding under rocks.

After consulting a map of the stacks, Adelaide led Brock to the basement where a bank of terminals was waiting, wedged in between the rows of shelves containing all of the bound chemistry journals subscribed to by the library.

Due to the late hour and the remote location, they had the area to themselves, save for two older male students. The men were sitting in the corner, huddled around a single terminal, apparently playing an online game of some kind. One of the men was blond, with sleeve tattoos and two studs in his upper lip. The other had light-brown hair with purple streaks woven into a braid down his back. He had an earring and was wearing a T-shirt that said, "Chemistry—it's like cooking, but don't lick the spoon." Behind the computer terminal they were using was a long table covered with chemistry and physics journals cluttered around the newest edition of *Physical Chemistry: Thermodynamics, Structure, and Change*, the standard text for advanced physical chemistry. Adelaide presumed they were graduate students taking a break.

"I'm going to start reading. I'm sure you can find a magazine or a book to kill some time."

Brock looked around. "Can't I help you find whatever it is you're looking for?"

She shrugged then nodded her head. "Actually, there is a way you can help." She pulled the printouts from her briefcase and set them out beside one of the terminals. "If I need an article that's not available online, I'll give you the citation and you can go find the hard copy and bring it to me. I positioned us down here because all the chemistry journals should be in these stacks."

He smiled. "Cool. Like a genius version of fetch. If I bring it back every time, do I get a biscuit?"

She shook her head. "No biscuit." Aware of the students across the room, she took her voice down to a whisper. "But maybe you get to find out why a team of cold-blooded killers are trying to obliterate us. Wouldn't that be better than a biscuit?"

Brock picked up a tattered copy of *People* magazine from one of the library tables. He plopped down in a chair not far from her terminal and watched as Adelaide settled in and began tapping keys. After a few seconds, she leaned back in the chair and closed her eyes.

"Can't log in?" he asked.

"What? Oh, I'm already in. I'm just trying to formulate a search strategy."

He scooted his chair up beside her. "Okay. I'll bite. Exactly what are you looking for?"

Talking more to herself than to him, she said, "If we assume that the explosion was not related to the particular manufacturing operation the public is aware of, then it's logical to assume that the anomalous toxins we found in the pond may be linked with a clandestine manufacturing operation."

He nodded. "Reasonable place to start."

"So, that means…I need to identify a type of manufacturing operation that is potentially explosive and also yields the unaccounted-for by-products we found earlier." She studied the graphs. "Hydrochloric acid, acetone, iodine, sodium hydroxide, and toluene." She thought about it some more and continued muttering to herself. "I'd think paint, but the iodine and HCl don't fit with that…"

Brock brushed her leg with the toe of his shoe and nodded toward the students. No matter how innocent the gesture had been, the feel of his body touching hers sent sensations shooting to places that weren't innocent at all. She forced herself to concentrate on his message. Using her peripheral vision, she noticed the students had paused their game and were plainly listening in on this exchange. They were looking at each other and then back at her and Brock.

He subtly nudged Adelaide—*Jesus, again with the touching*—and then made a show of looking over her shoulder at the screen. However distracted she may have been by those…sensations… she picked up on his cue immediately. "Please stop leaning over me. I can't concentrate."

Brock backed up. "Sorry. I was just trying to help." When she didn't respond, he moved to a chair close to the gamers. Adelaide adjusted her reports and monitor where she could see the action out of the corner of her eye while pretending to study the databases. In the late-night quiet of the library, she could hear almost everything the men were saying.

Brock nodded to their screen. "You guys playing *Counter-Strike*?"

The guy with the facial jewelry said, "You know MMPOGs?"

"Absolutely. I'm an *Overwatch* man myself, but I've played a lot of *CS: GO*."

The guy with the braid said, "We weren't big on *Half-Life*, but when Valve bought it and morphed it into CS, we were hooked."

Brock leaned in conspiratorially, "Hey, guys. As you may have noticed, we're stumped here. Judging from your books over there, you might be just the folks to help us. We've got a little chemistry problem. Either of you have any ideas about a manufacturing process that is potentially explosive and produces the stuff she was rattling off? The acetone and other stuff…"

The grad students looked at each other and back at him. The one with the long braid spoke. "What is she? Some high school chemistry teacher?"

Brock shook his head. "She's a hotshot engineer. But she's obviously out of her element, no pun intended. Between you and me, she doesn't have a clue what she's looking for. I'm going to be stuck here in the man chair, so to speak, while she struggles with this all night. Me, I'd rather be home watching ESPN, but you do what you gotta do, if you get my drift… At least I'm not having to watch her try on clothes at the mall."

They all had a good, we're-the-guys chuckle at that one. Adelaide pretended she didn't hear them and continued tapping keys on the terminal.

Facial Jewelry leaned in. "Why does she want to know about… what she's asking about?"

Brock rolled his eyes. "They're having some company competition thing where she works, and this is one of the contest questions. She's hoping to be the smartest kid in the class tomorrow when nobody else has figured it out."

The students seemed to find this amusing. The one with the purple hair leaned in to Brock. "Hey, man, we can get you out of here, like right now. We can tell her pronto what she's looking for. But what's in it for us?"

Brock paused for a minute, like he was mulling this over. "How about I get you some gift skins at the Steam Community Market?"

The two looked at each other and back at Brock. "Deal, dude. As soon as you make the transfer, we'll get you out of that man chair and back home to ESPN."

Brock took out his phone and tapped the keys. Shortly, the two misfits were apparently able to confirm that the goodies were in their online accounts. The one with the lip studs called to Adelaide.

"Excuse me, ma'am. Could you give me your email address?"

Acting like she had been lost in concentration the entire time and had no idea what was going on, Adelaide looked perplexed. "I beg your pardon?"

Brock spoke up. "It's okay. He's got something for you."

She recited the address and made a show of going back to her research as the man started typing. In a few minutes, he called over to her. "Ma'am, check your mail."

Adelaide kept typing and said absently, "Okay. Thanks." After a brief fist bump with the gamers, Brock walked over to Adelaide and peered over her shoulder as she opened a blank message from a university address with an attached pdf. When she clicked on the attachment, a publication from the Texas Department of Public Safety opened on her screen.

CHAPTER 27

BROCK WATCHED AS Adelaide typed for a few more minutes, referring back and forth between the DPS publication and the journals she was consulting before she logged out of the system. She was lost in her work, her beautiful face tense with concentration. When she absently wrapped her long black hair around her hand and tossed it over her shoulder, his mind wandered to thoughts of him running his hands... He caught himself. That part of this assignment was over.

He forced himself back to the present...to what he had seen in the articles she was reading. He couldn't follow all of it, but what he saw scared the hell out of him. He kept telling himself he must be misunderstanding.

Retrieving pages from a printer across the room, she nodded to him, signaling that it was time to make their exit. The students were once more lost in their virtual combat. He quietly picked up his backpack and followed her up the stairs and out of the library.

They walked silently out into the night, making their way back down the sidewalks that would lead them to the Explorer. After a time, Adelaide spoke.

"Aren't you the slick operator? Now I don't feel so bad about being conned by you. You worked those guys like you were hustling a shell game."

He kept his eyes forward. Until this operation, Brock had always been clear about the morality of his job—or at least he hadn't really thought about it. Now, he was floundering in the deep end of the ethics pool. He didn't respond.

The Explorer came into view, and Adelaide clicked the remote. As they climbed in, she asked, "Are you really that into online gaming?"

He snorted. "God, no. I worked a case a few months ago where an embezzler was hiding his stolen booty in online gaming accounts. When I finally figured out how he was doing it, I had to open several accounts of my own so I could chase him online and, eventually, turn him over to the FBI. I had a few bucks and some game materials left in a couple of accounts, so I improvised."

"How did you do it? With the embezzler? Make him think you were just some random guy he met gaming and hang around with him in cyberspace until you found out all his secrets?"

Brock let the silence hang in the air for a few beats. He finally said quietly, "More or less."

She pulled the folded article from the outside pocket of her briefcase then set the satchel on the rear floorboard. She turned to him, handing him the printouts. "East-Tex Consolidated is running a meth lab inside the mill and dumping the waste into the pond."

"What?" He pushed the button for the overhead light and scanned through the article. "I really can't understand much of this. Are you sure about this meth business? Maybe those guys were hustling me." He stared at the pages. *Could I have been working for a bunch of murdering meth cooks all this time and not known it? They'll for damn sure take away your secret magic decoder ring for that.*

She shook her head. "I verified the list with other academic sources."

He flipped back through the pages. "You think the meth lab is what exploded?"

"Absolutely. Paper mills dump toxic chemicals into the water and the air. They're a fire risk because there's so much flammable inventory around—the paper. Generally, paper mills have huge, awful fires and terrible toxic runoff, but not explosions. Explosions are different."

Brock held up his palm. "Just give me a minute to think." He stared out the window. What in the hell was going on? "I need to use the internet."

"Fine. I still have the password for the library system."

Brock shook his head. "This isn't the kind of research you do in a library."

She rolled her eyes. "Fine, Double O Seven. Use your phone. There's cell service here. What do you need to do that's so top-secret, anyway?"

Smart-ass-quick-witted Adelaide was a lot more relaxed than seriously-pissed-off-no-humor-at-all Adelaide. Not only was it extremely sexy, but he hoped with all his heart that this verbal jousting was a sign that she was warming up to him again, maybe even considering forgiving him.

In any case, he needed his laptop connected to the internet and not in some college library where he wouldn't be able to access the dark web without running the risk of getting caught. "I'm an investigator. I need to investigate. I need to get in some pretty obscure places in cyberspace and find out what I can about all the folks in this deal and figure out what they're really after."

"You mean besides killing us?" When he didn't respond, Adelaide sighed. "There's a sandwich place in Apple Springs. They have open Wi-Fi."

He shrugged. "Lead on."

While she drove, she worked hard at ignoring the chemistry between them. No matter how mad she was at him, how wrong he might be for her, there was no denying their magnetic attraction. Why did everything in life have to be so freaking complicated?

As they pulled up to the sandwich shop, Adelaide looked around. "Where do you want me to park?"

He craned his neck. There was an abandoned dry cleaner's across the street. "Let's try behind there. We'll be out of sight." Brock hefted his backpack onto the seat and took out his laptop. Using a USB cable to attach a device that was shaped like a deck of cards with an eight-inch antennae, he set the device on the dashboard and adjusted its position. Satisfied, he tapped the keyboard and pulled up a browser. She watched as he logged onto the restaurant's Wi-Fi system using the extender.

"You're getting their signal from all the way over here?"

He nodded to the device. "That's a high-gain antenna. They're really made for RVs, but they work well in all kinds of field situations."

She squinted at the screen. "What's that browser? I've never seen that before."

"It's called Tor. It's a little cumbersome, but it allows for completely anonymous browsing. It's open source, so anyone can get it."

Adelaide watched the screen intently, but she had trouble making sense out of what she was seeing. Brock was accessing a part of the internet she knew nothing about. As she leaned in to see the screen, she caught a whiff of his musky scent. Keeping her mind off *that* chemistry was getting harder and harder…

Half an hour later, he looked over at her. "Your pal Arthur Wesley was busted for cooking meth in college in Baton Rouge. He pled guilty and got a deferred adjudication. When he was twenty-five, the record was expunged. Apparently, his father had some connection to the governor's office."

She was stunned. Arthur Wesley cooking meth? That couldn't be right. "How did you find it if the record was expunged?"

"I didn't find the whole thing. I found reference to it." He tapped keys on the laptop and hit Enter.

When she leaned in to study the screen more closely, she was staring at a newspaper article containing a mug shot of a much younger version of Arthur Wesley. After pausing a few seconds to consider what she was seeing, she shook her head. "That's him, all right. Jeez. I've known him for the past decade. I would have never guessed that in a million years."

"Yeah."

Lot of that being surprised about your business associates going around, she guessed.

After a lull in the conversation, Adelaide said, "Back when Arthur was hired, the plant made out like, *Look at what good guys we are. We're hiring a local EPA guy to be in charge of our compliance and safety.* It put local folks at ease because Arthur was a home-town boy made good. It's horrible to think he was part of a plan to turn that awful paper mill into a giant meth lab."

"People do all kinds of things for all kinds of reasons, most of which we will never know or understand."

"But I know this guy. There's something we're missing. Something just doesn't add up."

Brock turned the laptop back to face him and went back to tapping the keyboard. After a few minutes, he looked up from his work.

Adelaide cocked her head. "What did you find?"

Brock stared at the screen. "As you say...curiouser and curiouser."

She leaned over for a look. Being that close to him, she was having a hard time not burying her face in the crook of his neck and forgetting about East-Tex and all their bullshit. But it only took a split second for her to realize that wasn't an option. East-Tex wasn't going to forget about her. "How so?"

"Darren Blackwood was arrested for something in Miller County, Arkansas, last year. No trial, no conviction, nothing. He was never formally charged after the arrest."

That prospect perked her up. Blackwood caught running drugs could be very good news for the plaintiffs. Arthur's crime—the only one they knew of for sure—had occurred years before, and sadly, Arthur was gone. But Blackwood was very much alive and smack in the middle of the East-Tex operation. "Miller County is Texarkana. That's just across the state line. What was he arrested for?"

Brock shrugged. "I can't find an offense code associated with the arrest, so I can't tell what he supposedly did."

"Anything else on Blackwood besides that?"

Brock returned to typing. He looked at the screen and nodded. "Yeah…there is. He declared bankruptcy last month." He scrolled through the pages of the filing. "Looks like a ton of medical debt. A bunch of cancer treatment invoices."

Adelaide couldn't stand Blackwood or his East-Tex compadres. But it was hard not to feel sorry for any parent with a sick kid losing everything to endless piles of medical bills. "That fits with what I overheard at the town meeting. His son apparently has leukemia and a seizure condition."

"I heard it, too. Jesus."

"So, Darren Blackwood hires Arthur Wesley to cook meth in the paper mill then sells it himself across the state line in Arkansas to pay his kid's medical bills? Why shoot Arthur and kill the goose that was laying the golden eggs? That doesn't make any sense. No cook, no product."

Brock nodded. "Good point."

"Besides, meth is extremely flammable. Arthur Wesley was

one of the top environmental engineers in the country. Even assuming he would participate in such a thing in the first place, I can tell you, if Arthur Wesley was cooking that meth, it for damn sure wouldn't have exploded."

"But if you're right, *someone* has been cooking meth in that plant. Maybe Blackwood was selling it when he got caught and arrested. But why take all that risk of carrying the drugs to Texarkana? That doesn't make sense, either."

"Neither does the bankruptcy. If Blackwood was selling meth as far back as last year to pay medical bills, then why would he have to take Chapter 7?"

Brock shook his head. "We're definitely missing something."

Adelaide looked around. "Do you need anything else from the internet?"

Brock paused for a couple of beats and shook his head. He slumped back in the seat. "Not that I can think of. The more I find, the more confused I am."

She cranked the engine. "Then we may as well get back to the silo. I'll feel better when we're underground and off the grid. This whole thing is starting to freak me out."

He shut down the laptop and stuffed it into his backpack. "You're not the only one."

CHAPTER 28

WHEN THEY WERE finally back in the safety of their underground hiding place, Adelaide plopped down on the couch.

"I am so damn tired. I feel like I've been up since Christmas," she groaned. Rufus jumped up on the sofa and nestled in beside her. She scratched his chest. The dog rolled onto his back and splayed his legs, showing her his pink belly.

Brock came and sat beside them on the edge of the large suede sofa. "You want your belly rubbed, pal?" As he stroked the dog, Rufus's mouth gaped open and his tongue lolled out to the side. His eyes closed, and he began to snore. Brock smiled. "He's down for the count. Works every time."

He leaned his head back on the cushion and massaged his temples. His side was burning, and he felt like a jackhammer was banging behind his eyes. "It's the stress. Fieldwork is rough. It always wears on me. I do have to admit, though, in all these years, I've never been chased by murderous meth cooks, watched a man get shot in the head, or hidden out in a Cold War missile silo. This is a whole new level of stress, even for me."

"You? I'm a frigging engineer. The most dangerous thing that happens to me at work is my laptop runs out of power or an attorney gets snotty with me on cross-examination. I'm the nerd.

Nerds are supposed to pencil-whip bad guys with science, not use evasive driving maneuvers to keep from being shot by gun-wielding drug dealers."

They sat in silence for a time. Finally, Adelaide turned to Brock.

"Look, I'm sorry about the cracks I made earlier. You did a good thing tonight with those guys in the library. It was impressive work. You saw an opportunity, and you seized it. It would have taken me all night to find what you got out of them in five minutes."

"Years of field experience teach you to always be alert to resources in the environment. Their pierced ears pricked right up when you read off that list of waste products. It was just a matter of building rapport, determining a need, and offering a trade."

She looked at him sadly. "All in a day's work."

What had years of pretending to be someone else done to him? A sudden wave of guilt washed over him and then grabbed him like an undertow. He felt like he might be yanked under and drowned in a sea of doubt and recrimination.

He took a deep breath and composed his thoughts. "Here's the truth. Yes, I was hustling you when you almost busted me putting the tracking device on your truck at the rest stop. I had been following you since you moved into the Swiss Chateau. Hell, I was right behind you in that cloud of dust you were throwing up after the alarms sounded. Yes, I was hustling you when I sent Rufus over to help me worm my way into sitting with you during dinner at the barbecue joint. Yes, I was following you that night after the community meeting."

When an image of the huge white-haired man with his knife to Adelaide's throat flashed through his mind, a surge of rage raced through his body. Just thinking about it made him feel the overwhelming need to protect Adelaide, to keep her safe—the same need that had overtaken him that night. "But I sure as hell wasn't hustling you when I saw those guys attack you in the alley.

I would have stepped in to stop that even if it meant blowing the whole operation. And, whether you ever believe it or not, what happened at the Caddo Inn had absolutely nothing to do with this case, East-Tex Consolidated, or anything but you—you and me. It makes me sick inside that you may never believe that, but it's the truth."

She looked at him for a long time. "Thanks for saying it. I want to believe you—that what happened was real, that I'm not needy enough, desperate enough, stupid enough to have been that confused about what was happening in the most intimate part of my life. But with all the craziness going on now, I don't know what to believe about anything."

Brock's heart ached at the thought that she could actually believe what had passed between them was nothing more than part of an undercover operation. He wanted desperately to prove to her that what they had was real. Maybe he was the one fooling himself…maybe she didn't feel for him what he felt for her. When it came to Adelaide, he had lost his horizon.

He shook his head to clear it and walked across the living area to a gallery wall of family pictures featuring the silo owners and their two children. There were pictures of the four of them swimming and snow skiing. He looked at shots of the kids at birthday parties and school functions and snaps of Mom and Dad dressed in formal wear, dancing together.

A hollowness deep inside of him ached as he studied the images. He'd never known any of the moments in those pictures… never in his entire life. Those were experiences he'd only seen on television, in the movies. Now he realized how desperately he wanted to make those moments for a family of his own…only he had no real idea how to do that. But somehow, he knew it had to start with Adelaide.

She walked up beside him. "What?"

He ran his hand over one of the frames. "I've been in the

field so long…living on the road, being someone I'm not. Look at these folks. They have a real life. Some part of me has always wanted that."

She massaged her shoulders. "Wanted what?"

He shrugged. "A wife, a couple of kids, a real family of my own." He nodded at the pictures. "Like these people."

Adelaide snorted. "Be careful what you wish for."

"How do you mean? I'm just saying I'd like to have a wall like this."

"Oh, really? Well, let's see. The patriarch there is under investigation by the IRS for tax evasion. They're thinking he'll get by with a fine and some community service, but word is that Club Fed is not off the table. He's had three affairs that are common knowledge in the Tri-Cities. God knows how many they've kept quiet. His wife just got back from her second trip to rehab, which they all affectionately refer to as *camp*. The darling little girl is seventeen now and way too generous with her feminine favors. The boy is in military school after he got kicked out of Highland Park for setting the gym on fire with a DIY IED directed at a coach who benched him for punching a teammate. You should be very careful about remembering that there is more going on in people's lives than you can scam out of them in a few days."

He stood dumbfounded at her rant. *What am I doing wrong here?* Things would seem to be going along fine with Adelaide, then he'd say something that would strike a nerve for reasons that completely confounded him. "I…um…I'm not sure what I said wrong."

She shook her head as she stood up. "Undoubtedly. I'm way too tired to be having this conversation. I'm going to bed. Thanks for your help with the grad students. Good night."

She turned and headed toward the bedroom.

He wanted a chance with this woman…a chance at a life

he'd never even imagined. He might be on his third strike in that ballpark, but he was sure as hell not giving up until he had to.

He stepped in front of her and put his hand on her arm. "No. We're not doing this anymore. Talk to me. Tell me what I said… what I did that upset you."

She shook her head and gazed at the wall of family photos. "Don't you get it? You want what every man wants—his own family…to further his bloodline, perpetuate his name. It's in our DNA. Society has little use for sterile women. If we aren't breeding stock, we're useless."

He gently stroked her cheek and turned her face toward him. "Adoption is a great option. There are so many fantastic kids looking for a home, looking for someone to love them. There's a hell of a lot more to parenting than producing eggs and sperm."

She pulled away. "I consoled myself with that idea for years when I was growing up. Later on, I came to learn that adopting is nothing more than a consolation prize for desperate women who can't have kids of their own."

The words hit him like a flail, but he fought to keep a straight face as she continued.

"In the Highland Parks of the world, it's all about the DNA. Dallas society is so inbred, sometimes I'm surprised that everyone at the country club doesn't have hemophilia or six toes on their left foot. Men and their families aren't interested in raising 'someone else's children' when it's just as easy to marry their sons off to a woman who isn't damaged goods and can do her part to further the dynasty. Besides, they can't ever be certain they're not getting some inferior DNA in the mix that might drag down the precious family name." Hurt and resentment oozed from her voice.

Brock was so stunned by these comments, he didn't know what to say. What did that make him? Someone with inferior DNA? Maybe that was why he'd chosen a career where he was always being someone else…because he didn't feel worthy. Maybe she was right. The pain in his heart was excruciating. He stared at her. "That's not true" was the best he could come up with.

"Oh, really? I don't think so, either, but I guess that depends on who you ask." She walked over to the pictures. "I was engaged to a guy I met in college. He was the perfect Highland Park catch. Handsome, filthy rich family, just finishing law school. His father and mine knew each other professionally. They were, to say the least, the 'right' kind of people. What more could you ask for? He gave me a three-carat emerald cut diamond on the Valentine's Day before he graduated. Our engagement party was held at the Meadows Museum. Our picture was in the *Morning News*."

Brock remained silent. But he could already guess where this was going.

"It wasn't like I kept my medical history a secret from him. I told him when we first got serious. He didn't seem to care…went on about adopting…"

"What happened?" His mouth was dry, and he was afraid she could hear it when he talked.

"Well, it seems my fiancé neglected to mention to his family our bright future in the world of infertility. Anyway…for what eventually became obvious reasons, he saved that little morsel of information until we were well into the invitation phase of the wedding."

What a bunch of monsters! He'd dealt with these people all his professional life—country-club crybabies with a narcissistic sense of entitlement and superiority that could choke a goat. He was never surprised by them. "Uh-oh," he stammered.

"He didn't even have the balls to dump me himself. His father called my father—at the office, mind you—and said that 'the family' had decided it was not in their best interests for his son to 'continue with the engagement.'"

Brock stared at her, mouth agape. This was a new low, even for a bunch of socialites.

She went on. "As if that wasn't bad enough, he offered to reimburse my father for any wedding costs that were nonrefundable. My dad told his old man to pound sand on them paying for anything. Dad said he considered the nonrefundable fees a small price to pay to avoid being related to such horrible people."

Brock realized he was still staring. Her father seemed like a pretty cool guy. All he could think of to say was "Good for your dad."

"Oh, I left out the best part. His father threw in that I could keep the ring. Big of them—under Texas law, the damn thing was already mine. Anyway, I'm not sure what they thought I was going to do with it. I guess he viewed it as a parting gift, like the lawn furniture and laundry soap they give the losers on daytime game shows."

Brock shook his head in stunned disbelief. For lack of a better response, he asked, "What did you do with it?"

She laughed bitterly. "The ring? I donated it to Greenpeace. They auctioned it off for ten grand."

Brock fumbled for words. This whole diatribe left him feeling like he'd been gut-punched by Mike Tyson. He swallowed hard as he searched for a response.

"That's obscene. Whatever the definition of the 'right' kind of people, those godless, soulless monsters surely aren't right for any place but hell. I'm really sorry that happened to you."

She nodded. "Thanks for saying so. My takeaway from the whole thing is that men talk a good game about adoption—right up until they are about to get locked in for life with a woman who doesn't lay eggs…" Despite her bravado, he could hear her voice beginning to crack. "Then their biological urges kick in and they head for hills, on the hunt for a real woman." Tears brimmed in her eyes and started to seep down her cheeks. She discreetly wiped them away with one of her fingers and walked around the corner. Seconds later, he heard her bedroom door slam shut.

He felt like he was wading into unknown depths, but something propelled him forward. He followed her and knocked on the door. Her voice was muffled as it seeped through the wood. "What?"

He cracked the door. "Can I come in?"

She was standing by the dresser with her back to him, but he saw her shoulders trembling. Her voice was strained as she said, "I guess so…" She turned to him. Her eyes were red and her cheeks were wet. "What is it?"

He took her hand and led her to the bed. "Please, sit down." She sat and he pulled a chair from the sitting area up opposite her so he could look into her eyes. He gathered himself, choosing his words carefully.

He had never told anyone what he was about to tell Adelaide. The only other person on the planet who knew the whole story was Vance—and he'd been there, lived through it with him. Every fiber of his being told him now was the time and this was the woman. He swallowed hard. His heart was pounding in his chest, and his palms were clammy.

"I wasn't raised on a farm in Iowa. I don't have a brother or sister…at least not that I know of. I said I didn't want to talk about it when you asked about the farm and that billboard because I had no idea what you were talking about. I've never been to Iowa."

She stared at him with an expression he read as either intrigued or horrified. He clenched his jaw and soldiered on. Telling this story was harder on him than getting cut in that alley. "Not only have I never been to Iowa, I have no idea who my mother or my father is…or was. When I was about three years old, a passenger found me abandoned on the back seat of a DART bus at the Five Points intersection in Dallas, not far from Vickery Meadow. I don't remember it—don't know how I ended up there…nothing."

She took his hand. "Oh, Brock…I'm so sorry."

He smiled a sad smile. All these years, he'd worked so hard

at making sure no one ever knew this story. Finally telling it was terrifying and liberating at the same time. Absently, he took the St. Christopher medal in his fingers and slid it back and forth on the chain. Suddenly, it dawned on him what he was doing. He looked down at his hand. "They found this with me. Someone had tucked it inside one of my pockets."

Adelaide leaned in to study the medal. "I'm not Catholic…I don't know much about St. Christopher medals, but this one looks somehow unusual to me."

He nodded and fiddled with the pendant some more. "The traditional depiction is St. Christopher with the Christ Child on his left shoulder and a staff in his right hand. This one is reversed, and St. Christopher is holding a sword instead of a staff. I've searched for years to see if that could provide any clue to who I…" He paused and collected himself. Shaking his head, he continued. "The first thing I do remember was a foster home when I was about four. The year or so before that is a complete blank. I was essentially unadoptable. I was already too old when I entered the system. Orphanages are like dog shelters—everyone wants puppies."

Adelaide winced at the crude analogy.

"I bounced from place to place. When I was eight, I ended up in this hellhole of a group home out in the country, east of Dallas. Vance was thirteen when I arrived. The foster parents were…well, let's just say they were the last people who should have been trusted with kids, let alone vulnerable kids. One day, Vance walked in on me and our foster dad in the basement."

He clenched his teeth. For a moment, he was that little kid again, in that awful place. The terror of it tore through him like tornado cutting a swath through a trailer park. How could he still be afraid of that memory after all these years? He struggled to steady his voice. He was too far into this to turn back… "Truth told, I don't think it was a coincidence at all. I'm sure Vance had been in that basement. I believe he knew exactly what went on there. Funny, we've never talked about it. Not a word in all these years..."

For the first time in his life, it struck him as strange that neither of them had ever once mentioned a single syllable about that day to the other—a day that had changed both of their lives forever. She put her other hand over his.

He took another deep breath. "Anyway, when Vance saw what the old man was doing, he grabbed a tire iron and beat the crap out of him. Then we ran away. Somehow, a couple of weeks later, he managed to get us on a Greyhound bus to Arkansas. Made up some story about going to see our grandparents. Fooled the clerk into thinking some people in the bus station were our folks."

Brock was lost in the vision of his past. He looked down as he felt Adelaide interlace her fingers with his and squeeze his hand.

"We lived on the streets for a while. We finally got picked up by the cops when Vance got busted shoplifting some donuts from a convenience store. He told some wild tale about us being brothers from Ouachita County and our parents having run off and left us. We ended up back in foster care, but in Arkansas this time. It wasn't great. The people were really poor and uneducated, and they were just doing it for the money. But it wasn't...it wasn't like in Texas.

"When he aged out, Vance scraped up a little money and went to the local junior college. He made pretty good grades and got himself a scholarship to a third-tier state university up the road. I graduated high school by the time he finished with a criminal justice degree.

"He went to work in security in this chemical plant that made precursors for over-the-counter drugs. Like cold pills and such. He met a bunch of people in that industry. Eventually, he worked his way up to head of security for the whole company. When he got that far, he decided he could make it on his own. That's when he started InfoGlobal. Naturally, his first clients were the people he had met during his time with the chemical company. Once he was up and running, he wanted me to come with him. I started out as a staff investigator. Two years ago, he made me a minority shareholder."

She touched his face. "I'm so sorry...what I said about adoption...I would never have..."

He stroked her hair. "I know. I'm not telling you this for any other reason than I want you to understand why I lied to you, why I do this work. Vance and I have made lives for ourselves. We've taken care of each other and found our way. We have a good business, nice places to live, cars, IRAs. Christ...freaking IRAs. Two throwaway kids with European sports cars and retirement plans. But now—now it seems so dirty and wrong—what these clients and companies like them are doing, have done, to people like Grace, like the people on the Families in Need list..." He rubbed his thumb across her index finger. "Like you."

She pulled him toward her. He sat next to her on the bed and she hugged him. "I'm so sorry." He held her tight and kissed her. She didn't resist. Very gently, he removed her blouse and bra. Desire coursed through his body as he felt her respond to his touch. He felt heat rising in his body. He unbuttoned her jeans and helped her out of them. She slowly, tenderly unbuttoned his shirt and pushed it down over his shoulders. The feel of her body next to his bare skin was intimate in a way he'd never imagined. Her body was firm, but her skin was silken. He kissed her breasts, her mouth. Her wavy black hair was full and rich and luxurious as he ran his hands through it and kissed her neck. She rolled on top of him, undoing his pants. He loved the feel of her weight pressing against him. Then, they were naked together... physically, emotionally. He could feel the quickening rhythm of her breathing, the heat of her desire for him. This time, their lovemaking wasn't desperate like at the Caddo Inn. This time, it was soft, gentle, patient. He loved the feel of her accepting him, letting him inside her, surrendering to him. He wanted to give her everything she could ever desire. For the first time in his life, sex was a way of communicating, being close, showing...love? The world of Dallas arm candy seemed a lifetime away. Adelaide was real...this was real. Afterward, she lay spent in his arms and dropped off to sleep. Brock watched her for what seemed like hours, firm now in the knowledge that protecting her, keeping her safe mattered more to him than anything ever had. He couldn't imagine the pain he'd feel if they made it through all this and she decided once and for all she could never trust him again. He was exhausted but he fought sleep...he didn't want to miss a moment of this time with her, this feeling. He couldn't bear the thought he might never have that again.

CHAPTER 29

RUFUS WADDLED UP to the bed and whimpered. In the windowless room, Brock had no idea what time it was. He checked his phone. Three in the morning. A sliver of light slid into the room from the kitchen. He gently stroked Adelaide's hair. He didn't want to leave her, even for a minute. Rufus impatiently pawed his arm. He scratched the dog's ear and whispered, "Okay, buddy. I get the message." He quietly got dressed, slipped out of the bedroom, and hooked Rufus up.

They hustled up the spiral stairs and outside. The poor beast desperately needed a pit stop. Once outside, Brock pulled his cell phone from his back pocket and dialed Vance's number. His partner picked up on the first ring. "Where the hell are you? I've been worried senseless."

"Not over the phone. Listen…I'm in deep shit here. Someone hacked into the signal for the GPS I put on her car. As soon as I realized it had been compromised, we hit the road. I think we're safe for the minute, but I don't know how long that's gonna last. Who the hell could have hacked that signal? It had to be somebody from the agency…"

"The agency?" Vance sounded perplexed.

"Who else could it be?"

Vance was silent for a few seconds. "Jesus...I can't imagine. That shit's supposed to be encrypted..." He paused for a beat. "You better get yourself back to Dallas. Just come straight to my house. We'll sort it out."

"It's not that simple. The water samples from the pond...she tested them. There's a meth lab operating inside the mill."

"What? Meth lab? That's ridiculous."

Brock pressed on. "What are the lawyers saying?"

Vance cleared his throat. "They're still looking into it. I need you to tell me where you are now."

Brock couldn't believe what he was hearing. "*Looking into it?* Are you on acid? Someone's trying to kill me! I've had enough of this crap. When the sun comes up, I'm going to the Rangers office in Tyler."

"What in the hell is wrong with you? Has that Reese woman got your balls in her purse? This is sure not the first time some asshole took a potshot at you."

"Potshot? These bastards are assassins. I'm telling you, the mill is behind this, and if we don't get our shit together, we're going to be ass-deep in alligators when this busts open—which is just about any minute now."

"When did you ever get this wound up over a piece of ass?"

"She is not a piece of ass. And you leave her out of this." In fact, Adelaide Reese was the furthest thing from a *piece of ass* he'd ever known. What he felt for her was something he'd never imagined and didn't understand at all, so how could he possibly describe it to anyone else? Besides, it was none of Vance's business. He continued. "This isn't about her. I'm talking about us... you and me."

Vance was undeterred. "I need you to dump those water samples."

Brock shook his head. He felt like he had fallen down the rabbit hole and landed in an alternative universe. "Jesus Christ.

Do you get that our clients are cooking meth in the mill where they are killing people? Not like in the abstract with pollution but in the freaking here and now with guns."

"Listen, buddy. That woman was trespassing on mill property when she illegally collected those samples from a client that employs us to protect their interests. And you were there with her, I might add. Now she's trumped up some bullshit about a meth lab to ruin them. I'm the boss around here. I'm not asking. I'm ordering you. Get rid of the damn samples."

Brock had taken a left turn at the corner of Confused and Baffled and was now speeding past the last exit on the expressway to Really Pissed Off. "You're *ordering* me?"

Vance's voice took on a tone Brock had never heard before. "You listen to me. You need to remember whose team you're on and what park we're playing in. This is the big leagues, buddy, and we're the stars. Our undercover ops save our clients tens of millions of dollars every year, and we take a hefty fee out of those savings."

Brock interrupted. "But at what cost, Vance? We could go to prison for this...lose everything."

Vance was quiet long enough that Brock wondered if they had lost the connection, but then he heard his partner draw a long breath. "While you've been playing house with this Reese woman, I've been doing some investigation. You remember investigation, don't you?"

Brock was too stunned to respond.

"Your girlfriend there is a hustler...only she's not as good at it as we are. She got caught."

Brock heard his phone chime with a text message. He fumbled to open the file. There, on the screen, was a grainy newspaper picture of Adelaide in handcuffs, wedged between two police officers under a headline that read, "Expert Witness in Lake Charles Toxic Tort Charged with Evidence Tampering."

Brock felt his breath leave him, like he'd been kicked in the chest by a bull. Visions of Adelaide confiding her plans to trespass on mill property flashed through his mind. And all that camo gear she had… She was apparently doing a lot of sneaking around. As Brock struggled to make sense of what he saw, Vance went on. "There's something else you need to know. Raines and his team definitely have a mole inside the mill operation. Last week, Remy planted some false intel. He poured it into the rumor mill and lit the fuse. Guess what the bullshit was? Meth being manufactured inside the mill."

Brock's mind was reeling. He felt like he was on a jet in a flat spin, careening toward the ground. "What?"

"Remy floated a rumor that meth was being manufactured in the mill. And, lo and behold, guess what showed up in those water samples? We're not sure who the leak is, but we're about to find out. Little Miss Smarty Pants is playing you, buddy. I don't care if she can suck the felt off a billiard table, you dump those samples and get your ass home."

Brock was flabbergasted and his head was whirling. "Why would Remy start such a potentially disastrous rumor about the mill?"

Vance laughed. "It was brilliant. There's no meth operation in the mill. Raines gets the info, goes postal, and Remy puts on his picture-of-cooperation face and shows the world what a bunch of fools Raines and his band of thieves are."

Brock was struggling to put it all together. "This doesn't make any sense. I was with her when she collected the samples and when she tested them in the lab. She really had a hard time figuring out the meth thing. We…she actually got some help from a couple of chemists at Travis State University who pointed her in the right direction. She hasn't talked to Raines. I've been with her. She's not making this up. Our clients are wrong."

"When did you get so much holier than thou?" Vance ranted. "You didn't seem to mind these clients' brand of business while you were buying the Porsche and vacationing in St. Barts. We take their money and keep their secrets. What? Suddenly you can afford ethics now? You need to buck the hell up. You've gone all soft because some putz in Wisconsin ate a handful of pills when the going got rough."

Brock couldn't believe Vance would mention Milwaukee. An accountant with three kids was in a coma on a ventilator because of one of their ops—one of *Brock's* ops—and that was something to throw around as ammunition in a professional disagreement? Brock and Vance had been friends almost their whole lives, and Brock had never seen this side of his best—hell, his only—friend. He was stunned as the tirade continued.

"Listen up. I'm the majority partner in this agency, and I decide which ops we run and which clients we service. You dump those water samples and get back to the office. This op is over."

Brock shook his head. "Vance, what if they really are cooking meth inside that mill? In the face of this lawsuit, the blowback on that'll make Chernobyl look like a kitchen fire. And we'll be the poor bastards who get cooked—"

Vance interrupted him, his voice almost a whisper. "Don't give me any shit on this. Just do what I'm telling you and get home."

Brock took a deep breath. "What about the murder? What about her? Those thugs from the mill are still trying to kill her."

"She's our adversary. Don't you get that? She's trying to ruin our client. She collected those samples illegally from mill property, and she's making up a bunch of shit about meth because Raines got word from the mole about it and she's his flunkie. She's tampered with evidence before. Face it, bud, she's not what she seems. What happens to her is not our problem." He was on a roll, his anger building by the second. "Those thugs from the mill would have prevented all of this if you'd kept your eye on the damn ball and done your frigging job instead of—"

"Instead of what?" Vance was silent. Brock swallowed hard. "I can't leave her. I won't have another Milwaukee on my conscience."

Vance's voice had a tone that made Brock's blood run cold. "You remember what it was like in Arkansas? And those weeks in Dallas? Who made sure we ate, found us a place to sleep? Who came into that basement? I've always been the one who made the tough calls—some of them you've never had any idea about. Remember that the next time you pick up some chick in that sexy little sports car and screw her in your hotshot apartment. And for Chrissakes, remember it now. Dump the damn samples, dump the broad, and stay away from the cops."

Brock heard a click. "That's the lawyers. I've got to take it," Vance said, and the line went dead.

CHAPTER 30

BROCK SAT DOWN on the ground, leaning back against the Quonset hut. Rufus waddled over and looked at him, cocking his head to the side and perking up one ear. "Jesus, pal. What in the hell am I doing?" Brock asked. The dog grunted in answer and snuggled up along his side. He rubbed the terrier's velvety ears. "It's okay. Don't worry. I'm confused, too." Rufus began to snore. *If only life were so simple…if I could just curl up and go to sleep…* He closed his eyes and tried to think.

Was Vance right? Could Adelaide be playing him? He stared down at the image of her in the grainy newspaper photo. Tampering with evidence? Could what he was feeling be nothing more than lust? He'd never really loved anyone in his life, except for Vance…he guessed that was love, but he couldn't be sure. Outside of that relationship, he'd never been close enough to anyone to know what love meant.

Then Adelaide came along. What had happened to him? Had he gone from confident undercover operator to lovesick patsy?

Why not dump the samples? If that was so important to Vance, why not just do it? If they actually contained evidence of a meth operation, the whole pond would be full of it. There were plenty more samples where those came from. But if there was no meth, why was Vance so determined that he get rid of the samples in the first place? Vance was right about one thing…he had always taken care of things for both of them. He was older and wiser, more daring…

Brock made his way to the SUV. Carefully, he opened the tailgate and pulled Adelaide's sample case out and set it on the edge of the cargo area. Tapping the button for the truck's indoor lights, he pulled a Swiss Army knife out of his pocket, fanning open the series of gadgets hinged inside. He fiddled with the tools until he heard the satisfying sound of the lock clicking open. He carefully extracted one of the sample jars and studied it in the light.

What in the hell was he doing? The reality he had always known was morphing into something he'd never imagined, and it wasn't stabilizing. Adelaide a woman he thought he loved—had been playing him all along. Vance was threatening him. He had broken confidentiality. He had put his license—and Vance's—in serious jeopardy. Had he lost his mind?

Adelaide woke up and rolled over toward Brock…or toward where he had been last she knew. But she was alone in the bed. Disoriented by the sensory deprivation of being underground, she took several seconds to get her bearings.

"Rufus!" She whistled for the terrier. "Come here, boy!" She listened for the tinkling of his tags, the pitter-patter of his nails on the hardwood floors…nothing. She got up, flipped on a lamp, and pulled on her clothes. "Brock? Rufus?" The residence was forty feet underground and perfectly insulated from outside noise with thick concrete walls that bounced sound like a handball court. Any noise coming from inside the apartment would have been crystal clear… But all she could hear was a supernatural silence. As she made her way into the main room, she could feel it… something was wrong.

∽

Brock pulled the tray of jars out of the case and unscrewed the cap of the first sample. He took a deep breath and tipped the jar over, watching as the water streamed over the glass lip, through the air, and down into the red clay of the field surrounding the silo.

∽

Visions of the Caddo Inn flashed through Adelaide's mind and the awful feeling she'd had then when she found him under her car hit her...she felt sick to her stomach. *Nononono...*

She pushed the feeling aside and calmed herself. Things between them were different now. For that matter, they were different than they had ever been with any man in her life. *Don't jump to conclusions and ruin the best thing that's ever come your way.* She ran a glass of water from the kitchen sink and took some long swallows. The dog hadn't been out since before dinner. *He must be taking the beast for a walk...* She headed toward the stairs to the surface.

∽

Brock dropped the glass jar and repeated the procedure for each of the remaining samples. Then he heard it...the unmistakable sound of a door opening. He whipped around and saw Adelaide, framed in the light of the vertical tunnel, her face racked by surprise and what? Terror?

For a couple of beats, she seemed too shocked to speak as she pulled the door shut and walked blankly toward him. When she finally found it, her voice was deadly level. "What are you doing with my samples?"

His first impulse to go to her, to comfort her, to explain was suddenly knocked back by the freight train force of the picture of her in handcuffs, the news about the mole. She was his adversary now. She'd been his adversary all along.

"Jig's up, Mata Hari. You really had me going there for a while, but we know about the mole. And about your life as a fraud, about your tricks over in Lake Charles. The samples are gone, and your tenure playing me as a patsy is over."

Adelaide's face showed only confusion. Her eyes wandered from her open case to him with the pile of empty sample jars at his feet. "What are you talking about?"

"Guess what? The meth lab story is bullshit. It was planted by Remy Stone to smoke out Raines's mole in the plant. Guess it worked."

Still sounding detached, she shook her head. "I don't have any idea what you mean."

"We know about you tampering with evidence over in Lake Charles…about you being arrested." His voice was building. Rage was rising in him like magma making its way to the surface through a volcano about to blow. He had trusted this woman, trusted her like he'd never trusted any woman before, and she had been conning him from the start. "All your bullshit about me and my undercover work…you were hustling me all along."

Mention of Lake Charles seemed to snap her out of it. Her eyes flashed with anger. "I wasn't hustling you. You don't know a damn thing about what happened in Lake Charles." She slammed the tailgate, jumped in the SUV, locked the doors, and fired up the engine. Throwing the truck into gear, she spun the tires and sped away, leaving Brock and her empty sample jars in the dirt.

After the dust settled, Brock looked around. He was essentially stuck in the middle of nowhere. His backpack was locked in the silo. He stared down at his phone, still showing the image of Adelaide in handcuffs. He studied the photo more carefully. The date of the article was three years before. Something he'd said earlier ran unbidden through his head. *I'm an investigator. I need to investigate.*

He typed in search terms on the phone's screen—*evidence tampering, Reese, Lake Charles.* The phone struggled under the yoke of the crappy connection that came with the sparse, low-performance rural service. Then he saw the first hit. The service was too weak to pull up the article, but the Google blurb told him everything he needed to know. *Engineer Cleared of Evidence Tampering Charges. Two employees of Louisiana Paper Manufacturing, a subsidiary of East-Tex Consolidated, were arrested on charges for planting manufactured evidence in the vehicle of Adelaide Reese, expert witness for the firm suing the mill for…*

Brock's heart was racing. She didn't do it… Thank God. But what did that mean? Vance must have been mistaken… Then he heard Vance's voice in his mind… *Little Miss Smarty Pants is playing you…*and *Those thugs from the mill would have prevented all of this.* It hit him like lightning. *Oh God, oh God, oh God…*

He looked around wildly. Running to the rusted-out pickup parked beside the silo, he swung himself into the driver's seat floor and hotwired the old truck. As the engine kicked over, he sat up in the seat and whistled for Rufus. When the bulldog leaped into his lap and made his way to the passenger seat, Brock threw the old Ford into gear and raced down the road after Adelaide.

CHAPTER 31

ADELAIDE SPED THROUGH the night. She saw lightning in the distance. Thunderclouds blocked any view of the stars. As she drove the last miles into Huntsville, rain began to fall. First, as lonely, fat drops splattering on the windshield, and then later, as driving rain that slapped her face as it came through the broken windshield, making it almost impossible to see past the hood of the Explorer.

After forty-five minutes of white-knuckle driving, Adelaide turned onto a street about three blocks from the university.

Back at the silo, she had been seized by adrenaline driven by terror. The world had turned upside down. Who was this man? How could she have been so wrong? What was he capable of? But for the last hour, driving through the awful weather had totally occupied her conscious mind.

Now that she was off the highway, a maelstrom of questions surged through her mind. How had Brock found out about Lake Charles? And if he had found out about it, why didn't he know the whole story? What in the hell did he mean about a fake story about the meth? The confusion was like salt rubbed into the wound of her broken heart. She had truly thought she'd made a once-in-a-lifetime connection with him…a connection she'd never imagined possible. The idea that it was all a sham, just part of the day's work for him, caused her a pain she'd never experienced before…and made her so angry she could hardly breathe. She was heartbroken, mad, and totally baffled.

The one thing she was sure of was that someone was trying to kill her, and she didn't know who to trust. Every fiber in her being told her to get herself some life insurance before she made another move. She remembered seeing a twenty-four-hour FedEx store a few blocks from the Travis State campus.

Across the street from the copy shop, there was an all-night diner. *Earl's* was spelled out in red neon script on a large sign in the shape of a coffee cup. The diner had a side parking lot that was mostly empty, save for a couple of Bondo-laden beaters parked near the building.

Adelaide steered the Explorer into the diner lot and backed into a spot in case she needed to make a hasty exit. She grabbed her briefcase and set the alarm as she jogged across the street to the copy shop.

The store was a cool, gray fluorescent pod floating in a sea of darkness. Adelaide was soaking wet from her sprint across the street. She shivered from the blast of the air-conditioning that hit her as she walked through the glass door. With all of its shiny metal machines and equipment, the store made her think of an alien spaceship. In the center, behind a gray counter, a bald man in a purple pullover stood loading brochures of some kind into a box. He looked up as she approached.

"How can I help you tonight?"

She pulled the sheaf of graphs from her briefcase. "I need to scan these and then do some emailing."

The clerk led her to a workstation complete with a terminal, scanner, and printer. He pointed to a touch screen attached to a card reader and told her how to log in. She dug a FedEx copy card out of her briefcase and slid it into the slot.

Her first order of business was to open a new Gmail account with the name meth_lab_at_east_tex_mill and install an email scheduler plug-in to the new account. She scanned her wrinkled printouts, checking the images to verify the graphs and charts were clear and readable.

Lightning was slicing through the darkness as thunder roared. It seemed to Adelaide like the store was ground zero in the electrical storm. She struggled to concentrate as she carefully loaded the article that she had gotten from the gamers on the hazardous waste generated by meth labs. Next, she attached the pdfs she had made of the graphs of the NIR analysis of the pond water along with a screenshot of a map showing the location of the samples she'd collected at the pond. Last, she added the file containing the video of the murder. She wrote a brief technical explanation of the meth waste findings and details of the attempts on their lives, describing Big Foot and Yeti and identifying them as the mill employees who had made a scene at the community meeting. Satisfied, she saved the message, scheduled the transmission, and logged out.

As she headed to the exit, a bolt of lightning hit right outside the front windows of the store. The glass vibrated so violently, she froze, waiting for the big panes to shatter. Almost instantaneously, thunder struck, and the store went dark.

∽

Brock's heart was pounding against his chest wall like a pinball ringing bells and flashing lights as it ricocheted from place to place. Where the hell was Adelaide going? How could he have doubted her? He had to get to her before something awful happened. He would never be able to live with himself…

The wiper blades in the old truck streaked and smeared like they hadn't been changed since the Hoover administration, making it almost impossible to see out of the cracked windshield. He prayed the local deer population was bedded down out of the rain.

Night surveillance was hard. You could follow someone most of the day without getting busted if you kept a decent distance and they weren't looking for you. But when you were chasing someone on a country road in pitch darkness, your headlights announced your presence like a brass band. Brock didn't really care if Adelaide saw him or not. He was there to do his damnedest to keep her safe. His only fear was that if she made him, she'd try to lose him and get hurt doing it. When he saw her pull into the diner parking lot, he dropped back around the corner and watched as she ran into the copy shop. Once she was inside, he pulled the truck into the lot and waited.

As he watched her through the glass storefront, his heart ached in places he'd never known existed and ways he'd never known were possible. Just as he had finally gotten close to her, broken down her barriers, and convinced her to trust him, this happened. The horrible guilt he felt at ever doubting her, at having been co-opted into using her, violating her trust…all of that was overshadowed only by the desperation he felt at the idea of losing her for good. But, in this moment, all of those were abstract issues to face later. For now, all he knew for sure was that no matter what, he had to keep her safe.

He was jolted by a thunderous crack as lightning struck a transformer station next to the diner. The power went out just as she exited the store, plunging the entire block into total darkness. He lost sight of her until the glare of the Explorer's headlights illuminated her as she sprinted toward it. He jumped out of the old truck and ran toward the SUV while Rufus cowered on the floorboard of the pickup, terrified of the storm.

CHAPTER 32

JUST AS ADELAIDE reached the driver's door, a man cloaked in shadow stepped behind her and slapped his gloved hand across her mouth, placing the cold steel barrel of a pistol to her head. Through the whipping wind and the rain slapping on the pavement, Adelaide heard the man behind her commanding, "Be still, or I'll blow your brains out." A second man off to her left seemed to be struggling with another victim…

In the next instant, a scratched and dented black panel van pulled up next to the Explorer and the side door jerked open. The attacker shoved her into the back of the van, knocking her facedown onto the dirty rubber floor. Adelaide tasted blood in her mouth as she heard another body thud down next to her right before the tires squealed and the vehicle surged forward.

As the driver slewed the van onto the road, one of the attackers grabbed her wrists and pulled them behind her. She felt his knee on her back as something hard cut into her wrists, binding them together. Terror turbocharged her heart rate. The force of the van's violent turn surged through her body, and pain racked her shoulder as she was hurled against the side of the vehicle. She struggled to position herself to see who else was in the back of the van. By rolling her body slightly to the side, she managed to turn her head so she was facing the other victim. The form was obviously that of a man slumped motionless on his side facing away from her. Then she saw it. She blinked several times, wondering if she was hallucinating. But, no matter how many times she closed her eyes and opened them again, there was the silver medallion, carelessly slung over his shoulder as he lay with his back to her, apparently unconscious. Her heart raced with relief…with hope.

She wasn't alone. She couldn't imagine how he had gotten here…how he had found her. A shuddering wave of dread washed over her at the unbearable thought that he might be dead.

The van was a grimy sty. She could see old fast food containers and a broken beer bottle under one of the front seats.

They drove through the rain for what seemed like an hour, maybe longer. Unable to see out, she had no idea where they were or which way they were heading. When the truck finally stopped, the men opened the sliding door and dragged the pair out onto a gravel parking lot. Brock seemed almost limp, but she heard him moan as the men dragged him out of the squalid van. He was alive! Tears welled in her eyes when she caught her first glimpse of his face. He appeared to be having trouble walking as their captors frog-marched them through the rain into an immense windowless building.

Once through the door, the man holding Adelaide hit a switch. A flickering emergency light buzzed to life, dimly illuminating a large cement-floored warehouse. As far as the eye could see, leaky blue drums of hazardous waste bearing the mill logo, and the universal poison symbol of a black skull and crossbones, were stacked from floor to ceiling. Pools of toxic liquid had collected in low spots on the floor. The place stank of chemicals and mildew. Adelaide was as worried about breathing the air as she was about being shot by the kidnappers.

They passed through the warehouse area into an old office suite. Brock's captor flipped another switch, and a bare overhead bulb came on. The warren of rooms was dotted with the scattered remnants of ratty, beat-up office furniture. Two blue plastic chairs sat side by side in the middle of the room.

For the first time, Adelaide's captor spoke. When she heard his voice, a shudder ran the entire length of her body and she broke out into a cold sweat. Big Foot shoved her into one of the chairs. With her hands cuffed behind her, she had no way of breaking her fall. Pain shot up her arms as her weight landed on her bound wrists. She heard Yeti command Brock to sit as he dumped the semiconscious man into the other chair.

The two giants assumed their positions right in front of their prisoners. Yeti spoke simply.

"We want the video."

Neither of them responded. Brock appeared to be coming in and out of consciousness. Their attackers must have hit him in the head during the kidnapping. She couldn't control the trembling that rippled through her as she ran down the list of awful options. Concussion? Skull fracture? Blood clot? She forced herself to calm down and try to analyze what was happening to them. No way she could help either of them if she fell apart.

Adelaide racked her foggy brain to concentrate on what the kidnappers were saying. Something about this was all wrong. How would they know it was a video? Even if they saw her taking pictures, how could they know it was video and not just still photographs?

Before she could reach any conclusions, Yeti made a fist with his huge, pink hand. His massive biceps flexed as he punched Brock square in the face. Brock's head snapped back and then lolled to the side.

"Oh, God! No!!!!" Adelaide screamed.

Yeti laughed at her while Big Foot sneered and smacked the back of Brock's head, knocking it forward. Helplessness grabbed her like a strong current pulling her under. She felt like she was drowning in a bottomless ocean of fear and desperation… She was sure the world was going to fragment into a million pieces and shatter her along with it.

Then, Brock moaned. While his eyes never opened, she felt like she had been momentarily flung to the surface, giving her one more chance at a desperate gasp of air. He slumped in the chair and slid halfway to the floor. But he was alive. She forced herself to hold on to that idea as Yeti grabbed Brock's shirtfront and dragged him back to a more or less sitting position.

Big Foot removed his glove and ran his finger down Adelaide's lips, over her chin, and down her neck. He hesitated as he let his hand drop slowly down the middle of her chest, between her breasts. She thought her skin would crawl off her body. She wretched and dry heaved. Big Foot laughed.

"It's your choice, Little Miss Smarty Pants. You can tell us now…" He laughed again. "Or you can tell us after we've done things to you that'll give you nightmares for the rest of your life." For some reason, Big Foot found his own threat riotously funny.

Yeti chimed in as he placed a gun to Brock's temple. "Maybe you'd like to tell us where the video is, so we don't have to kill your boyfriend."

Her lizard-brain instinct was to scream out everything they wanted to know…give them whatever they wanted to save Brock. She couldn't let them hurt him. But the tiny, faraway voice of her rational self, still audible in her head, told her they were both as good as dead the second she gave in to that. As she stared horrified at the spectacle before her, she noticed a slight movement out of the corner of her eye. She forced herself to keep looking straight at the gun and study the movement with only her peripheral vision. She made herself speak. "I don't know anything about a video. I have no idea what you are talking about."

Her denial elicited a laugh from Big Foot and Yeti. Yeti drew back his fist again and hit Brock on the side of the head. Adelaide screamed, but there was no response from Brock except for another moan. More slumping. She felt horribly responsible for this—he was in this mess largely because of his interventions to save her. God knows, he'd been less than perfect, but if he hadn't stepped up to try to rescue her, he wouldn't be unconscious and tied to a chair. If she didn't say the right thing, do the right thing, he could end up dead...and she could end up spending the rest of her life without him.

Adelaide struggled against her bindings. As she did, she caught another glimpse of movement. Brock had a small piece of the broken beer bottle from the filthy van. Not only was he alive and conscious, he was slowly sawing through the plastic cuff that bound his wrists. Excitement surged through her, hope quelling her ever-rising panic.

Big Foot grabbed her hair and forced her face toward him. "Oh, you'll tell us, or you'll end up like your pal, Wesley. He couldn't get along. You saw what happened to him. If you don't fork over the video, you'll be joining up with him soon."

Yeti wasn't going to be left out. "We know you were there at the pond. We chased you. I know you have the video. And I know you're going to give it to me."

Who the hell told them it was a video? Adelaide wondered again. Maybe they were just assuming?

Big Foot pulled a switchblade from his back pocket. The knife popped up and locked into place with a deadly snap. "You'll give it to me when you want me to stop cutting your boyfriend."

Adelaide was out of her mind with rage. Anger had overtaken her. She screamed for him to stop. The piercing tone of her cries halted Big Foot in his tracks. He turned his head in her direction. Yeti stared.

"We knew this was coming. We knew you might catch us. We loaded all of our evidence—the video of the murder and proof that the fire was part of a meth operation—we loaded all of it into the cloud, in a scheduled email. If we don't reset the schedule every two hours, the files will automatically be sent to the media, the EPA, the DEA's Meth Tip Line. Neither of us has the whole password. I only have half of it. I was waiting for Brock so we could do the reset at the copy shop, but he didn't show, and I left. That's when you grabbed us. I can't stop it alone. No one can. You kill him, and you're screwed."

The two thugs looked at each other in bewilderment. In a matter of seconds, their expressions turned to terror as a man emerged from the warren of other offices.

In his forties, he was dressed in khakis and a button-down shirt. Short and oddly proportioned, he was almost bald, with a bad case of unibrow and crooked teeth. He was pointing a gun at them. Adelaide didn't know anything about guns, but this one was large and boxy and a flat blue-gray steel. It made her blood run cold.

The man dismissed the thugs with a tip of his head. Big Foot and Yeti disappeared through the door. Using the newcomer's interaction with the duo as a distraction, Adelaide snuck a quick peek at Brock's progress with the flex-cuff. It was hard to see, but she thought he was almost done slicing through the plastic.

The man looked at Adelaide and Brock for a time, as if he was considering what he wanted to say. Finally, he spoke.

"It's too bad the boy wonder here lost consciousness. If he were awake, I'd tell him he should be more careful about using the company cell phone. Not a good way to stay under the radar. Once he turned it on outside of that damn silo, I had him. He led us right to you. Worked almost as well as the GPS." He shook his head as if to get himself back on track. "No matter. I guess we'll just have to kill you slowly, hoping that you might 'remember' that whole password, if there ever was one. Or maybe our Brock will come to in the nick of time." He smiled a terrible smile, exposing his small yellow teeth. Adelaide noticed that Brock tensed momentarily when the man spoke. It was subtle, but she was certain he recognized the man's voice.

As long as Brock continued his charade of unconsciousness, he couldn't see what was happening in the room. She looked straight at the man.

"Whatever you do to me with that gun won't change the fact that I can't stop the broadcast."

He shook his head and made a *tsk, tsk, tsk* sound. "Well, then, maybe we'll just have to write this off as a training exercise. I'll just forget the gun for now and get the boys back in here so they can take turns practicing with that switchblade."

The very mention of Big Foot and Yeti made her stomach roil. As she bit back bile, the man ran the back of his finger down her face, continuing his terrifyingly calm monologue.

"Your boy *Brock* and I—we go back a long way. He's doesn't have any ethical trouble working these undercover gigs, being a professional liar. Funny where people draw the line. But *Brock* just doesn't have what it takes to make the big bucks. Never has. I could never understand why all the shit he went through as a kid didn't toughen him up, but I think he was just weak from the start. That's why I never cut him in on the real action. I couldn't afford to have him going all righteous and weak-kneed on me. I realized a long time ago that doing the heavy lifting for chemical dumpers might pay the bills, but it wasn't the way to the real money. That's when I figured out a way to sublet some space from the plants and conduct a little manufacturing operation of my own." More of the yellow teeth.

Adelaide was struggling to follow along. Who was this man? Was he behind the meth operation?

He was showing off now. She was sure he was bragging to her because he planned to kill them both in short order. Regardless, the longer this maniac blathered on, the longer Brock had to saw through that plastic.

"Darren Blackwood stumbled into our little operation a couple of years ago. Fortunately for everyone, he came to see things my way and didn't have to end up like poor Arthur. It got a little dicey last year when he got busted making a delivery up to Texarkana, but some of our friends over in the sheriff's office were able to smooth that over. Now he really owes us. Funny how your high-and-mighty ethics go by the wayside when your kid needs chemo and you need to stay out of prison."

Adelaide had to stall, to buy Brock a little while longer to get free. But even with his hands loose, she couldn't imagine what he would do against a captor with a gun.

"Why kill Arthur Wesley? What did he do?"

"How in the hell were any of us supposed to know that Wesley had been a meth cook in college? I guess that's not the kind of thing you put on a job application. When he went to meet with the contractors to arrange the repairs after the fire, he knew immediately what he was seeing. He was a former fed. He was going straight to the DEA when the boys caught him. They had to improvise, and lo and behold, there you were snooping around that pond." He stopped talking and appeared to be considering his next move.

Adelaide summoned up her courage. "Kill me or don't. It won't change the fact that I got water samples from that pond. I have NIR analysis on them that is going straight to the DEA Meth Tip Line with that email broadcast that describes who I am and pinpoints exactly where the samples came from. Those fireworks will start going off in less than an hour."

The monster smiled. "Well, isn't that ironic? You see, my dear, you and lover boy aren't the only ones working on a short fuse around here. I can't take a chance of some other yokel at the plant discovering what we're doing in that building and going all Nancy-Reagan-Just-Say-No on me." He consulted his watch. "There's a bomb set to go off right around the time your broadcast hits cyberspace. It'll blow the whole place to kingdom come. Darren Blackwood will die in the explosion. You and *Brock* will be dead. Arthur Wesley has already left us. My money is in the Caymans, and shortly I'll be joining it. Too bad it had to end, but as they say, que será, será."

Adelaide felt a lump in her throat and her mouth went dry. But visions of a massive toxic plume shifted her from panic to analytical problem-solving mode as she realized the terrifying scope of what he was saying. "If you set off a bomb in that facility, it could affect hundreds, maybe thousands of people downwind from the blast. The pollution that will be dumped into the water is nothing compared to the toxins that will immediately be discharged into the air. Why do that to the people of the community? What did they ever do to you?"

"What did they do to me?" He shrugged as if he hadn't considered this before. "Nothing that I can think of…they're just in the wrong place at the wrong time." He looked over at Brock. "Like your pal here. *Brock* knows all about being in the wrong place at the wrong time. Hell, he was conceived that way."

Adelaide was confused and having a hard time following what he was saying. He used a strange tone every time he said Brock's name.

"Oh, you didn't know? I guess while he was playing spin the bottle with his socialite subject, he neglected to mention the details of his humble pedigree. I guess he stuck with that Iowa farm boy story he cooked up for his journalist cover."

How could he know about Brock's journalist persona? Then it hit her. Could this awful little man be Brock's partner? The facts started to coalesce in her mind. *Oh, God.*

The man went on. "It's a lot more appealing than the truth—that when his whore of a mother decided that a kid was just too much trouble, she left him on a city bus."

The sound was visceral. Like the roar of a charging bear. The element of surprise was enough to give Brock the momentary advantage as he flew out of the chair and hit the horrid little man like a defensive end tackling a running back at the two-yard line. Brock knocked his partner off his feet and into the wall. The gun skittered across the floor. Adelaide's survival instinct took hold. The entire world shrank down into a laser point—nothing in the universe mattered but her and Brock getting out of that warehouse alive. She reached the gun with her foot, dragged it toward her and pulled it under the chair. Shakleton clawed the wall for purchase and regained his footing, then ran into the warehouse. Brock was on him like a wild animal, clutching the fleeing man's shirt and punching him over and over before he got him down on the ground and straddled him. He landed blow after blow until Vance Shakleton quit moving and went limp.

Brock ran toward Adelaide and snatched the gun out from under the chair. He checked the load and stuck the barrel in his waistband.

"I don't know where the other two are." He scanned the dirty floor for the broken piece of glass. Unencumbered by the need to work clandestinely, he sliced through the plastic in seconds. He walked over to his still-unconscious partner, rolled him onto his back, and rifled the man's pockets for car keys. Hitting pay dirt, he took the fob with one hand and grasped Adelaide's arm with the other just as Big Foot and Yeti came walking in.

Big Foot was rolling his cigarettes up in his T-shirt sleeve. The duo had apparently taken a smoke break after being dismissed by their boss. Brock pulled the gun before the pair could get to them.

"Stay where you are."

Yeti charged toward Brock and Adelaide with Big Foot tight on his heels. Brock fired point blank into the charging attacker. Yeti recoiled from the impact of the bullet and fell into his cohort as they both slammed into one of the stacks of toxic waste barrels.

As the tower teetered, Adelaide grabbed Brock and pulled

him clear. Brock stuck the gun back in his waistband before he pulled Adelaide under his arm and rushed her through the dank warehouse and toward the front door. As the avalanche of blue barrels tumbled down, Brock and Adelaide darted out of the fetid, poisoned warehouse. She gulped the fresh air, relief flooding her brain. The ecstasy she felt at their escape soon crumbled at the thought of the ticking bomb.

Brock held up the fob he had taken from Vance's pocket and hit the panic button. Adelaide felt Brock yank her arm as he pulled her toward the sound of the honking horn coming from a brown Ford Taurus. Adelaide struggled to pull her door closed as Brock gunned the engine and they sped out of the gravel parking lot in a cloud of dust.

CHAPTER 33

BROCK'S INSTINCTS HAD taken over when they were thrown into the van. He was still running on pure adrenaline. In his line of work, that was par for the course, but now he wasn't just worried about himself—he had Adelaide to protect. Plus, he was terrified for the people inside the plant and downwind. As he skidded the car toward the road, he tossed Adelaide his cell phone. "Call nine-one-one. Then call your guy at the EPA."

Adelaide dialed while Brock sped toward the plant. They were at least twenty minutes out from the mill. If Vance Shakleton was telling the truth about the timing of the bomb, then they would still be driving when T minus zero came. When she finished the last call, Adelaide stuck the cell phone in the Taurus's cupholder. "EPA and the locals are scrambling."

She checked her watch. "We don't have any hazmat suits. If that bomb goes off, a bunch of extremely nasty stuff is going to be released into the air. It's not going to be safe to be downwind. We need to get to the north of the plant. Right now, we're south."

"Hopefully, they're going to find the bomb and get it defused."

"*Hopefully* doesn't help when you're breathing aerosolized toxins."

He was thinking out loud. "I hope to God they're evacuating

the plant…it's a workday. There must be three hundred people inside…then there are all the folks in Pine Grove—"

She cut him off. "Brett's on it. There are protocols for these situations. Trust me, Brett Pierce is hell on wheels in an emergency. He'll get it done. But, right now, we have got to get out of the way and upwind of that mill."

"I'm with you. But I don't know these back roads well enough. You're going to have to find a paper map or use the GPS on my phone and tell me where to go."

She rummaged through the glove compartment and found an old Texas highway map. She studied it for a minute before she used his phone's GPS to pinpoint their exact location.

"In about a mile, I want you to take 58 up to the loop outside of Lufkin. Cut over east and then north to 1669 South. From there, we can approach the plant from the upwind side. All the other roads are likely to be turned one-way as part of the evacuation."

He nodded as he hit the flashers and sped north. Pegging the speedometer, he sailed through curves in the road. At times, he was sure the Taurus was going to swerve up onto two wheels. Thinking about Vance threatening to kill them, about the ultimate betrayal by the closest thing he would ever have to a brother, made the bile rise in his throat. The terrible realization that he had put Adelaide—hell, he'd put everyone within god-only-knew how many miles of the mill—in mortal danger by trusting his partner made his stomach turn. *What have I done?* He forced himself to concentrate. He needed all of his energy to stop the bomb—to stop the senseless ruin it would rain down on countless innocent people.

They saw helicopters overhead. Soon, fire trucks from volunteer fire departments were speeding along with them. Brock slowed down to let them pass. "Looks like you got the right people on the phone."

Adelaide looked at her watch for the hundredth time. "The

broadcast I set up at the copy shop should have gone out five minutes ago."

"You really set that up? I thought you were just jacking with them."

"No...I just made up the part about you having half of the password. The rest was true. It'll likely be lost on law enforcement in the face of this emergency, but the news stations will be glued to those tip lines hoping for cell phone video of the evacuation or the explosion. They'll get the message."

They cut south on 1669. As they approached Pine Grove, a huge explosion threw fire what seemed like a mile up into the clouds. Adelaide dialed Brett Pierce.

"It just blew. I'm north of the plant. We saw the explosion."

There was a pause before Brett's voice crackled through the phone. "I'm getting that from the guys in the choppers. Stay upwind, but get over there ASAP. I need you to suit up and help out until I can get my people on the ground. I'm calling the locals and telling them that you're taking over when you get there. They should have a suit for you at the roadblock."

"Will do. I don't have any ID. Just tell them I'm in a brown Ford Taurus." She hung up. "Take me as far as we can go before we hit a roadblock."

He sped on until a barricade blocked the highway. Adelaide gave the state trooper manning the roadblock her name.

"Mr. Pierce called. We're ready for you."

She turned to Brock. "I've got to go. Where are you headed?"

Things were moving too fast. He didn't want to leave her. "I'll come with you."

She shook her head. "I'll be okay. This is what I do. You've got to get back to the diner. Rufus is stuck somewhere alone."

Her mention of Rufus shook him. How could he have not been thinking about Rufus? With all that was going on, Adelaide was worried about his dog. *Adelaide...*

"Ma'am," the trooper said, "we need you to come with us. We have a suit for you and an ambulance is waiting. The medics will check you out on the way to the site."

She was halfway out of the car. He desperately wanted her to stay, to talk, to let him say the things he hadn't had a chance to say. But there was no time.

She turned back and looked at him for a moment. She put her hand on his and simply said, "Trust and honesty are everything in this world...in my world, anyway. And we both know we can't ever have that." She shook her head and wiped tears away with the back of her hand. "Thank you—for helping me, for...everything." And then she was gone.

CHAPTER 34

THE BOMB HAD made everything federal. Sometimes Adelaide felt like she should have just moved her new EPA trailer-turned-office from Pine Grove to the federal courthouse in Marshall. It seemed that she was testifying before grand juries more often than she was supervising cleanup operations at the mill—and managing the cleanup occupied almost all of her waking hours.

Just as well... Whenever she left work, memories of her time with Brock permeated every part of her mind...and her heart. While Thinking Adelaide knew better than to ever trust him again, Feeling Adelaide wanted him just as much as she had that night in the missile silo. Dealing with a massive toxic waste spill was easier than refereeing that argument between her head and her heart.

She had just finished yet one more morning of testimony and was heading back to the site. She juggled her briefcase and laptop as she exited the courthouse, then almost dropped them both when she saw Brock coming up the sidewalk. He stopped in his tracks when he saw her. Her heart fluttered, and her mouth went dry. She felt like she was in sixth grade again, when the first boy to ever ask her to dance headed across the gym toward her...

They stood opposite each other in silence until the awkward-ness overcame her. She managed a smile. "Hey."

He opened his mouth but no words came out. Finally, he said, "After I left you at the roadblock, I tried the number you gave me that night in the hotel...several times. But I never got anything but a message that the voice mail hadn't been set up."

She nodded. "It took me a few days to get a new phone and set up the mailbox..." He stayed quiet, his eyes locked on hers. *Those damn blue eyes.* She shook her head. "I don't want to lie. I saw the missed calls. I didn't call you back because I've never been able to figure out what to say. Every time some lawyer mentions you in a hearing, they call you Brandon or Mr. Eaton. I still can't think of you as anything but Brock."

He gestured toward a park bench along the sidewalk heading up to the courthouse. "Would you like to sit for a few minutes?"

Her heart raced as she was flooded with memories of Caddo Inn, the silo, the feel of him touching her...kissing her. The look on his face when she'd said those terrible things about adoption, when she'd found him dumping her samples. Images of him saving her life at the warehouse. She nodded. "Sure."

They walked to the bench in silence. When they were seated, Adelaide said, "How's Rufus? Ava told me she busted him out of the hunting truck and did a little babysitting."

He laughed. "She's something. That's for sure. When I was headed back toward the copy shop, I got snagged in evacuation traffic. I realized it was going to take me hours to get through the mess and back to Rufus. I was worried sick about him. I knew he'd stay in that truck waiting for me if it killed him. Thank God the windows were broken out or the heat would have done him in. I fought my way through the university switchboard and finally got her in the lab. She promised to run right out and get him. She took Rufus to her office where the little guy was fed, watered, and walked. Three of the grad students were playing with him when I got there. Now he has this strange interest in polymers."

She bit her lip. "Yeah. She also told me that Rufus somehow managed to show his gratitude by sending her a beautiful dogwood tree." She smiled. "Rufus has class."

More silence.

"The Texas Rangers are investigating the Fairfield County sheriff's office. The place was hip-deep in corruption linked to the meth trade. The county commissioners have appointed an interim sheriff to run things until they can hold a special election."

Adelaide nodded. "Yeah. I met him. He seems like a nice guy. He's retired from the FBI. Those connections are really helping with all the liaison work the sheriff's office has with the feds. I was happy to hear it looks like that jerk Jackson's going to have plenty of time in a cell to ruminate on not letting me and the mayor into the mill that day."

Brock said, "One of the lawyers told me yesterday that the big albino guy and his sidekick copped a plea on the kidnapping and the assault in the alley. At first, they were holding out on admitting they killed Arthur, but they even cratered on that in the end. What the hell were they going to say with your video in evidence? Their lawyer was most interested in getting them into a facility with some decent medical care. I hear they're both pretty messed up from that bath they took at the warehouse."

"Getting dunked in twelve barrels of toluene will cook your nervous system, for sure. Doubtful they'll ever fully recover. It's just good enough for them."

He looked off into the distance. "Vance got moved to the jail today. He's been in the hospital ever since the warehouse."

She studied him. "Besides what he said that morning, I've only heard bits and pieces about exactly how he figured into all of this."

"I hadn't gotten all of the background either until last week. Some investigative journalist from the *Republic Tribune* got it.

Sounds to me like it leaked from the prosecutor's office, maybe some from the grand jury. I don't think it's been in the paper yet, but the reporter called me for a comment. When Vance was working security at the chemical company, he had a thing with a woman named Sybil who worked in the plant. I knew about Sybil. She always struck me as troubled, and it was my impression she had been a stripper at one point before they met. The version of events I heard was they met at work, dated for a while, broke up, and went their separate ways.

"It seems what really went on was that Sybil was tied up in the meth trade, and they met when Vance caught her stealing pseudo-ephedrine from the plant. She apparently traded him sexual favors in return for him turning a blind eye to her thefts. In the course of their liaison, Sybil got pregnant. The exposure to the toxic chemicals in the plant coupled with her drug use and neglect of her prenatal care resulted in a child born with severe spina bifida. After the birth, Sybil abandoned the child at the hospital and disappeared. The child required round-the-clock medical care that Vance wasn't able to offer her. Ill equipped to be a single parent and not knowing what else to do, Vance picked up Sybil's contacts and started his own meth operation to pay for the little girl to live in an exclusive long-term care facility for severely ill children up in Massachusetts."

The story made her heart hurt and reminded her that nothing was ever simple in this world. "What's going to happen to the child now?"

Brock shook his head. "She only lived a few days past her third birthday. But by then, Vance was deep into the meth business. Without the nursing care costs, he was suddenly awash in cash. It was too much to resist, and he was lost to the dark side. It just spiraled from there."

She shrugged. "And the rest, as they say, is history."

He nodded. "I had no idea about the child, and I swear, I

didn't know anything about the meth. I would never have had anything to do with that. And, just for the record, I didn't see a dime of it. It wasn't like he was tossing that excess revenue into the agency kitty. I think that was just between Vance and Blackwood and Stone and the creeps from the sheriff's office."

"I know you didn't. Vance said as much while he was pointing that gun at us."

"The feds must have a little sympathy. Way I hear it, they've drummed up some community service thing to let Blackwood off in exchange for his testimony."

She nodded. "And from what I understand, he's singing like Pavarotti. I hate what he did, but I can't help feeling sorry for the guy."

Brock was quiet for a minute. "How's Grace Hinkle doing? What's happening with the lodge?"

Adelaide smiled. "Talk about a bright spot in the darkest night… Addison got the lien holders to take the insurance money and walk away. She's selling the place as is to a couple who are turning it into a bed and breakfast. She and her husband are getting enough out of the sale to move to Houston and start over. He's getting a transfer to the Houston office of the water well company, and she'll be right there in town with MD Anderson Cancer Center, so she can get the very best treatment. The whole thing should close next week. It couldn't have worked out better on that front." She turned to him. "Grace told me that you came by to visit her and see if you could help out. That was really kind of you."

Brock looked away. "She's a nice lady." He paused then cleared his throat and turned to look her straight in the eye. "I'm sorry. I'm sorry for all of it—for all the lies. I think I worked undercover for so long the line between real and not real got blurred. I think that's why I liked the work so much. When I was undercover, I was anybody but that poor little kid left on the bus." He scrubbed a hand over his jaw. "When Vance sent me that picture of you being arrested for evidence tampering...I never should have believed him. I kept thinking what he was saying didn't make sense. But he saved my life when we were kids. No way I would have survived without him. Not only was he my business partner, he was the only family I ever had. We were arguing, and I couldn't sort it all out fast enough.

"But after you drove away, I kept looking at that picture of you in handcuffs. I just couldn't imagine you doing anything like that. When I checked the web and saw how you had been cleared, my blood ran cold. It was then that I remembered Vance called you *Little Miss Smarty Pants*...and he said something about *those thugs from the mill would have prevented all of this*...and it all came together in my head. I remembered hearing the dark-haired guy with the long beard say the *Smarty Pants* thing that night in the alley. Then the veil lifted. I knew something horrible, beyond anything I could have ever imagined, was going on behind my back."

They were quiet for several moments before he went on. "The thing about the mole leaking information about the meth lab. I can see now—it was just a flimsy impromptu cover to counter you discovering it yourself. I knew when he told me that something about what he was saying didn't fit. I should have seen through it all then. Adelaide, I'm so sorry...for all of it."

She nodded. "I know you're sorry. You saved me in that alley..." Her mind was once again flooded with terrible images of that night. She shook her head. "And you came after me, got yourself kidnapped in the process... If you hadn't, they would have killed me in that warehouse."

He reached out and stroked her cheek. "I couldn't let them hurt you."

She swallowed hard. "And I'm sorry about all those things I said about adoption. I never felt that way. I was just angry, so hurt by what my ex-fiancé and that horrible family of his did to me."

He nodded. "I believe you."

She collected her thoughts. "I want you to know…I am sorry about Vance. The fact that he went bad in the end doesn't change what passed between the two of you in a lifetime together. I can't imagine what this must be like for you, but I am deeply sorry it's happening to you."

He nodded. "Thank you."

They sat in silence for a time. She felt his eyes on her…hopeful, searching. She shook her head and smiled a sad, regretful smile. "I keep seeing you pouring those samples out. Destroying evidence, believing those lies about me." He lowered his gaze. "Sometimes," she went on, "there's just too much water under the bridge."

She got up and gathered her briefcase and laptop, then turned to him as he stood.

"You saved my life. I'll always remember that. And I'll always remember you…" she said softly.

Wordlessly, he bent down and kissed her forehead. She smiled wistfully before she turned and walked away, a lone tear escaping down her cheek.

CHAPTER 35

DAMN LAWYERS.

Since the explosion at the mill, it seemed like his whole life was spent with lawyers. Platoons of them, with serious faces and expensive suits—and meters that never stopped running.

One of them was sitting across his desk from him right then. Ted Oldham was the new lead counsel for InfoGlobal. Brandon thought of Ted as Thing One. Next to Thing One sat a worried-looking forensic accountant. Brad Monet was overseeing the spate of problems with the money. Thing Two. Brandon picked up a legal pad and pencil, leaned back in his chair, and nodded.

Thing One started. "Well, there's good news and bad news."

Jesus. "What's the good news, Ted? The Martians have landed?"

Thing One didn't have much of a sense of humor. "I spoke with the US attorney's office this morning.

They have made a decision not to come after you or any of the staff investigators. It's reasonable to believe the DAs in Dallas and Fairview Counties will follow suit."

Great. Just friggin' great. I live in a world now where the good news is that I'm not going to federal prison. Christ help me with the bad news. "And..."

"Well...East-Tex Consolidated has filed a lawsuit against

InfoGlobal and you personally alleging that you violated their confidentiality and breached your contract when you failed to stop Ms. Reese from collecting water samples in their pond."

He couldn't help himself. He laughed out loud. "They let Vance Shakleton cook meth in their mill while they poisoned the water supply for twenty thousand people, and they're pissed because I didn't stop Adelaide Reese from proving that?"

Thing One cleared his throat. "I know it seems...extreme. One of my associates is crafting an answer to the original petition now."

Brandon shook his head. "To hell with crafting anything. How about our answer is 'Screw off, you polluting bastards'?"

Thing One swallowed hard. "Uhhh..."

Brandon tossed the pencil onto the desk and leaned forward. "File a general denial and let that pot cook. No way those assholes didn't know what Vance was doing. Hell, Blackwood was in on it. They're bluffing. Next."

"The state board is still considering sanctions based on the complaint filed by East-Tex against the agency license."

Brandon settled in his chair. "Are they looking at my license in particular or just the agency ticket?"

"Just the agency."

"Same answer. Screw 'em. If I still have my license, then they can take the InfoGlobal ticket. I'll start over if I have to. Anything else?"

Ted Oldham cleared his throat again. "I think that covers the main issues for now."

He turned to Thing Two. "Brad? Bottom-line the money to me."

The accountant pulled out a wide spreadsheet. "The good news is that Mr. Shakleton kept all the drug money for himself. I see no evidence that any money from a source other than legitimately billed hours by the agency ever passed through Info-Global accounts."

Brandon leaned forward. "Does that mean the feds can't claim any of InfoGlobal's assets as the proceeds of a criminal enterprise? We get to keep what we have?"

Thing Two nodded. "I don't have it in writing yet, but I believe it will be the case, and if it isn't, I think you have a strong defense against any claims."

He breathed a sigh of relief on that front. But Thing Two pulled out another spreadsheet, screwed on his most concerned face, and fidgeted in his chair.

Here we go... "Go on, Brad. Spit it out."

"With the reduction in revenue from the...disturbance in business, cash flow is taking a significant hit. Plus, we obviously have concerns about collections from East-Tex on their outstanding bills—which are substantial. Current payables are being supported by capital reserves, but those won't last long. In short, sir, you are going to need to approximately double current cash flow in the next three months if you want to keep the agency operating in its current form." Thing Two lowered the spreadsheet and swallowed hard.

Brandon put his palms on the desk and rose from his chair. Being as this morning's funfest was running him about a grand an hour, he wasn't interested in pleasantries. "Well, thanks, guys. I think that's all we need for today."

Thing One and Thing Two nodded, gathered their briefcases, and exited.

Well, at least I probably won't be locked up. He'd spent plenty of sleepless nights worrying about attending bankruptcy hearings in an orange jumpsuit. *Now I know I'll be wearing a coat and tie.* One after another, the chemical companies that made up the backbone of InfoGlobal's business were dropping off the client roster like clay pigeons at a trap and skeet range. Some were probably tied in somehow with Vance's meth business and were trying to get the hell out of Dodge before the feds got onto them. Most of them were probably as guilty as East-Tex, so he wasn't sure they were much of a loss.

This whole thing was a Technicolor nightmare that felt like it would never end.

He shuffled through the latest stack of mail on his desk. Spotting the distinctive seal of the Texas Department of Public Safety Private Security Bureau, he sliced the letter opener through the envelope. He was staring at a form letter advising Vance about a new DPS policy requiring fingerprint-based criminal background checks every year before license renewal. Vance's was due next month.

The irony overcame him. He tossed the notice on the desk and started laughing…then he laughed harder…and then he couldn't stop.

And then he was crying and laughing at the same time. Tears streamed down his face. Everything they'd worked so hard for was crumbling around him. He was so mad at Vance sometimes he wished he'd killed him when he had the chance at the warehouse. Other times, he missed his friend so much, he would find himself thinking of making a visit to the jail.

What did all this say about him? What kind of an ace detective doesn't even know what's happening in his own office with his own partner? And then that would make him think of her.

Thinking of Adelaide almost broke his heart. Visions of her during their nights together dissolved into the look on her face before she turned and walked away outside the courthouse. The recurring kaleidoscope of images scalded his soul.

The pain of knowing that he'd found something most people never even imagine in a lifetime…then wasted that one precious chance by trusting a crazed drug dealer who, in the end, didn't care about anyone or anything besides money and power was indescribable. How could he have believed the things Vance said about her? She was the most honorable, authentic, generous person he'd ever met. He'd never be able to forgive himself for being so stupid.

Wiping his eyes, he saw a mailer that had spilled out from what he had lately dubbed the Leaning Tower of Postal. The postcard featured a color snapshot of a young girl with blond pigtails wearing a blue flowered jumper under a banner that read, MISS-ING in large red letters... *That poor, terrified child—out there somewhere in the world at the mercy of some monster.*

Suddenly, he saw the situation plainly. Either he got his shit together and figured it out now, or he faced bankruptcy and losing it all. This was his defining moment.

He fingered the St. Christopher medal. He hadn't come this far to give up on the agency, on his career—or on a life with Adelaide. Hope surged through him, bringing a renewed energy.

He had an idea.

CHAPTER 36

THE DAMN PHONE was making her crazy. She was afraid she couldn't keep herself from biting the head off the next person who rang her line. Between the OSC, the DEA, and the rest of the alphabet soup involved in the cleanup, Adelaide was on her last nerve. Every time she picked up the receiver, some other government drone was whining on about yet one more inane request. At this rate, she wasn't even going to make it through the pile of daily progress reports before it was time to head out to the weekly community meeting at the high school. Her frustration-tolerance tank was running on empty.

She buzzed her assistant on the intercom. "I'm drowning in paper in here. Would you just hold all the stupid calls?"

The assistant laughed. "That means you want me to hold *all* your calls, right?"

"Unless it's Club Med offering me a free vacation, just tell them I ran off and joined the circus."

She ended the call and started shuffling paper. Halfway through the pile, she took a break and refilled her coffee cup. Outside of her trailer-office window, Adelaide watched as the shifts changed. A woman pulled up to the gate in a pickup truck, got out, and opened the rear door, retrieving a little boy from his car seat. The child looked at the woman with adoring eyes as she hefted him onto her hip and handed him a stuffed alligator. The woman pointed and spoke to the child, who smiled brightly as his father exited the mill gate. The man kissed his wife and swung the child into a bear hug. The child laughed and grabbed his father's ears.

In all the excitement, the little boy dropped his alligator and began to sob. The father picked up the alligator and handed it back to the child, but the baby only cried harder until his father passed him, grasping, to his mother. Once safely in his mother's arms, the child stopped crying and rested his head on her shoulder as she stroked his head and whispered in his ear.

She'd met the parents at one of the community meetings and knew the toddler was adopted. Watching them, Adelaide realized there was no one on the face of the earth who could have comforted that child the way his mother did. That little boy had absolutely no idea about DNA. All he knew was that Mommy kept him safe.

She realized, in that moment, that she hadn't just believed men wouldn't want a sterile woman but that somewhere deep inside, she'd believed she couldn't be a real mother. In that simple exchange, she had seen something that reminded her love was what made a mother, not shared genetics. Brock had seen that. He'd loved her just as she was. But now, she'd lost her chance with the only man she truly wanted.

The vision of him pouring out her samples ran through her mind again. *Vance showed him a picture of me in a newspaper and told him a lie about me, and he not only believed it...he broke into my sample case and destroyed evidence—my evidence.* But, Adelaide wondered, if the situation had been reversed, if Ava had sent her evidence that Brock was a dirtbag, would she have been wrong to trust her oldest friend over some guy she'd met a few days before?

As she turned to watch the family's pickup truck pull away, she was startled by the clock. If she didn't get a move on, she was going to be late for the community meeting.

One by one, she plowed through the reports. Each of her five team leaders provided a daily summary of their activities and progress. Soil Remediation was coming along nicely, but Ground Water Testing was behind. Government Compliance and Reporting was bogged down...what a surprise. Air Quality had a handle on things but was struggling to keep up with their part of the cleanup plan. Accounting was demanding a meeting. Accounting was always demanding a meeting.

By five twenty, she was crossing the parking lot, schlepping her briefcase. That was when she saw a handsome man in a snug black T-shirt, black jeans, and high-top sneakers leaning against the hatch of her SUV. Brock! *Brandon*, she reminded herself. Next to him was a panting bull terrier.

A surge of joy ran through her as Rufus bounded up and stood on his hind legs. She squatted down and ruffled his ears while he lapped her face. Satisfied, Rufus turned and trotted back to his master. She called out, "Excuse me! What are you doing leaning on my car?"

Brandon stood up straight. Smiling, he dusted himself off. "I'm here to tell you that I'm not going to accept this 'water under the bridge' business."

She walked toward him. "You're not, huh?"

He shook his head. "Nope. In my opinion, you and I are not beyond hope. From where I stand, we're all about hope. We're just beginning." She feigned consideration, and he continued. "Think of the story we're going to have when one of our grandkids asks how we met."

She was stunned. "Grandkids?"

He nodded. "Grandkids. You heard what I said." He put his hands on her shoulders and held her facing him. "Damn it, I love you. I've loved you since I saw you in that stupid green suit. And I know you love me...I can't be that wrong about you."

As if on cue, Rufus yapped. Brandon laughed. "Rufus can't be that wrong about you, either. Rufus is never wrong about people."

She was smiling in spite of herself. "It's not that simple..."

He nodded emphatically. "Yes, it is. It is just that simple. I love you, you love me. We get married and adopt a houseful of kids. If we can survive a machine gun attack, a kidnapping, and a bombing, then what, exactly, do you think will sink us?"

She wanted him so much, her heart felt like it was leaping out of her chest. Yet, deep down, she thought of what his job...the constant lies...would do to them. "But what about the agency? The undercover work?"

"Our ownership agreement made it clear that if either of us could no longer perform our duties in the partnership, the other could buy out all of the outstanding stock. With Vance on his way to prison, I own the whole agency now. The guys all work for me. And I decided—no more undercover, no more corporate espionage."

Adelaide was confused. "How will you make a living?"

"You are looking at the chief investigator for the newest firm in the Dallas area specializing in missing and exploited children."

She broke into a wide smile as tears flooded her eyes.

He pulled a small velvet box from his pocket. Her heart raced as he held it out for her and carefully lifted the hinged lid. She peered inside.

"Go on..." he prompted.

She carefully lifted the medallion and held it against her palm. The half circle was filled with the face of St. Christopher suspended on a beautiful silver chain.

Instinctively, she looked to his chest. There, framed against his black T-shirt, hung the other half.

Gently, he took the pendant in his hands. "I don't have a ring yet. I was hoping we could pick that out together. But this medal...it's the only thing I have that links me to who I was, to where I came from. It was the symbol of a home I never had. I hope you'll wear it until we find you the perfect ring." He rubbed the saint's image with his thumb. "I always believed it would show me the way." Then he looked up at her with those amazing blue eyes. "All these years, I didn't realize how lost I was until I met you. Now..." He slid the necklace over her head and let it rest around her neck. "Now, if you'll have me, you and I are going to find our way together."

Tears flowed down her cheeks as she reached out for him. She could feel her heart opening to him, accepting him. She felt safe, secure in a way she had never dreamed possible. She took his face in her hands. "There is no one in the world I'd rather find my way with than you."

Then it hit her.

"There is one thing we have to get out of the way first."

He brushed her hair back from her face. "And what would that be?"

She smiled. "We've never been introduced."

He extended his hand. "Brandon Eaton. Nice to meet you."

She dropped her briefcase as he took her into his arms. He kissed her and held her close. Then she pulled back. "Wait a minute."

He looked so confused, she could hardly contain a smile. "I don't go around kissing guys I've just met."

He stepped back. "Hmm. Well, I guess we'll have to get to know each other first." He nuzzled her neck.

She laughed. "That's enough for the introductions. Kiss away."

He stroked her hair and looked into her eyes. "You know, all these years I've told myself I didn't need to be close to anyone, that I was better off on my own. Now, I know—I need you. I need to be close to you, near you, to have you in my life always."

He kissed her again, long and deep. She held on to him, feeling his strength and reveling in how right it felt.

"Welcome home," she whispered against his cheek.

Enjoy this excerpt from the award-winning third book in the
Deadly Secrets Texas Trilogy!

BURIED SECRETS

CHAPTER 1

SAMANTHA JORDAN LOOKED out over the crowd. What a zoo.

The first buses had arrived in the dark. As the earliest rays of light peeked over the horizon, the protesters climbed down from their chartered coaches and retrieved their picket signs from the luggage bays. They formed up and began to circle the construction site singing what they claimed were Comanche burial chants.

Never in all her years of education had anyone told her that abandoned Piggly Wigglys were historically significant architectural resources. Because Samantha had no legal basis upon which to deny the building permit, she had approved the demolition of the old grocery store and the construction of the new hipster lofts. It should have been no big deal. Except for the politics.

And the skeletons.

"You gotta love that First Amendment."

Startled, Samantha turned and found a tall, handsome man in black jeans and a white oxford button-down with a lightweight black sport coat surveying the crowd. He wore a pistol on his hip and a gold shield on a chain around his neck.

She checked his badge. Nicholas Ballard. Though Samantha had spoken briefly to him on the phone, she'd never actually met the man. His voice, deep and mellow over the phone, was even more appealing in person. But she wasn't falling for it. Hot guys always thought they could charm away any conflict with female colleagues. That strategy never worked with Samantha Jordan.

"Actually, I do."

"Do what?"

"Love the First Amendment. Protesting is their right."

"Well, aren't you a good sport—especially about a bunch of folks who are here specifically to complain about you."

Samantha shrugged. "Unfortunately for them, the federal judge their lawyer complained to this morning sees things my way."

Samantha's phone chimed, and she checked the message. Returning the phone to her suit pocket, she looked up at Nick. "The court order was just entered."

He surveyed the scene. "I'll get my people ready to escort you through the picket line."

Samantha rolled her eyes. "Hold on there, Wyatt Earp. Before you turn this into the O.K. Corral, how about I go over and talk to the protest organizer and see if I can't work this out?"

"I don't think—"

Before he could finish his sentence, Samantha waved to a man dressed like Indiana Jones. Dylan Pierce was the head of CAR, the University of Texas at San Antonio Center for Archaeological Research. Together, she and Dylan waded into the crowd. Samantha looked back to see Nick scrambling behind her, elbowing his way through the growing mass as she and the archaeologist approached the leader of the Comanche protesters, who was standing under an old pecan tree.

Samantha shook hands with the man. "Mr. Eagle Feather, the court order has just been entered authorizing us to resume work on the site." Samantha held out her iPad, showing him an image of the order. "Dr. Pierce's team is ready to get to work. SAPD is here to escort us across the picket line if necessary. But I would much rather leave the police out of this."

Eagle Feather looked at Nick and the waiting ranks of police officers, many on horseback, and then turned his gaze back to Samantha. "We'll open the line, but we want press coverage of us doing it."

"Not a problem." She picked up her phone and spoke briefly with her public relations officer. Finished, she stuck her phone in her pocket. "Janie'll get the press in gear and then come up here to get us when they're ready."

Eagle Feather headed off to organize his people.

Nick looked at Samantha. "Great. Maybe I should just send all the cops home for the day. Let you work it out. If it gets dicey, you can hit them with one of your diplomas."

Samantha shook her head. "Bad idea. My diplomas are on the wall in my office. They won't do me much good here. But I do think it would be great if you could marshal your people over by the buses. We'll make a show of your officers withdrawing once the press is in place. If we withdraw the police and the protesters make any trouble, then it will be a PR nightmare for them. Eagle Feather's a pro. He's not going to let that happen."

Nick looked around the site. In addition to the crowd noise, worksite generators were cranking up to provide power to Dylan Pierce's team. Nick put a finger in his ear and shouted over the racket. "And just what do you want me to do if a riot breaks out?"

She took a map from the outside pocket of her briefcase and pointed. "Look at the layout."

Nick leaned in to see better, his arm pressing against hers. As subtly as possible, she adjusted her position to break the contact. Trying to ignore the warmth spreading up her arm from the brief touch, she made herself concentrate on getting Pierce's team across that picket line. "If you stage your people over by these buses, your folks will look unobtrusive for the media. Meanwhile, they will also be well positioned to move in on the site by streaming right down this alley behind Barbe Street—which would, incidentally, have them coming out right inside the picket line."

Nick studied the map and shrugged. "All right. We'll do it your way, but we're going to come in and put a lid on any trouble before it escalates." Samantha heard the crackling chatter of police traffic as Nick picked up his radio and spoke to his officers.

It was summer in San Antonio, and soon the Texas sun and tropical humidity were going to make the construction site feel like a cross between a toaster oven and a rain forest. Samantha needed to get this situation handled before the heat made everyone that much more unreasonable. "Just try to stay calm, please. What we can't afford is anything that will show up on the news looking the least bit like a remake of the Council House Massacre."

"The what?"

She shook her head. How could he not know this? "Who briefs you on community relations? Dirty Harry? Honestly. The remains uncovered two weeks ago—you know, the skeletons that started this whole problem with the Comanche Nation? It appears they are the remains of Comanche people who were killed in March of 1840 when they came to San Antonio for a peace council. Instead of getting peace, they were shot dead by the Texians in the council house where the negotiations were taking place, not ten minutes' walk from here."

Nick scowled. "So I'm on the hook for what a bunch of yahoos did a hundred and eighty years ago? Oh, please."

Samantha stared at him. "Don't *oh, please* me. The optics of SAPD officers on horseback using mace and nightsticks on Native Americans in the shadow of the Alamo would be atrocious. I have no intention of that PR train wreck happening on my watch. You best keep your people under control."

Across the crowded site, Samantha saw Janie working out

choreography with Eagle Feather and Pierce. Shortly, Samantha's phone chimed. She checked the message and turned to Nick.

"Please get your folks moving. This show is hitting the road."

Nick spoke into his radio, and the police working crowd control withdrew and gathered around the corner by the parked buses. Samantha joined Pierce, and they led the CAR team through the picket line, which opened like a well-rehearsed marching band. Once the team had passed, the opening zippered shut, and the protest continued. Samantha motioned for Joseph Eagle Feather to join her at the press podium as Nick emerged from the alley and fell in behind her.

Then the ground exploded.

CHAPTER 2

AS CONCRETE PILLARS and iron framing from the old building crashed around them in a deadly avalanche, Nick grabbed her and pulled her under his arm, shielding her head with his hand. Samantha struggled to regain her footing as he half dragged her through the chaos into the cold storage shed of the old grocery store. The deafening explosions and the crashing sound of the falling debris clattered through her head. Clouds of dust burned her eyes and choked her as she struggled to breathe. Racked by blast after blast, the dilapidated old shed began to crater in on itself.

Nick yanked Samantha's arm and shoved her into an old walk-in freezer, then dived in on top of her. His weight forced the breath out of her lungs as she hit the ground with a bone-rattling thud. Fighting for air, she squirmed out from under him as he rolled onto his back and kicked the door closed with his alligator boot. Seconds later, the freezer was buried in falling debris. Chunks of concrete slamming into the metal chamber made it sound like they were trapped in a junkyard car crusher. The filthy floor was rough and hard. She tasted dirt and grit and smelled things she'd rather not think about.

After what seemed like an eon, the crashing stopped. When Nick activated the flashlight on his cell phone, Samantha saw graffiti on the walls and trash all over the floor. Beer cans and other detritus she tried hard to ignore littered the space. The heat inside the metal box was stifling, and it was only going to get worse.

Nick turned to her, putting his hand on her shoulder. "Are you all right?"

He helped her as she pushed herself up into a sitting position. His touch was strong but gentle and somehow comforting, but she forced herself to concentrate on her physical condition. She hurt all over, but she was pretty sure nothing was broken. She worked the stiffness in her right elbow. "I think so." She massaged her shoulder and looked around. "What in the world happened?"

"I'm not sure. Some kind of explosion."

Nick pulled on the door, which mercifully opened inward. A mountain of huge chunks of broken concrete with twisted lengths of rusty rebar protruding from them like octopus tentacles blocked their exit. Nick yanked his police radio off his belt and began a series of mayday calls.

Samantha's heart sank when she didn't hear any crackling static coming through the radio. She tried her phone. A deep pang of dread shot through her gut as she watched half of a single bar flicker away. The metal freezer compartment was going to work just like a car trapping heat in the Texas sun. They couldn't last long in there.

Nick checked his cell and shook his head. "There's no signal." He studied the mound, illuminated only by a few eerie rays of light peeking through the rubble. "We're going to have to dig ourselves out. At least move enough of this rock to get a radio or cell signal to the surface."

Samantha stared at the sinister-looking pile of shattered concrete. "How do we know there won't be another explosion?"

Nick shook his head again. "We don't. If it was a bomb, there could be others."

"Maybe it was a gas leak."

"Possible. I don't have any way of knowing from down here."

"If it was gas, the leak could be continuing. A spark could blow us sky-high."

Nick sniffed the air. "I don't smell anything. Standard emergency procedure calls for City Public Service to immediately cut the gas and electric service at the nearest trunk line."

Before Samantha could respond, the freezer was rocked by another explosion followed by the sounds of more rubble slamming against the metal shell. Nick pulled Samantha to the floor and crouched over her, shielding her. She buried her face in his shoulder as they waited out the terrible storm. She could smell his sweat mixed with aftershave and feel his breathing. It was strange to be so close to a man she barely knew, but somehow he made her feel safe. Thank God he'd pushed her into the shelter of the walk-in. No one could have survived the avalanche of concrete and rebar that had rained down outside the freezer.

When the deafening barrage subsided, Nick helped her to her feet and she walked toward the freezer door. The architect in Samantha took over as thoughts about the compressional strength of the metal framing and the structural integrity of the freezer raced through her mind. Her eyes darted around the ceiling of the metal compartment desperately searching for clues to the freezer's ability to survive the blast.

"Bring that light over here." He must have sensed the urgency in her voice because he leaped across the space. "Shine it toward this corner." Samantha studied the walls of the freezer unit. *Crap.*

"What are you looking at?"

She pointed to the place where the two walls joined the ceiling. The metal wall was buckling. *Crap. Crap. Crap.* She could feel the stress prickling the skin all over her body. Her hands trembled as she tried to calculate a solution. She examined the open freezer door. "We need to tear this rubber gasket off so the seal isn't airtight. Then we need to close the door. Now." Samantha clawed at the gasket. "The door may help support the wall when the frame gives way under the stress." Nick yanked the gasket loose and tossed it aside while Samantha quickly slammed the freezer door.

She looked around and did a quick mechanics problem in her head. "Get toward the back. The point of maximum stress seems to be near the door. That's where this place is going to collapse first."

No sooner had she spoken than the corner of the freezer began to crumple. She and Nick crowded as far as they could against the back wall. Then she smelled it—the undeniable sulfur stench of natural gas.

Nick's eyes darted around the room like a fly dodging a swatter. "This is not good. Up top, they are going to assume the gas has been cut. They'll start using heavy equipment to move the rocks. One spark and we're toast."

He snatched the radio from his belt and began issuing mayday calls. Again, his demands for help were met with silence. Samantha pulled out her phone and began tapping on the screen.

"You have service?"

She worked to steady her hand as she shook her head. "I'm checking for signal strength."

He looked over her shoulder as the bars on her iPhone disappeared and were replaced by a number. "Negative one hundred eight? What does that mean?"

She used the flashlight on the phone to look around the dirty room. "It means there is a signal—it's just not strong enough to support a call." As she surveyed the room, the creaking sound of the bending metal grew louder, and the corner of the freezer nearest the door buckled another foot. *If we can't send an SOS, we'll either be crushed or blown to hell and back.*

Find out what happens next...
Buy *Buried Secrets* now on Amazon.com!

FREE *BURNING SECRETS* BONUS

Get your free *Burning Secrets* bonus including a letter from the author and a bonus chapter with Adelaide and Ava. Also, you can see the surveillance log that Brock kept while he was following Adelaide and take a look at the actual pamphlet that helped Adelaide figure out a meth lab was leaking toxins into Pine Grove's water supply.

Get your *Burning Secrets* bonus at denisedianahuddle.com

ENJOYED *BURNING SECRETS?* YOU CAN MAKE A DIFFERENCE!

Please leave your honest review of the book. As much as I'd love to, I don't have the financial capacity like New York publishers to run national ad campaigns for my books.

But I have something much, much more powerful! Committed and loyal readers.

If you enjoyed the book, I'd be so grateful if you could spend five minutes leaving a review on the book's Amazon.com page.

Thank you very much.
Denise

ACKNOWLEDGMENTS

I would like to thank the following people who have been of help to me in this project.

Chris Parks, attorney and author of *Poco Bueno*, came up with the idea of setting the story of Brock and Adelaide around a polluting paper mill in East Texas. Chris was also instrumental in creating the scene where the mystery doctor shows up at Grace's lodge to treat Brock's injury. I can't thank him enough for all his help.

My friend, bestselling author Mariah Stone, and her husband, Michael, are so willing to share their vast expertise, and their input always inspires and amazes me. I'm lucky to know them.

Laura Barth is consistently kind and considerate while she firmly keeps me in line and always pushes me to improve. She makes every book she edits for me a new learning experience.

Beth Attwood is an eagle-eyed copy editor and proofreader. Any remaining errors are mine alone.

**Greed. Lies. Corruption.
Sarah Chandler must rely on the enemy to
save her brother and escape a killer.
But will joining forces mean losing her heart...or her life?**

TEXAS RANCHER SARAH Chandler is having a tough month. First her brother, Stone, goes missing and now an oil company has had a well blow out on a ranch she manages.

Special Forces veteran Ethan Tanner is not what she expected in a landman for the oil company—intelligent, funny, and gorgeous! And she can't deny his heroism when he runs through flames to rescue his men. But painful experience has taught her to keep men at a distance. When they discover a murder victim while investigating sabotage on the ranch, they become the killer's next targets!

Evading their pursuer in a cross-country car chase, and ending up on the most-wanted list, they search for evidence that could expose the killer...and maybe help them find Stone.

They can't escape the sexual tension between them. But when Sarah learns the real reason Ethan is helping her out—and the truth about his dark history—their growing connection is tested.

Is she sleeping with the enemy...or could Ethan be her only hope of survival?

Buy *Stolen Secrets* (Book 1) on Amazon.com

BURIED SECRETS
(BOOK 3)

Danger. Corruption. Passion.

**When an explosion unearths human remains—and almost
lands *them* in the morgue—historical preservationist
Samantha Jordan and San Antonio police detective
Nick Ballard reluctantly team up to investigate.**

SINCE THE CASE is as cold as the corpse, Samantha uses the
cutting-edge science of genetic genealogy to unravel the dark history of a gruesome unsolved murder and identify the body. But
Nick is obstructing her at every turn. Then a targeted hit and run
and a break-in force them to seek refuge in San Antonio's forgotten historic sites and underground tunnels.

Despite their differences, Samantha is falling for the jaded
detective. And Nick cares for her more than he should. But
coming clean about his past—and the reason he's been dragging
his feet during the investigation—could end his career and put
his deceased partner's family in jeopardy.

As the final puzzle pieces fall into place and Samantha dis-
covers the truth, Nick will have to face his own demons and the
corruption rampant in the SAPD to save her from a cunning killer.

Can love survive their buried secrets?

Buy *Buried Secrets* (Book 3) on Amazon.com

ABOUT THE AUTHOR

Denise Diana Huddle was born and raised in San Antonio, Texas. She graduated from the University of Texas at Austin with a degree in geology and a minor in accounting and went to work as the land manager for her family's oil business.

After thirteen years as a landman, Denise got her private investigator's license and worked for the next twenty years as a PI and forensic genealogist servicing oil companies and law firms nationwide.

Now retired, Denise splits her time between Mobile, Alabama, and San Antonio with her significant other and their rescue dogs while she writes mysteries inspired by cases from her colorful career. Two decades of discovering hidden secrets and unraveling complex family histories has left her with a lot of stories to write.

Subscribe today to Denise's newsletter and join the Crimes & Passion Club for a free true crime story, bonus chapters, and more!

www.ingramcontent.com/pod-product-compliance
Lightning Source LLC
Chambersburg PA
CBHW061952170626
46813CB00006B/2618